Master Plan

By Ian Stuart

IAN STUART

Master Plan

A CRIME CLUB BOOK
DOUBLEDAY
New York London Toronto Sydney Auckland

A CRIME CLUB BOOK
Published by Doubleday
a division of Bantam Doubleday Dell Publishing Group, Inc.
666 Fifth Avenue, New York, New York 10103

DOUBLEDAY and the portrayal of a man
with a gun are trademarks of Doubleday,
a division of Bantam Doubleday Dell
Publishing Group, Inc.

Library of Congress Cataloging-in-Publication Data

Stuart, Ian.
  Master plan / Ian Stuart. — 1st ed.
    p. cm.
  "A Crime Club book."
  I. Title.
  PR6069.T77M297 1990
  823'.914—dc20   89-48674
  CIP

ISBN 0-385-41188-x

Printed in the United States of America
July 1990
First Edition

Master Plan

ONE

THE YOUNG WOMAN crouched in the stern of the inflatable dinghy, had cut the outboard motor twenty minutes ago; now she shipped her paddle and let the boat drift with the tide. There was no moon tonight and thin cloud obscured the stars, so that she couldn't see the mountains which in daylight dominated the island just ahead. But she knew they were there. It was as if the scene were imprinted on her mind's eye, the white houses strung out along the shore, the huts by the jetty, the crofts and, behind them all, the steep slopes of Bheinn Fhada. Round the headland at the south-western tip of the island, by the entrance to Loch Damph, were United's fish farm and cannery. She hated them both; for her they were a symbol.

It was very quiet out here, the only sound the gentle lapping of the surf on the beach a hundred yards away, and the dinghy floated silently, silky black water sliding under it as the tide carried it slowly in towards the shore.

For a minute or two the girl sat motionless, peering into the darkness as she searched for a landmark. She was young, no more than twenty or twenty-one, with straight dark hair and thin features, the sallow skin stretched tight over her narrow cheekbones and her eyes deep-set behind her glasses.

No light showed in the village, or in the houses dotted about the slopes beyond it, and she began paddling again, steering the ungainly little craft towards the land.

It grounded with a slight rasp of rubber on sand, and a tremor went through her. She told herself she wasn't afraid; this was her first mission and it was only natural that her nerves should be tense. Moreover it was a sign of the faith Roy and the others had in her that they had sent her alone.

Getting out, she moored the boat, took a plastic bag from it and started walking diagonally across the narrow beach, her feet making a gentle sighing sound as she dragged them through the dry sand.

It was nearly two hours since she had set out, and by now her eyes were accustomed to the near-darkness. She walked confidently, not stopping until she reached the stretch of rough turf which bordered the beach. There she paused for a moment, looking round. Away to her right she could make out the shapes of the cottages at that end of the village, but her business wasn't there, and she set off along the narrow road, heading obliquely inland and away from the village.

She moved silently now. When she had covered a quarter of a mile she stopped again. Just ahead was the dim shape of another house with a slate roof and a single chimney thrusting up at one end. It was newer than the houses in the village, but built like them and, although she couldn't see it in the dim light, the girl knew that a tiny wood and glass porch protected the front door from the westerly gales.

She went forward slowly, her eyes straining to see. And while her nerves were still on edge, the fear she might have felt was overcome by her excitement. It pulsed through her, buoying her up, overriding any doubts. She had worked and waited for this moment, and now she was here. She was *doing* something. She thought of Moira, asleep over there in the village. Moira would approve.

The curtains at the front of the house were undrawn and the windows stared back at her blankly. There was a patch of garden, but no fence or gate to mark the boundaries of the plot, and she circled it, gazing at the black squares of the windows, as if by doing so she could see into the rooms beyond.

Returned to the front, she opened the outer door of the porch and stepped inside, pulling it to behind her. She paused again then, her heart pounding and her ears straining for the slightest sound. But she heard nothing and, stooping, she took out the contents of the plastic bag and placed them carefully on the floor. She worked quickly and efficiently, intent on the task she had rehearsed so often in the house in Edinburgh, Roy at her shoulder ready to pounce if she hesitated or made the slightest mistake.

In a few minutes it was done. Straightening up, she replaced the tools she had used in the bag and walked back the way she had come, calmly and without hurrying, as Roy had told her to do. She felt no excitement now, not even any triumph, only satisfaction that her mission was accomplished and now she could go home. She had always been law-abiding, observing speed limits and parking restrictions and never driving if she had had more than a single drink, yet it hardly occurred to her that what she had just done constituted a serious crime. Such considerations were irrelevant.

The tide had just turned, and the noise the dinghy made as she pushed it over the sand seemed so loud it must wake the people in the nearest houses. Then the surf was round her ankles and the boat was floating. Scrambling aboard, she picked up her paddle and dug it deep into the black water.

She was over a mile from the village when the bomb exploded. The sound carried clearly to her on the still air, and the flames of the fire which followed lit up the sky. The girl took the weighted bag from the bottom of the boat, held it over the side and let it drop. It sank with a faint sucking sound. If she were stopped now, there would be nothing to link her to the explosion. Only when she was what she considered a safe distance from the island did she ship her paddle and start the dinghy's outboard motor.

That same night a truck loaded with cattle was driven along a narrow road across the border from Eire into Northern Ireland, and a cargo of oranges which had never existed left a Southern Italian port for Iraq. The movements were unconnected, and the people involved in one of them knew nothing about the other, yet both were part of the same design. It was only later that the design became clear.

Lorimer looked round the crowded room and wondered what he was doing there. The answer, of course, was simple: Grantley had told him to come. But why? The Old Man never did anything without a reason, and Lorimer felt a twinge of foreboding.

United's chairman was twenty feet away, talking to two young men wearing expensive suits, the old boys' ties of minor public schools and sycophantic smiles. Even at that distance you could feel the strength of his personality. Sir Aidan Grantley had been blessed with most of the advantages an Englishman could inherit or acquire—wealth, sufficient ability at games and an education at Eton and Oxford—but the chances were he would have been successful without any of them. He had won his place at the head of one of the world's great companies on merit; nobody, even his enemies, disputed that.

Once a year a score of the group's brightest and most promising prospects were summoned to the top floor of United House to drink the company's liquor and be subjected to the critical gaze of its top brass. Grantley disliked the parties, but they were a tradition, jealously fostered by Philip Rayment, the personnel director, and he didn't feel strongly enough about them to have them stopped.

"You'd better come," he had told Lorimer. "It'll be good experience for you."

Lorimer couldn't see how; he didn't delude himself that he was an executive in the making. So he had said simply, "Right."

That had been a week ago.

Colin Bagguley, the chairman's other p.a., was in his element at this sort of junket, saying the right things to the directors and seeing that they were kept supplied with drinks and exuding *bonhomie* to the young hopefuls. Good luck to him, Lorimer thought.

Their roles were quite distinct: Lorimer was Grantley's troubleshooter. The job had taken him to some odd places and involved him in some fairly hairy situations, but he enjoyed it. He found it hard to remember now the boredom of the days when he had worked for Gerald Borrett before the Old Man whisked him up here to the fourteenth floor. Since he and Rosalind had split up he had no family responsibilities; if anything happened to him, it wouldn't make much difference to anyone for long.

"They tell me you're an uncouth Scot," Grantley had said when he offered him the job. It wasn't true, but there was a grain of truth in it, and Lorimer always suspected that that, as much as anything else, was why the Old Man had picked him. Grantley didn't like yes-men.

Philip Rayment hadn't approved. He wanted all senior jobs in the group to go to young men (women should only be secretaries) with public school and Oxbridge educations and accents to match. It didn't matter if their chins receded and they brayed when they laughed, they could be relied on to know how to behave decently, even if they didn't always do so. Rayment approved of Bagguley, who had been to Radley and Oxford, and disapproved of Lorimer, who had gone from an Edinburgh day school to Heriot-Watt, whose manner was often forthright, to say the least, and whose speech still retained the accents of his native city. Worse, he played soccer, and for a semi-professional team. To Rayment, whose only games were bridge and a languid, inexpert brand of tennis, rugger was acceptable provided it wasn't taken too seriously. Soccer, even if it was played at Eton, was not.

The young aspirants stayed rooted to their places while the directors moved about amongst them, pausing for brief, meaningless conversations before moving on. Lorimer sipped his Scotch and thought what a bore it was. Apart from the Old Man, Rayment and Colin Bagguley, there was no one here he knew. The three women were young and attractive, but they had been cornered by two senior members of the board and so were unavailable.

One or two of the more conscientious directors were making little notes in their diaries, names and assessments to be remembered if and when their owners came up for promotion. The others probably forgot whom they had met before they left the building. It was a farce, why had the Old Man wanted him to come? He wasn't one of the select few, to be assessed for his potential like some prize calf, and Grantley couldn't have thought he would enjoy himself. More likely he had wanted him here out of a misguided sense of mischief: if he had to suffer, why shouldn't his p.a.? But that wasn't like him. Whatever his faults, and he had plenty, Grantley was neither selfish nor vindictive.

Lorimer hoped it wasn't because the chairman wanted his opinion of one of the young hopefuls; the last time that had happened it had nearly got him killed. And Shelley . . . He made himself not think of her.

Perhaps he was too ready to look for hidden motives where the Old Man's actions were concerned. If so, it was Grantley's fault, he shouldn't be such a devious sod.

The chairman's voice just behind Lorimer said, "Meet one of your fellow-countrymen, Robin. This is Graham Lorimer, my other p.a."

Lorimer turned. The man with Grantley was in his late thirties, well over six feet tall and burly, with sandy hair and strangely dark, penetrating eyes. At first glance he might give an impression of self-indulgence, even of softness, but his jaw was firm and his bulk mostly hard muscle. He looked like a man who took plenty of exercise and enjoyed it.

"Robin Forsyth," he said, holding out his hand and taking Lorimer's in a firm grip.

"Mr. Forsyth's the chairman of Excelsior and Morgans and a director of two investment trusts," Grantley explained. "He's joining us as a non-executive director next month."

"I'm looking forward to it," Forsyth said in accents which would have delighted Philip Rayment. A lock of hair fell forward across his forehead and he pushed it back with a boyish gesture. "Where are you from?"

"Edinburgh," Lorimer said.

"Oh. I'm a wild highlander, Inverness-shire."

They chatted for a few minutes before the chairman led Forsyth away to meet somebody else, leaving Lorimer to wonder if he need stay to the end of the party. No one was likely to miss him if he slipped away soon. Then he saw that Grantley was coming back, and this time he was alone.

"Enjoying yourself?" he enquired ironically. His expression changed and he said quietly, "I want you to go up to Iniscaig tomorrow."

Lorimer told himself that he should know better than to be surprised. Nevertheless he wondered what had happened for the Old Man to want him to go to the Hebrides at a few hours' notice. "Trouble?" he asked.

"Some bunch of fanatics blew up Burton's house last night."

Lorimer was startled. Burton was the manager of United's fish processing plant on Iniscaig. "Was he there?" he asked.

"No, luckily he and his family had gone to spend the weekend with some friends in Oban. But there's not much left of the house. Somebody rang the *Scotsman's* offices and said they'd done it as a protest against the exploitation of Scotland by the 'English' government in London. They call themselves Dorn nan Something-or-other, apparently it means the Fist of the Gaels."

"Dorn nan Gaidheal," Lorimer said. He had dabbled in Gaelic during his first year at university, and a little of it had stuck.

"It looks right up your street. You'd better fly up on the shuttle and hire a car in Glasgow. I imagine there's somewhere to stay on Iniscaig."

"There's the Islands Hotel."

"You know it?"

"I stayed there a couple of times when I was at university."

"All right. Find out what's going on and what the police are doing. Push, if you have to, Gray; I'm damned if I'll have a group of lunatics getting away with blowing up our people's houses."

They didn't sound like empty words, Lorimer thought. You got the feeling that they were a warning which it would be unwise to ignore. And it was typical of the Old Man to speak of the house as if Burton owned it; that it was United's property was irrelevant to him, it was the Burton family's home.

As one of Britain's largest companies, United possessed considerable power and influence. Normally that power was kept under wraps, rarely seen and never abused. Now Grantley was telling him to use it if necessary. It was an indication of the anger he felt. Lorimer reflected wryly that a year ago the chairman would have warned him not to tread on too many feet; perhaps that he hadn't done so now was an indication of something else.

"Robin Forsyth's a good man," Grantley remarked, changing the subject. "We're lucky to get him."

Lucky? Lorimer thought, surprised for the second time in three minutes. Not many men would turn down an invitation to become a director of United, and it wasn't like the Old Man to display such corporate modesty. He wasn't personally vain, but he had great pride in the group. Forsyth must be a more valuable acquisition than he had realised. After all, non-executive directors were appointed for their expertise or connections, and to supply a more objective view than the rest of the board, who were involved in the day-to-day running of their company, could have.

"He has a lot of connections in Scotland," Grantley went on. "He may be able to help with this business."

Lorimer thought he understood now why the chairman had introduced them and why he had told him to come this evening. He hadn't known about Burton's house being blown up, but he had wanted the two men to meet, perhaps for Forsyth to have a look at him. "I'll remember," he promised.

Grantley nodded. "I shouldn't hang around here any longer. I'll expect you back in two or three days."

Lorimer reflected that he had heard that before, and the forecast had proved wildly optimistic, but this time all he had to do was assess the position and see that the police were doing all they could. It shouldn't take very long.

Grantley went off to speak to the managing director of one of United's subsidiaries and Lorimer finished his drink. As he walked to the door he saw Philip Rayment watching him and frowning. Rayment probably thought he was sneaking away.

TWO

ACCORDING TO BURTON when he had come in to United House three months ago, Iniscaig was a hundred miles from nowhere, a sort of purgatory beyond the limits of civilisation. But to Burton anywhere more than a couple of miles from neon lights and a chippy was at the edge of the world. He was the sort of man who went to the Costa del Sol for his holidays in order to feel the sun on his back while he ate fish and chips and drank English beer.

It wasn't how Lorimer remembered the island. His memory was haunted by a vision of mountains rising steeply from a sandy beach, clear blue skies and seemingly endless evenings when you could read a newspaper out of doors until nearly midnight; of convivial nights in the bar of the Islands Hotel after hard days walking and climbing; and of quiet, hospitable people not given to bombast or exaggeration. Both times when he was there it had been June, of course. Also he had been only nineteen the first year, and he had never been to the islands before; you had to allow for that. Just as you had to allow for his being a little in love with the hotelkeeper's daughter. He couldn't even remember her name now. Moira something. Moira MacNeil, that was it. How innocent it seemed, looking back.

She had been a year or two younger than he was, with dark hair and dark eyes, colouring common enough in the Northwest. Some people said it was a legacy from the Spanish sailors the islanders had rescued from one of the Armada's ships which had gone aground and sunk off Iniscaig three hundred years ago. They must have had a high old time, those Spaniards. But more likely the islanders owed their colouring to their Celtic blood.

You couldn't blame Burton. He had only taken over last November, and it had been a hard winter this year; he might feel differently about the island now he had seen it in the summer.

There had been no factory on Iniscaig fourteen years ago, and the fishermen had had to take their catches to Mallaig or Kyle to sell them. When United established a salmon farm on Loch Damph, and built a processing plant and cannery there, it had brought badly needed employment to the area. Young people no longer had to go to the mainland for work, rarely to return, and new houses had been built, the first on Iniscaig for many years.

Standing on the deck of the Caledonian MacBrayne steamer from Oban as it passed the western tip of Liavaig, Lorimer watched the pale blue mountains coming nearer. Their jagged peaks stood out against the almost cloudless sky, and he was conscious of a sense of satisfaction that years ago he had climbed those peaks, that he had known them at close quarters and not only from a distance as most people did; you had no real feeling for the hills until you had explored their high slopes and seen what lay on the other side.

It was a long time now since he had done any climbing, not since the year he finished at university. Then he had gone off to the Sudan for a year, working for VSO at a remote valley in the South, and soon after he came back he had met Rosalind. Rosalind hadn't been interested in climbing. Now there was nothing to stop him taking it up again, but he knew he wouldn't. Climbing belonged to his youth. To innocence.

Far away to the north he could see the sawtooth outline of the Coulins on Skye, while astern loomed Liavaig's toxic waste processing plant with its administrative block, its incinerators and its tanks, the incinerators and tanks painted a dull grey, the colour of war. Lorimer wondered whether it was the plant's size and its inappropriateness to its setting, or a primitive subconscious fear, which made it seem not only out of place but vaguely menacing.

Its building had aroused bitter opposition from the conservationists and others; United had objected to its siting only three miles from its fish farm, foreseeing the possibility of pollution. But it had been overruled. Disposing of other countries' toxic waste was a profitable business for the companies involved and for Britain; the government, under pressure to allow a new plant to be built, had agreed to the site where there were fewest local people to complain.

Lorimer looked away. He could make out the village now, a string of white dots sheltered on the north and east by the mountains. There were more dots beyond them, crofts scattered across the level ground at the foot of Bheinn Fhada. Somewhere there was Burton's house—or what was left of it.

It was good to be coming back. Iniscaig must be one of the most peaceful spots on earth. Tranquillity clothed it like a halo. Violence had no place here, and it was the most unlikely setting imaginable for any sort of political demonstration. Unless it had changed since he was last here. You thought of such places as remaining the same for ever, but thirteen years was a long time, even in the Hebrides, and it was inevitable that the building of the cannery by Loch Damph and the plant on Liavaig had brought changes. Perhaps, too, he was looking back through rose-coloured spectacles, and Iniscaig had never been quite the paradise he had believed it to be.

The ship's bows turned a few points and Lorimer saw the pier jutting out from the shore. The old wooden huts were still there at the end of the street, but now there was a larger brick building beside them. A small pick-up truck was parked by one of the huts, and Lorimer could make out three men, one of them in a sailor's cap and guernsey, waiting on the jetty with two women for the ferry to come alongside. A gull swooped low over their heads, screeching, then soared away. The sound died and quiet settled again, almost tangible.

Slowly, without fuss, the ship eased alongside the pier, a ramp was lowered and two passengers went ashore, their feet clumping on the gangplank. Lorimer started the engine of his hired Maestro and followed them. As he passed, one of the crew was handing two parcels to the man in the guernsey. They spoke in Gaelic, their voices rising and falling musically.

Why had Dorn nan Gaidheal chosen this place to burn down a family's home? he thought bitterly. It didn't matter that he knew the reason, he felt personally outraged.

Along the narrow strip of turf which separated the road from the beach, a dozen chickens were pecking at the grass, their heads lifting and ducking in a purposeful rhythm. One of them stopped and looked up, regarding the Maestro with a beady eye before it resumed its pecking. Lorimer hesitated. He had arranged on the phone to meet Burton at the factory later; should he drive straight to the hotel and check in there, or go to see the damage to the Burtons' house first? But there was no hurry for that, and doubtless the manager would prefer to show him himself.

The Islands Hotel was halfway along the single row of houses which extended for two hundred yards beside the shore and constituted Iniscaig's only street. A whitewashed building, flat-fronted and slate-roofed, it differed from its neighbours on each side only in its size and the glass panels in its door. There was a name board over the door and AA and RAC plaques on the wall beside it. Lorimer wondered if Burton and his family were staying there, and hoped rather guiltily that they weren't. But where else could they find accommodation on Iniscaig at such short notice?

Parking the Maestro, he went inside. The lobby was deserted, but when he rang the bell a young woman came through a door from the back. Lorimer recognised her at once. She was no longer quite as slim as she had been all those years ago, but she was still as dark, her hair curling softly round her face, and her eyes had the same expression, slightly melancholy when nothing was amusing her. When it was, they lit up and sparkled. She wasn't beautiful, but something warmer and more comfortable.

Clearly she didn't remember him, and he felt a pang of disappointment he knew was ridiculous. For a woman, perhaps, it was different, but he didn't want to look twenty still.

"I'm Graham Lorimer," he told her. "I phoned and booked a room."

"Oh yes, Mr. Lorimer." Her voice hadn't changed either, it was soft, with the lilt of the islands in it.

"You're Moira MacNeil."

She had turned to reach for a key hanging from a peg on the board behind her. Now she looked round, surprised and puzzled. "I was," she said. "I'm Moira Cameron now. Were you staying here before?"

"Twice, a long time ago."

"I'm sorry, I should have remembered you." Moira's expression changed suddenly and her eyes brightened. "You're Gray!" she exclaimed. "Och, it never occurred to me when you phoned. Fancy you remembering my name."

"I've often thought about Iniscaig and wondered whether you were still here," Lorimer said.

"Oh yes, I'm still here." Moira laughed. "I expect I always will be."

She started leading the way up the stairs and Lorimer followed her.

"The first time we came it was my first year at university and I'd never been to the islands before," he said. "We spent a fortnight here, walking and climbing."

"I remember. There were five of you." Moira smiled. "Andy, George, you . . ." She stopped, unable to recall the others' names.

"Mike and Colin."

"That's right. Colin was the big one."

He had been six feet four and sixteen stone, a cheerful giant who worked and played rugger and golf with the same enthusiasm. Now he was dead, a captain in a Scottish regiment blown up by the IRA in his car in Northern Ireland. They had buried him in a village graveyard in Tweedale with full military honours, and Lorimer had gone to the funeral.

"Where is he now?" Moira asked.

"Dead. He died two years ago." Strange, Lorimer thought, it seemed much longer than that.

"Och, I'm sorry." Moira unlocked a door and opened it. "This is your room."

It was the one Lorimer had had before.

"I'd like to kill the bastards," Burton said. He was a brawny man with sandy hair and hard, pale blue eyes, and he looked as if he meant it. "If we'd been at home, the kids might have . . ." His voice tailed away as he thought of the possibility he couldn't bring himself to put into words.

"How many have you got?" Lorimer asked.

"Two girls, nine and six."

"Where are they now? And your wife?"

"They've stayed on with the people we'd gone to see in Oban. Ken Jarvis is Barbara's cousin."

"And you?"

"Steve Barnett, he's my number two, and his wife are putting me up for the time being. They insisted."

Lorimer was slightly ashamed of the relief he felt. But he and Burton had almost nothing in common except their sex and their working for United, and for the next day or two they would see enough of each other during working hours without being thrown together in the evenings. He silently blessed Barnett and his wife.

Burton had taken him to see the damage to the house. The manager seemed to have forgotten that it belonged to the company and that United had a direct interest in its destruction; he kept referring to it as "ours," and it was clear that he meant his and his wife's. The fire must have been intense; most of the roof had fallen in and little remained except the four walls, their whiteness stained by heat and smoke, and a heap of charred debris. No ordinary fire, even one started with paraffin or petrol, would have caused such devastation, Lorimer thought. The arsonists must have used some sort of incendiary device.

Now they were back at the side of the loch. He looked at the rows of pens moored by the shore. The only fish farm he had seen before consisted of a small pool formed by damming a stream in Essex and diverting some of the flow. The trout they raised had provided the owner and his wife with some sort of living until a farmer had allowed a drum of chemicals to leak into the river a mile upstream. That had been the end of the farm; somehow it hadn't seemed worth starting all over again for such meagre rewards.

This was no more like that venture than Everest was like Bheinn Fhada; there must be at least a score of those big pens, covering the best part of a couple of acres. The late-afternoon sun shining on the salmon's backs, cast a faint, iridescent glow across the surface of the water.

"How much do you know about what we do here?" Burton asked.

"Not much," Lorimer confessed.

"Meaning nothing."

"More or less."

"All right, a few years ago fish farming in Scotland was a bit of a joke, and nobody took it very seriously. Now Scottish farms produce all sorts of fish, salmon, trout, oysters, mussels, you name it. This year the turn-over will be around £100 million."

Lorimer was impressed, he hadn't realised that it was such big business. But United wouldn't be in it if it wasn't.

"There are hundreds of farms," Burton went on. "We're one of the biggest. If we sold the salmon we produce straight on, they'd bring in getting on for £20 million. But we don't, we smoke a lot here, and we do our own canning. And it's not just salmon, we handle trout and shellfish too. We used to buy in the oysters and mussels, now we've started producing our own. The scampi come from local fishermen.

"We produce most of our own smolts in fresh water at the other end of the island, there's a good stream there, and buy the rest from small farmers who specialise in them. They're raised in those pens and fed on dry pelleted feeds until they're big enough. Some farms use tanks on land and pump sea water into them. We're developing our own wet feeds and fish silage, but so far they're still in the experimental stage."

"How long do they take to grow big enough?" Lorimer enquired.

"Twelve to twenty-four months." Burton paused. "Counting everybody here and up at Glen Morlaigh, we employ just over a hundred and sixty people. More women than men."

Lorimer nodded. That was one of the facts he had checked during the flight to Glasgow; he couldn't overlook the possibility that one of those one hundred and sixty had started the fire.

"Come back to the office," Burton said.

The manager's room was light and airy. Through the window behind him Lorimer could see the sun shining on the sea, a broad shimmering silver band across the deep blue-green water, and the shore of Liavaig three miles away. There were no mountains on Liavaig, nothing to soften or diminish the ugliness of the waste disposal plant. If Dorn nan Gaidheal had campaigned against that instead of burning down an innocent family's home, they might have gained a sort of credibility. But they hadn't.

"Do you know anything about the Fist of the Gaels?" he asked.

"All I want to," Burton replied bitterly.

"I can believe that." Lorimer suppressed a little spurt of impatience; Burton had suffered a pretty traumatic experience. "But had you heard anything about them before?"

He would ask other people, a lot of them, and maybe Moira or her father would be able to tell him something, although he doubted it; it was hardly likely that the group was based on Iniscaig. Perhaps the police knew something. Grantley had told him to push if he had to, and he wondered how ready they would be to talk. After all, there was no reason why they should put up the shutters.

"I'd never heard their bloody name until this," Burton said violently. "They're like those nuts who burn down houses in Wales, they don't want anybody here but the bloody Scotch. We're exploiting them, they say. Christ! This damned island was dying on its feet before we came here. All they had were a couple of fishing boats and a few cows and sheep. We've brought jobs. And money. The people who live here know that, you don't find them complaining."

"So where do they come from?"

"God knows. Edinburgh or Glasgow, most likely." Burton shifted in his chair as if he were having difficulty in restraining the bitter fury which had built up inside him like a head of steam in a boiler. "They'll kill somebody before long."

They hadn't this time, Lorimer thought. Was it luck that the Burtons were away when their house was fired, or had the arsonists known it would be empty? Because if they had, they must have somebody on the island. Maybe even here in the factory.

"How have people here reacted?" he asked.

"Okay. They're a good crowd, and it's shaken them."

"There's no one you know has got a grudge against you or the company? You haven't sacked anybody, or given them a rough time?"

Burton frowned, and he didn't answer at once. "No," he said after a few seconds. "You mean, it may have been somebody here and not the Fist of the Gaels?"

"Or the Fist is a one-man band, and it's here on Iniscaig."

"There's nobody."

Lorimer was fairly sure that the manager was lying, but he let it go. "Who knew you were going away for the weekend?" he asked.

"I don't know. Lots of people, I suppose; there wasn't any secret about it."

"Try to think."

"Well, Steve knew—it meant him being on call—and one or two of the others here. I said, it wasn't a secret. Barbara may have mentioned it when she went shopping or something."

Half the island had probably known, Lorimer told himself. Burton was an important man on Iniscaig, which meant that his movements were of more general interest than they would have been in a larger place. Also the family must have been seen boarding the ferry on Friday.

"When you hear about things like this happening you don't understand what it means," Burton went on. He seemed to be looking into himself, a normally inarticulate man trying to find words to express what he felt. "You saw what it's like, there's damn all left: just four walls and some rafters. No furniture, nothing. Nothing of ours. We hadn't anything valuable, but a lot of the things that have gone we'd had since we were married. Before then, some of them; there was a chair that belonged to Barbara's grandfather. And the kids' things. It's like part of your life being rubbed out. For nothing. That really gets me: it was all done for nothing."

Lorimer nodded. All the same, he doubted whether Burton would have felt any differently if the arsonists had achieved something worthwhile. And perhaps to them it hadn't been for nothing. You couldn't tell with fanatics, sometimes all they wanted was publicity for their "cause."

"I'll be seeing the police," he said.

"They won't be able to tell you anything."

"Maybe not, but I have to talk to them. Who's in charge?"

"Don't ask me. There was a constable came over from Liavaig, Macdonald or something, then an Inspector Wallace from Fort William."

There didn't seem to be anything more Burton could or would tell him now, and Lorimer stood up. "Right," he said, "if it's okay with you, I'd like to have a look round and talk to some of the other people here."

Burton got up from his chair. "I don't mind. I'll show you," he offered.

"There's no need for you to bother," Lorimer told him. "You've enough to do without me taking up any more of your time."

The manager shrugged. He knew Lorimer wanted to talk to people without his being there; it didn't bother him. "You'll find Sid Benstead in the office at the end of the corridor," he said. "He's our production manager, he'll look after you."

"Thanks," Lorimer said. "See you tomorrow then."

He walked out of Burton's room and down the bare, featureless corridor, past a row of doors, each with its label, towards the one at the end marked "PRODUCTION—NO UNAUTHORISED ENTRY." The manager was a bit of a rough diamond, able but intolerant, and not in the habit of mincing his words. He probably prided himself on not suffering fools gladly. It wasn't difficult to imagine his getting people's backs up; was it possible that he had aroused such hatred in somebody on the island that they had revenged themselves by burning down his home? Certainly he had been hiding something when he said there wasn't anybody who could have a grudge against him.

Burton wasn't a Highlander, he wasn't even a Scot, he was an outsider with little patience for or understanding of other traditions and ways of life. To Englishmen like him, Scotland wasn't a country but a few counties tacked on to the north of England, its separateness acknowledged only for the purpose of football matches and abuse. Such people, decent enough according to their own lights but insensitive and lacking the imagination to put themselves in others' places, existed in every nation. The trouble was they always seemed to fill the positions of power. And they were responsible for half the troubles of the world.

Burton had rung through to let Benstead know that Lorimer was coming. The production manager was waiting for him, kitted out in a white coat, a white peaked cap and rubber boots, asked if he wanted him to accompany him and, when Lorimer told him he would be all right on his own, left him to it.

By the time Lorimer drove back to the hotel he was inclined to agree with Burton that the staff at the factory were as shocked and puzzled by the fire as he was. And no one had admitted having heard of the Fist of the Gaels before.

It was too early in the year for the holiday season to have started, and the only other people staying at the hotel were two middle-aged Englishwomen. Keen hill-walkers, they came clattering into the lobby in their boots, rucksacks on their backs, as Lorimer was coming down the stairs. They smiled cheerily and went on up to their rooms.

Lorimer entered the bar and Moira Cameron came through from the kitchen to serve him. He asked her for a pint of heavy and watched her pour it, her left hand resting on the tap, the other holding the glass. He remembered her like that thirteen years ago, talking and laughing with the five of them, yet always with a hint of shyness underlying her gaiety. Naturally she was more mature now, and perhaps the suggestion of melancholy was clearer in her eyes, but it was surprising how little she had changed; she must be thirty-one or -two, yet she looked no more than twenty-five. Perhaps that was why the time since he had last seen her seemed to have shrunk, so that instead of someone he had known only casually many years ago, she had become a friend he hadn't seen recently. That and the way he had remembered her all this time.

"Does your husband work on the island?" he asked her.

Her head was lowered, her eyes on the beer climbing the sides of the glass, and she didn't answer immediately. When the glass was full she turned off the tap and pushed the glass across the counter to him. Lorimer handed her a pound note. Her back half turned to him as she put it in the till and sorted out his change, she said, "Duncan died last year."

"Oh." It had been a perfectly natural question, and there was no way he could have known, but still Lorimer felt awkward. "I'm sorry," he said.

For a minute or two neither of them spoke and the silence hung in the air, almost tangible.

"There was a fire on the island the other day," Lorimer remarked, to break the quiet.

"Yes."

"Had you heard of the Fist of the Gaels before?"

"No."

Moira was very still, looking not at him but out of the window beside him, so that her eyes were focussed beyond his right shoulder. Perhaps she was thinking about her husband, Lorimer thought. He sipped his beer.

"Do you know the Burtons?"

She looked at him then, as if surprised that he should know the manager's name and that it was his house which had been burnt down. "Not very well. I see Barbara in the village sometimes, and the girls. I don't see him."

That was odd. Burton liked his pint, and there wasn't another bar on Iniscaig; Lorimer had taken it for granted that he came here most evenings. He had a feeling that for some reason Moira didn't want to talk about the Burtons or the fire.

But the next moment she looked at him directly and asked, "Are you thinking that maybe somebody on Iniscaig burnt down their house?"

"No. Do you think it's possible?"

"I do not. There's nobody here would do such a thing, whatever they thought about Mr. Burton." Moira flushed.

"People don't like him?"

"There are some who don't." After a moment she added, "We never thought anything like that could happen here."

Who would have done? Lorimer thought. He remembered the sense of shock he had felt when the Old Man told him.

"Are you a policeman?"

He laughed; it hadn't occurred to him that she might think that. "No,

I'm not." Some instinct, or perhaps the way she had spoken about Burton, warned him not to tell her that he worked for United. "Why?"
"Nothing." Moira smiled uncertainly. "Are you married?"
"We're separated."
"Oh."
There was another silence, this time neither awkward nor so long, but rather it was as though they were sharing thoughts of what might have been and now never would. It was broken when the two English-women entered the bar.
"Isn't it a glorious day?" the taller of them said, beaming happily. "There's still a lot of snow on the tops and the sun was shining on it; it was so beautiful. We've walked miles and miles, haven't we, Mary? Now we'd like two lagers and lime, please."
Moira poured their drinks and they carried them over to a table by the window.
"I must help with dinner," she told Lorimer. "Will you ring the bell if you want anything?"
She went out, leaving him wondering why she had prevaricated, if not actually lied, about knowing Burton, and why she disliked him so much.

THREE

DETECTIVE INSPECTOR GORDON WALLACE was forty-one years old, five feet nine tall, and lean. He was also, Lorimer decided after he had been in his company for two minutes, dour. His face seemed to be composed of a set of almost flat planes in which his eyes were sunk and from which his nose protruded above an ungenerous mouth. He wasn't a mean man, and it was his misfortune that he looked one.
Lorimer thought wryly that Grantley hadn't seen Wallace when he told him to push if he had to; he suspected that trying to put pressure on the inspector would be about as productive as trying to push over Ben Nevis. He saw the other man watching him and realised that he had been smiling.

"I just remembered something my boss told me," he explained.
Wallace said nothing.

Outside, rain driven by a force-six wind lashed the town, whipping the waters of Loch Linnhe into restless waves and stinging the faces of the few people braving the weather in the streets. Across the loch the hills of Ardgour were hidden in a leaden mist. It was hard to believe that yesterday had been fine; but in a few hours, Lorimer knew, it might well be warm and sunny again. Who was it that first said the Highlands had the best climate in the world and the worst weather? It wasn't merely the weather; the whole climate could change from hour to hour up here.

The inspector had listened while he talked, his non-committal manner giving away nothing of what he was thinking. But although he hadn't erected a screen of official secrecy and refused any comment, Lorimer didn't delude himself: Wallace would tell him just as much as it suited him to do. He was sitting silently now, waiting for Lorimer to continue.

"These people, the Fist of the Gaels, do you know anything about them?" he asked.

"No."

"Nobody seems to."

"You think that's surprising?" Wallace's tone hadn't changed, but Lorimer sensed the coolness of the professional for the outsider. "They may be a new group, just three or four people maybe. Or it could be a new name for an old one."

"Or it may not exist at all."

"That is a possibility." The inspector's expression was, if anything, more inscrutable than ever.

"You didn't find any evidence that the fire was started by somebody at the factory?"

"We did not. Have you any reason for thinking it might have been?"

"No. It seemed to me it was a possibility. Have you any leads?"

"We're following up certain lines of enquiry."

The other man's reserve was beginning to irritate Lorimer. "If the Burtons hadn't been away, somebody might have been killed," he said. "There'd have been two wee girls in that house."

"We're not forgetting that, Mr. Lorimer." The inspector's tone might be flat, his disapproval was clear. "Will you be staying up here long?"

Plainly, as far as he was concerned, the sooner Lorimer returned to London the better. Wallace was no fool, he knew that he had been sent here to see how the land lay, and to put a bomb under the local police if it seemed necessary. It didn't make him like it.

"A day or two," Lorimer replied.

As if he had come to a decision, the inspector leaned forward in his chair. "You don't have to tell us that we could have had four murders on our hands," he said. "What happened on Saturday night was a serious crime, and we're treating it seriously. Your man Burton may not be exactly popular on Iniscaig, he's a mite too impatient for that, but I doubt there's anybody on the island dislikes him enough to blow up his house. We're not talking about a lad with a box of matches and a can of petrol just now, the fire was started with some sort of incendiary device, and there aren't that number of people on the island could make it, or know where to get hold of one. It's very likely these people came from Edinburgh or Glasgow. As I said, we're following up some lines, but they'll take time." For Wallace it was a long speech.

"And in the meantime you don't want me getting in your hair," Lorimer said.

The inspector regarded him without smiling. "That's not how I would be putting it," he said. He stood up. "Good-bye just now, Mr. Lorimer."

"Good-bye," Lorimer said.

He walked back along the nearly deserted street to his car. The wind tore at his hair and rain stung his cheeks. His mother used to say that God had given the Highlands so much beauty that He had given them the rain and mists too, so that the Highlanders should not become too proud. Days like this made him think there might be something in that.

He hadn't much to report to Grantley. The manager's house was a ruin, no one had heard of the Fist of the Gaels before the fire and the police appeared to be satisfied that nobody at the factory or on the island had started it. At least the police weren't dragging their feet; Wallace hadn't said so, but Lorimer suspected that the anti-terrorist people in Edinburgh were involved. Possibly they had taken over the case, and he was only the dog's-body on the spot. Lorimer wondered if any of the men he knew on the Anti-Terrorist Squad at Scotland Yard were involved: it might be helpful to have a contact. But there was no way of telling.

He should finish on Iniscaig tomorrow. He would have liked to stay longer, to revisit some of the places he remembered from thirteen years ago, but once he had talked to a few more people there would be no justification for his remaining. Perhaps one day he would return, he thought. But in his heart he knew that it was unlikely; Iniscaig wasn't a place to visit alone.

There was another reason why he would have liked to stay a little longer: Moira Cameron. She was more than just an attractive young woman; she had warmth and sparkle, yet at the same time a quality of calm. No wonder he had been in love with her when he was twenty.

He reached the Maestro and, climbing into the driving seat, he started the engine and drove through the rain to the ferry.

By the time the ship reached Iniscaig the sun was shining from an almost cloudless sky. Lorimer parked on the grass and crossed the road to the hotel. Moira was coming down the stairs.

"Are you doing anything this afternoon?" he asked her.

"Nothing in particular," she answered. "Why?"

"I want to have a look at the north side of Bheinn Beag while I'm here, and I thought maybe . . ."

"I'd like that," Moira smiled, and her whole face seemed to light up. "Good."

Lorimer went up to his room feeling more cheerful than he had all day.

When he came down again Alan MacNeil, Moira's father, was behind the bar. It was the first time the two men had met since he arrived yesterday.

"Moira was telling me you were here before," MacNeil remarked, pouring Lorimer's beer. "And now you're back because of the fire at the Burtons' house."

Lorimer reflected that he hadn't told Moira that; either she or her father had assumed it.

"That was a bad business. A very bad business indeed." MacNeil frowned. He was a stocky, grizzled man who looked more like a crofter or a fisherman than a hotelier. "We've never had anything like that on Iniscaig before. These lunatics with their bombs, they'll not be doing their cause any good at all."

"No," Lorimer said. As far as he was concerned, that was all to the good. He paid for his beer and drank some of it. "Moira hasn't changed much."

"No, I don't think she has," her father agreed. "Poor lassie, she's not had an easy time of it these last few months."

"Losing her husband," Lorimer said.

"Ay. Duncan was a good lad. He worked at the factory, did she tell you that? He was killed in an accident there last winter."

"I didn't know."

"Och well, it wasn't anything they would be telling you about down in London. But they had only been married a year."

"What happened?"

"There's a young lad works at the factory. Jamie's not very bright. It makes him a wee bit slow, but he's a good boy and he's willing, and people make allowances. He was in the despatch shed, stacking some of those big boxes of tins with a forklift truck. Mr. Burton came along and saw him. He was in a bad mood; he told Jamie to get a move on and not take all day doing it. The laddie was worried, and he started hurrying. He didn't stack the boxes properly, and a pile of them collapsed. Duncan was working there too. He was bending over, and one of them hit him." Alan MacNeil paused. "Those boxes are very heavy; it broke his neck."

Poor Moira, Lorimer thought.

"It wasn't Mr. Burton's fault," MacNeil went on. There was a curiously defensive note in his voice, as if he were protecting the manager. "He was as upset as anybody."

But Moira blamed him. So much was clear from what her father had said and from her manner last night. It didn't make any difference that Burton couldn't have foreseen what would happen when he spoke to the boy, nor that he had been appalled by the consequences—all Moira could see was that if Burton hadn't told Jamie to work faster, her husband would still be alive.

"I'm sorry," Lorimer said.

It was hot on the beach, and Lorimer could feel the warmth of the sand on his back through his thin shirt. Yesterday he had wondered if there was any point in bringing his car over to the island when he could easily walk anywhere he was likely to want to go; today he was glad he had. Moira and he had driven the twelve miles to the northern tip of Iniscaig, stopping on the way to walk a short distance up one of the lower slopes of Bheinn Beag. Now they were lying in the sun, relaxed.

"It was pouring with rain and blowing half a gale in Fort William this morning," he remarked.

"Och, it always rains in Fort William." Moira dismissed that town's weather. "You went there?"

"Yes." Lorimer didn't want to talk about the reason for his going. "It's great here," he said. "I wish I didn't have to go back to London tomorrow."

"You're going so soon?" Moira asked, surprised.

Lorimer wondered if he had imagined the note of disappointment in her voice, and hoped he hadn't. "There's nothing more for me to do here," he said. Then, feeling as awkward as he had done when she told him her husband was dead, he added, "Your father told me about your husband. I'm sorry."

"He said he had."

"You miss him very much, don't you?"

Moira nodded, keeping her head averted so that Lorimer wouldn't see that she was biting her lip. From anyone else the question might have seemed intrusive, but somehow coming from him it didn't. Was that because he was nearly a stranger? she wondered. Hardly, because he didn't seem like a stranger, more like an old friend she hadn't seen for a long time.

For a little while neither of them spoke, then Lorimer said, "I've often thought about those holidays here."

"They were a long time ago."

"I know." It was true, of course, but why did women always have to point out the truth you were trying to ignore?

Moira was wearing a white sleeveless blouse and a full skirt with a pattern of red and blue flowers. She had kicked off her flat white sandals and she looked very young lying there stretched out on the sand. Lorimer wondered what she would do if he touched her, put an arm round her or ran a forefinger down the inside of her arm. Kissed her. He thrust the thought away.

"Have you ever thought of leaving here?" he asked.

"I've thought about it," Moira said. "I might have gone once, then Duncan and I got engaged. Now my father and mother need me, and I suppose I'll stay. I don't mind, I'm happy here. Are you happy in London, Gray?" She turned on to her side to look at him.

"Most of the time."

"What do you do? Why are you here?"

Lorimer hesitated. It was the question he had been dreading. Because he suspected that once Moira knew, her attitude towards him would change, and he didn't want that to happen. "I work for United," he answered. "They sent me up here to find out what I could about the fire."

"Oh," Moira said flatly. The single syllable was charged with disappointment and disillusion.

"It was the company's house they burnt down," Lorimer pointed out.

"Yes." Moira sat up and straightened her blouse. "I must go back, I have to help Mother get things ready for dinner."

Hell! Lorimer thought. It still wasn't quite four o'clock, she didn't have to get back yet. He fought down an impulse to put his arms round her and hold her there by force. He knew that even trying to persuade her to stay would be useless, that helping her mother had been only an excuse for getting away from him. What was wrong with his working for United?

He watched helplessly as she got to her feet and stood brushing the sand off her clothes.

They walked across the beach to the car in silence.

"You blame us for what happened to your husband, don't you?" he ventured as they drove along the narrow road back to the village.

"Is there any reason why I shouldn't? Mr. Burton's your manager, if he hadn't spoken to Jamie like he did . . ." Moira stopped, defying the tears she could feel pricking her eyes to fall.

"He couldn't know," Lorimer said.

"He should have known, he knew what Jamie was like. Och, he's a bully, that man. I hate him. He shouldn't have let a boy like Jamie drive that truck, and he should have made sure nobody else was working there. He didn't care, all he thought about was getting the work done as quickly as possible."

Lorimer knew it would be pointless arguing with her.

When they reached the hotel Moira said stiffly, "Thank you for this afternoon, Gray. I enjoyed it." Getting out of the car, she walked quickly indoors.

Lorimer followed her.

That evening Alan MacNeil looked after the bar and, except for one fleeting glimpse through an open door, Lorimer didn't see Moira again before he went up to bed. He was pretty sure that she was deliberately avoiding him.

However, the next morning when he went to pay his bill she was behind the desk in the lobby looking tired and strained, as if she hadn't slept well. She said good-bye awkwardly, and Lorimer returned to London telling himself it was unlikely they would see each other again. He was surprised how much he minded.

Over the next three weeks he phoned Wallace twice. The inspector told him that the police believed Dorn nan Gaidheal was a new group, very small and probably based in Edinburgh. If they knew any more, Wallace wasn't saying.

. . .

It was part of Lorimer's job to go through the papers every day, looking for anything which might mean trouble for United. On the Wednesday morning a month after his return from Iniscaig, he picked up the tabloid on top of the pile that Dobbs, one of the commissionaires, had put ready on his desk.

"TOXIC WASTE LEAK. FISH SUPPLIES THREATENED." The headline spread across most of the page.

There wasn't much under it; the paper didn't believe in lengthy reports. Lorimer read what there was, put the paper aside and picked up the next one. The longest report was the *Times'*: fishermen on the Hebridean islands of Iniscaig and Liavaig were complaining that numbers of dead fish were appearing in their nets and being washed up on the shore. Their catches were already declining, and soon they might be almost entirely wiped out. They blamed the toxic waste processing plant on Liavaig. The plant's director admitted that there had been a leak from one of the tanks on Sunday night, but the material which had escaped was of very low toxicity and the amount involved small. This was the first such "accident" in its history, and the plant believed that it was the result of deliberate sabotage. The leak had already been traced and sealed, and there was no possibility of any danger to humans; the company's safety precautions were as good as any in the world.

Lorimer told himself that he had heard that before, if not about Liavaig. And how much was small? There must have been a pretty substantial leak for fish to be affected.

These days everybody shouted "Sabotage!" after a major accident. It was a popular scapegoat because it put the blame on some sinister, shadowy group, and people preferred to believe in conspiracies rather than in the fallibility of machinery on which they relied and the consequences of which they couldn't avoid. Then, if human or mechanical failure was responsible, by the time it was admitted the worst shock was over.

Whatever the cause of the pollution off Liavaig, United could be in trouble. Serious trouble. Burton had said that the factory on Iniscaig took most of its supplies of scampi from the local boats; if their catches were contaminated, heaven only knew what the outcome might be. Moreover the waste plant was only three miles from the fish farm on Loch Damph; could the currents carry the effluent there?

Lorimer asked the girl on the switchboard to get him Burton.

The manager was harassed and short-tempered, and sounded it. The last thing he needed was bloody fools from head office phoning him when he was up to his neck trying to deal with a problem he couldn't see or hear and which no one knew how to handle.

"What's all this about dead fish?" Lorimer asked. "How serious is it?"

"Christ, what do you think?" Burton's tone suggested that his blood pressure was rising again. "It's as bloody serious as it can be; if the currents bring the muck this way, we'll be lucky if we don't lose the lot."

"That's what I thought," Lorimer said.

"As it is, we're going to have to buy fish from Mallaig or the east coast ports, but God knows where we'd get any salmon. There'd be the hell of a shortage, and don't ask me what'd happen to prices." Burton paused, and when he continued it was more quietly. "It isn't only the shortage, it's the contamination. They didn't find the leak until Monday night and waste kept pouring into the tank and out into the sea. When they did find it they shut off the tank and hoped the tides would disperse the effluent and nobody would notice anything wrong. We don't know yet how bad the pollution is, but if it's affected the local catches over the last two days, we're in it up to our necks. Who's going to buy canned fish from here, even if it is as pure as your Aunt Fanny? Or anything else, for that matter? We don't know what we can use and what we can't. Sid Benstead's going up the wall."

Lorimer reflected that it was hard to picture Benstead, a cool, thin, bespectacled Yorkshireman, going up any wall, unless it was to paint it, but he could understand his problem. "Was it sabotage?" he asked.

"It looks like it."

"If it was a bomb, why didn't anybody hear it?"

"The tank's right on the shore, it was probably underwater. And the place is so automated there's practically nobody there at night. Anyway, it wouldn't have taken much explosive to blow a hole in the bottom."

So for nearly twenty-four hours effluent had poured straight into the sea, Lorimer thought, and, instead of dispersing it, the tides had carried it well out from the shore. Thousands of gallons of toxic waste.

"How long have you known?" he asked.

"Since yesterday. It's bedlam up here. The press, TV, the ministry, the ecology lot, they're all here. We're like bloody Canute, standing on the beach telling the stuff to go away. The DAFS people are talking about putting a boom across the entrance to the loch." The DAFS was the Department of Agriculture and Fisheries for Scotland.

Lorimer refrained from asking why he hadn't reported the trouble; Burton had enough problems on his hands already. He had a sudden vision of Grantley's reaction if he was confronted with a report that the manager of United's cannery had described the situation as "bloody serious" and said that the factory might have to close down. The press and television people and the whole conservation lobby could be relied on to inflate what might with luck turn out to be a fairly minor problem after all into a major disaster without any help from Burton. The cannery's output already in shops and warehouses, not only in Britain but all over the world, would be suspect, even if it had been despatched days before the leak occurred, and there would be pressure for the factory and everything connected with it to be closed, temporarily at least. Apart from anything else, a hundred and sixty people would be out of work in an area where every job was needed.

"Don't let anybody talk to the press or television," he said warningly.

"What sort of fool do you think I am?" the manager demanded.

"Sorry," Lorimer apologised. "I'll probably be coming up."

There was a moment's silence. Then, "I'm sending a report today," Burton said. He didn't sound overjoyed at the prospect of Lorimer's visit; he had enough on his plate already without people from head office getting in the way and telling him what he should do, and perhaps he hoped that making a report would stop him coming.

Lorimer grinned. He knew what Burton was thinking; in the manager's place he would have felt the same. "I'll keep out of your hair," he promised. " 'Bye."

He made another call, to the headquarters of the Friends of the Earth to hear what they had to say. It sounded good sense, but it didn't amount to much more than he already knew, and, picking up the pile of papers, he went across the landing to see Grantley.

The chairman was in his favourite position looking out of one of the two big windows in his room. He liked to stand there when he wanted to think; United House was several storeys higher than the neighbouring buildings, and he could see over them to the tower blocks in the City in one direction and southwards in the other. When his p.a. walked in he turned.

"What have you got there?" he enquired mildly, eyeing the bundle of newsprint.

"A problem," Lorimer replied. "It could be serious."

Grantley sat down at his desk and waved his assistant to a chair. "What is it?"

Lorimer explained.

The chairman listened without interrupting him. When Lorimer had finished, he swore quietly. "You think it was sabotage?" he asked.

"That it may have been," Lorimer agreed.

"Your Fist of the Gaels lot again? Anyway it's a mess." Grantley's expression was grim. "Why haven't we heard anything from Burton?"

"He's pretty busy dealing with things. He's sending a report today."

Grantley looked as if he considered those inadequate reasons. "You want to go up there again?" he asked.

"I thought maybe I should take a look."

"All right, Gray, do anything you think's necessary."

Lorimer hesitated. Before becoming the chairman of United Grantley had spent some time as a government advisor, and he still had contacts in very high places in Whitehall and at Westminster; it was an open secret that the prime minister sometimes sought his advice. It wouldn't be the first time that Lorimer had asked him to use his influence to obtain information, and he knew the chairman had no compunction about doing so if the reason was compelling enough. Grantley held the view that ministers and civil servants were there for the benefit of the rest of the population, not the other way round. It wasn't an attitude which endeared him to government departments, but that had never worried him. All the same, Lorimer was reluctant to ask him to use his influence now.

Grantley saw his hesitation. "What is it?" he demanded.

"I was wondering if you could find out what the word is in the ministry," Lorimer explained. "They won't want us publicly closing down a factory because of a leak at a toxic waste plant they pushed through and swore was a hundred percent safe."

The chairman eyed him thoughtfully. "There are times when you're disgustingly like a politician," he observed. "Very well, I'll see what I can do. But I doubt if it'll be much, they'll be anticipating a lot of awkward questions today—and that means they'll be pulling up the drawbridge and repelling all attackers." He picked up his diary and looked at that day's entries. "I might manage lunch. Get Helen to come in—and she can see about your tickets. Are you going to stay at the same place?"

"If I can get in," Lorimer answered. "According to Burton they've half the media as well as the conservation people and the ministry up there." He saw no need to tell the Old Man that he had his own reasons for being glad of an excuse for going back, and that even if there had been anywhere else on Iniscaig, he would still have stayed at the Islands Hotel if they had a room.

By the time he left United House that evening he knew that Whitehall was being even more reticent than usual and that Opposition MP's had requested an emergency debate on the pollution. Predictably, their request had been turned down. The Friends of the Earth, Greenpeace and the Nature Party were all demanding that the minister come clean and make a statement about what had really happened. So far he had said nothing.

There were reports and interviews with spokesmen for the waste disposal industry and the conservation groups on all the news broadcasts that evening. The man from the waste industry would only repeat that the material which had escaped into the sea posed no threat to humans; the fish had died, not because they were poisoned, but because they were starved of oxygen. Britain led the world in the disposal of toxic waste, and the industry's safety record was second to none, but if the accident had been the result of sabotage, as he understood it very probably had, nobody could guard one hundred percent against that. He sounded as if he wanted to think there were people going round with bombs, Lorimer thought.

The ecology interests and some members of parliament were not placated; they demanded that the plant be closed down at once, that no more toxic waste be imported from abroad and that new, stringent laws covering the disposal of Britain's own waste be pushed through without delay.

Lorimer half watched the Channel Four News while he grilled himself some lamb chops and cooked some new potatoes. Now that he was on his own, unless he was going out with friends, he generally got himself some sort of meal in the evenings. His cooking skills were limited, but he disliked eating out alone too often. Apart from the expense it seemed to him that there was something slightly pathetic about people eating alone in public when they weren't away from home. He suspected that it was illogical and most likely old-fashioned, but it made no difference.

Soon after the news ended Rosalind rang. Lorimer's wife didn't phone very often, and as usual when he heard her voice he felt a stirring of pleasure that was too near excitement for his peace of mind.

"You've heard about the leak at Liavaig?" she asked.

Lorimer admitted that he had.

"Isn't that near that place you were always talking about, Iniscaig?"

Rosalind was a production assistant on Barbican Television's "Mirror on the Week" programme, and Lorimer didn't delude himself that she was calling for the pleasure of talking to him; she was after information. When it came to her work, Rosalind was professional—and tough. Her ringing this evening probably meant that her boss was considering making a programme on the dangers inherent in handling toxic waste. Mark Preston's much vaunted inspiration must be running short; usually he was more original.

"I wasn't always talking about it," Lorimer objected.

"You were, *ad nauseam.*"

"All right, it's near."

"I thought it was." Rosalind sounded infuriatingly complacent. "And United's got a cannery or something there."

"Something."

"You must be worried."

"Why?"

"All that pollution. The fish. You'll have to close your plant."

"Why? The pollution's miles from the fish farm."

"Really?" Rosalind said innocently. "My map must be out of date. Did you know a group's claimed they blew a hole in one of the tanks at the waste plant?"

Oh God! Lorimer thought. "What do they call themselves?" he asked. But he didn't need Rosalind to tell him, he already knew.

"The Fist of the Gaels," she answered.

Lorimer said nothing. It looked as if the burning down of Burton's house hadn't been a personal attack on him, or even on United, but what it was claimed to be: a gesture. Wallace had said that the Fist of the Gaels existed, and Rosalind's news seemed to confirm it. Amidst all his other fears, he was surprised how relieved he felt about that: nobody on Iniscaig had burnt down the house as an act of revenge. Nobody? There was only one person he was interested in.

Dorn nan Gaidheal, however crack-brained and dangerous they were, would hardly have gone to the lengths of damaging a tank at the waste plant merely to contaminate the supply of fish to United's factory. Apart from anything else, it would have been too uncertain. They were fanatics, and they didn't care if innocent people suffered so long as they could make their point in the most public, dramatic way open to them. It didn't even matter that the people who suffered most were Highlanders. Extremists never cared too much if the people whose rights they were supposed to be defending ended up the biggest losers.

"Gray?" Rosalind said. "Are you still there?"

"Yes," Lorimer said.

"Have you heard of them before?"

"They burnt down our manager's house on Iniscaig last month. Did they say why they blew up the tank?"

"The usual stuff, as a protest against exploitation of Scotland by the English."

"They're round the twist," Lorimer said. "I'm going up there tomorrow."

"How long will you be gone?"

"I don't know. Only a day or two. Why?"

"I thought we might have dinner together when you get back."

"So that you can pick my brains and find out what I've learnt." Lorimer grinned. "Tell Mark United pay me, not Barbican."

"It's a shame you're turning into a cynic," Rosalind told him, managing to sound hurt. "We haven't seen each other for ages."

"Okay, I'll ring you when I get back," Lorimer promised. " 'Bye."

" 'Bye, love," Rosalind said. "Take care."

Lorimer replaced the phone and stood staring at it. Why, after all this time, should Rosalind's phoning and calling him "love" affect him like this? It meant no more than a bus conductor's calling an elderly passenger "love." They both knew that everything between them was over, and it was useless his trying to delude himself that it wasn't. Regrets were not only painful, they were pointless.

Oh hell! he thought.

FOUR

IT WAS OVERCAST, and a cool wind sent scuds of rain pattering against the ferry's superstructure. They stung Lorimer's face. To port was the open sea, with nothing between him and North America; to starboard Liavaig and the toxic waste plant.

A month ago when he arrived there had been no other vessels in sight. Now a fishery protection ship was anchored half a mile offshore, and farther in several small boats were bobbing up and down on the choppy water. As Lorimer watched, a helicopter flew low overhead.

The ferry turned towards the land and he saw a DAFS van, several cars and a large caravan parked at the end of the row of huts. There were three smaller caravans on a patch of waste ground fifty yards away; temporary accommodation for the men drafted in by the ministry, Lorimer supposed. A group was standing on the beach, staring out at the sea, while three more men were on the pier, waiting for the ferry to come alongside. It might not be Victoria in the rush hour, but it was more activity than he had ever seen on Iniscaig before.

No other passengers disembarked, and he drove straight to the hotel. The lobby was deserted, but when he rang the bell Moira came through from the back. All the way there he had hoped that by now she would have realised that she couldn't blame him for her husband's death, and things would be as they had been between them. Perhaps she had; she seemed embarrassed by his being there.

"Hallo, Gray," she said quietly. "I thought you might come back." Her tone betrayed neither pleasure nor disappointment.

"It's a mess," Lorimer said.

"Yes." Moira handed him a key. "You have the same room."

"I didn't expect you'd have one. I thought you'd be full with reporters and ministry people."

"We have been. Half the houses in the village have had people staying, but most of the reporters and the television people went yesterday. There's not much to interest them here any more."

Lorimer supposed that for them the story was already cold; nothing, they said, was as dead as yesterday's news. He carried his case up the stairs. Without the sun shining in, the room looked smaller and more drab, the furniture old-fashioned and slightly shabby. He unpacked the few spare clothes he had brought with him, washed and decided he had better see Burton first.

The little group, reduced now to three, was still on the beach, and as he drove past two other men emerged from the big caravan at the end of the huts. Lorimer wondered whether they had any plan for tackling the pollution. Would it be possible to pump in some neutralising agent, or spray it from the air? But even if that were feasible in theory, the sea was surely too vast an area. More likely, they would decide that matters must be left to take their course, in the hope that the currents would disperse the waste before it could do any real harm. Keeping your fingers crossed was sometimes the only practicable safeguard. That and prayer.

Beyond the first headland, the road ran beside the beach for a couple of hundred yards before climbing a second arm of Bheinn Fhada and

turning inland round the head of Loch Damph. Driving westward along
the loch's north shore, Lorimer could see more signs of activity at the
fish farm than on his previous visit. Men were working on the pens, but
he wasn't knowledgeable enough to tell what they were doing, and
when he had parked he headed for the main entrance to the factory.

Burton, looking harassed and embittered, greeted his visitor with a
noticeable lack of warmth.

"How are things?" Lorimer asked.

"How the hell do you expect?" The manager put the file of papers he
was holding down on his desk with a thud. "We're doing everything we
can, God knows if it'll be enough."

"You said on the phone they were talking about a boom."

Burton made a derisive sound. "That didn't come to anything. I could
have told them it wouldn't; the pollution's down in the water, not floating on the surface like a bloody oil slick."

"Has it reached here yet?"

"No, thank God." The manager appeared to relax a little, and he said
more quietly, "We're testing the water all the time, and so far it's okay.
The currents seem to be taking the stuff farther out."

Lorimer didn't need telling that that could change very quickly.

"We've rented a couple of pens at other farms and moved some of the
salmon there," Burton went on. "They're all we've been able to get so
far. We're looking for more, but people just haven't got empty tanks."

"They're sending Doctor Carter up," Lorimer told him. He waited for
the reaction: Vernon Carter was the group's chief scientist, and Burton
would like his coming even less than he did Lorimer's. Inevitably he
would see it as a reflection on himself.

He was right. "What the hell for?" the manager demanded. "I suppose they think we can't cope; I can't."

"It isn't that," Lorimer said pacifically. But it was: Grantley knew how
serious the contamination and its results could be for United, and he
had to ensure that everything possible was done to minimise the damage. The government, the press and his own sense of responsibility
demanded that, and it meant utilising the best brains that were available.

For several seconds Burton savoured his gall. Then, as if he were
doing his best to ignore it because the taste was too unpalatable, he said,
"Whoever blew that hole in the tank knew what they were doing. From
what I hear, they used just enough explosive and put it in exactly the
right place."

"You think it was an inside job?" Lorimer asked.

Burton shrugged. "Not necessarily, just expert. What are you going to do here?"

"Talk to the DAFS people and the police. Pick up any information I can. The chairman's going to want to know everything I can find out." Lorimer saw his companion's expression and grinned reassuringly. "It's okay, I won't get in your hair. I'm more concerned about how it happened and what's being done to clean up the pollution out there." He looked through the window at the grey sea and the distant shore of Liavaig and hoped that the minister who had allowed the plant to be built there would be made to crawl.

When he got back to the hotel he decided that he might as well go for a walk; it was either that or spend too long in the bar having too many pre-dinner drinks and thinking unprofitable thoughts.

The bar door was open, and he glanced in as he passed. Three men were sitting at one of the tables playing cards, glasses to hand. The remnants of the newspaper corps, he supposed. Alan MacNeil would be glad of their custom, and they would be gone before the holiday season really started.

Low clouds, driven by the wind, shrouded the peaks and hung like grey smoke in the corries, but to the west a streak of golden light just above the horizon hinted at the possibility of a fine evening. The rain had stopped, and Lorimer strode along, relishing the smell of seaweed and the feel of the breeze on his cheeks.

At the end of the street he took to the narrow strip of turf bordering the beach. The hens were at their perpetual task, pecking at the grass, and away to his left the wind stirred the dark grey water into white horses. They surged in with a roar, slapped the sand and receded in a rustle of frothing surf. It was good to be back, he thought, whatever the weather and the circumstances.

Grantley had had no success with the ministry. The Whitehall line was that the leak was a matter for the plant's owners and the police, the government wasn't involved. Officialdom was determined to stay aloof for as long as possible, admitting only that it was carrying out a full investigation to ascertain the nature, source and extent of the problem. It was what Grantley had expected; the leak was the sort of hot potato no politician liked finding on his plate.

Half a mile from the village Lorimer came to the *machair,* a wide expanse of tussocky grass growing out of the sand which extended as far as the headland, here only a few feet high. Cattle were grazing on the spiky grass. Skirting them, he scrambled over the rocks and came to a small bay.

The tide had just turned, and the surf was already in retreat, edging away from the highest line of wet sand. A hundred yards from where Lorimer was standing, the low waves were breaking over a black object lying at the water's edge. Curious, he started walking towards it.

When he was still fifty yards away he realised what the narrow, irregular shape was: only a human body looked quite like that. A body clad in a black wet suit. Something about the way it was lying, a sort of final abandonment, seemed to rule out any possibility of life, but he started running across the beach, his shoes sinking into the wet sand.

The body was lying face down, the surf racing up to it, then trickling away again almost furtively. As gently as he could Lorimer half dragged, half carried the black-clad figure out of the reach of the sea and turned it over. One look was sufficient to tell him that whoever it was had been dead some time, but it seemed natural to pull off the tight-fitting hood. As if, by doing so, he was freeing something. He had to use more force than he liked, and when the hood came away he stared at the dead face, shocked. Laying the head down again carefully, he straightened up and started running back to the hotel.

Moira was behind the bar when he came in.

"Is your father about?" he asked her.

Because he was out of breath the question sounded more brusque than he had intended, and Moira felt a flash of resentment.

"He's away to Liavaig just now," she replied shortly. "Did you want him for something?"

Lorimer saw the three newspaper men look up. "Can you come outside for a minute?"

Moira hesitated, but something in his manner persuaded her, and she accompanied him out into the street, deserted now. "What is it?" she demanded.

"Those three are reporters, aren't they?"

"Yes, they are."

"It's best if they don't know yet: somebody's been washed up on the beach beyond the headland."

Moira looked distressed. "You mean he's dead?"

"Yes. But it isn't a he, it's a girl. She's wearing a wet suit."

"Oh no!"

Lorimer told himself that when a community relied on fishing for its livelihood, the people were usually all too familiar with the possibility of death at sea. When it happened they were shocked and saddened, naturally, but not startled in the way Moira appeared to be. It was as if she knew without being told that she was personally affected. Was it simply that the victim this time was a young woman, or did she think she had known her?

"Alex and Gordon will be somewhere down by the jetty," she said quietly. "They will help bring her."

"We can't move her."

"Why not?"

"She didn't drown, she was shot."

Moira stared at Lorimer incredulously. "Shot?" she echoed. "She can't have been."

Lorimer thought that he wouldn't have seen the wound behind the dead girl's left ear if he hadn't tugged off the hood of her wet suit. Why had he? Even at the time he had known it was a pointless act.

"I'll call the police," he said.

They looked at each other.

"What's she like?" Moira asked through lips which had suddenly gone dry.

Lorimer didn't answer at once. He couldn't tell her that it had been hard to imagine what those pallid, bloated features had been like in life. "Young, I think," he said. "And slim. She wasn't very tall and she had dark hair." He paused. "You think you know who it is, don't you?"

"I don't know," Moira muttered. She made a visible effort to pull herself together. "Our policeman's Hamish Macdonald, you'll get him on Liavaig 44 if he's there."

Lorimer went back into the hotel and used the phone box in the lobby. PC Macdonald was there and promised that he would come over as soon as he had reported to Fort William.

Satisfied that there was no more he could do for the moment, Lorimer joined Moira in the bar. Without saying anything, she poured him a large whisky and watched while he drank it. The reporters had gone.

"Who was she?" he asked.

"I told you, I don't know. How could I? I haven't seen her."

"But you think you do."

There was a pause before Moira said, so quietly that Lorimer hardly heard her, "I think it may be Rona Smith."

"Who's she?"

"A student. She stayed here for a few days about six weeks ago."

"Why her?"

"You said the girl who was washed up was small and had dark hair—and she was wearing a wet suit."

"So?"

"There aren't many wet suits on the island. Some of the groups who come here from colleges and clubs have them, but there aren't any parties here just now. And Rona had one, she used to go swimming underwater." Moira hesitated. "I think she may have been one of those people, Dorn nan Gaidheal."

Lorimer gazed at her. "Why?"

"She asked a lot of questions, and she didn't say much about herself or what she had come here for. I thought it was some kind of research to do with her course at the university; she said she was reading geology. Then once when there were just the two of us here she talked a lot about how Scotland is exploited by the English. She was very bitter."

And she had been here six weeks ago, just before the Burtons' house was burnt down, Lorimer reflected. "You didn't say anything," he pointed out.

"How could I? It was only a feeling I had, I didn't really know anything." Moira saw Lorimer's expression. "What is it, Gray?"

"Dorn nan Gaidheal say they damaged the tank on Liavaig. Those tanks are right on the shore. It would be difficult to get to them by land because of all the fencing and that, but you could do it easily by sea; go in close with an inflatable dinghy, say, and swim the rest of the way. If that's what they did, the odds are they were wearing wet suits. Maybe she was one of them."

"Rona?" Moira frowned. "I don't believe it."

"Why not?"

"She wouldn't have done anything like that, she was too—responsible."

"You think she blew up the Burtons' house, you call that responsible? How did she know they weren't all asleep in there?" The suspicion which had been lurking uneasily at the back of Lorimer's mind ever since his previous visit forced itself forward so that he could no longer ignore it. "You hate Burton and everything to do with United," he said. "You don't like me, just because I work for them. Did she ask you when the Burtons would be away?"

"No!" Moira's distress and horror were genuine, Lorimer would have been prepared to swear to that. "I didn't know anything about it. I still can't believe she did it, or blew up the tank on Liavaig." She hesitated, then added quietly, "And it's not right I don't like you."

Lorimer was relieved, but he thought it safer to ignore that. "Then what was she doing back here just now?" he asked.

They were taking too much for granted. Ten to one the dead girl wasn't Rona Smith, not even a member of the Fist of the Gaels, but the victim of a jealous husband or boyfriend. Perhaps of some bizarre sex crime. From the appearance of her body, she must have been in the water for days; she could have died hundreds of miles away and had no connection with the island until she was washed up here.

No, those odds were too long. Jealous lovers didn't shoot their victims behind the ear, they blasted them from the front or stabbed or strangled them. There was something professional, almost clinical, about the way this girl had been murdered. It was like an execution. Make it two to one.

"I expect the police will ask your father to look at her to see if it is the girl who stayed here," he said. "They'll be there soon, I'd better go back."

Moira nodded.

A young girl murdered, shot through the back of the head, and her body wearing a wet suit washed up on a lonely beach only a short distance from where a nationalist group had sabotaged a toxic waste plant a few days ago: it was the sort of story any news editor would love. Moreover there were three reporters on the spot. Which made it all the more mystifying that there was nothing about it in the papers, Lorimer thought. Only a brief report that a young woman's body had been washed up on the island of Iniscaig in the Hebrides. She was believed to have drowned while scuba diving, and the police were trying to identify her. It was as if some Whitehall mandarin had issued a D-notice, banning publication in the interests of national security. Which was absurd.

The police soon established that the dead girl was Rona Smith and that she was a student at Edinburgh. According to the pathologist, she had probably died some time on Sunday night, death being caused by a single shot from a .38 hand-gun.

That was the night when the tank was holed, and it looked as if the dead girl had been involved in the sabotage, but why had she been shot? It didn't make sense, Lorimer told himself.

Effluent from the processing plant must have begun seeping out into the sea immediately the tank was holed. No, seeping was too mild a word, it must have poured out. Low-level waste, perhaps, but deadly to fish and potentially to man. So far it had only affected those fish which lived close inshore, shellfish mostly; it would take longer for the pollution to spread out far enough to kill deep-water fish, and hopefully it would be dispersed before that happened.

Fish usually died through a lack of oxygen in the water; how long had it taken for the contamination to affect those off Iniscaig? Two days at least, surely, if it was no more dangerous than the waste disposal people claimed. The raid on the plant had taken place on Sunday night, and the story about the dead fish was in all the papers on Wednesday morning. Given that pollution was a fashionable subject, that was still fast. Especially when you considered how little interest the London press usually showed in Highland affairs. It must have been the link with toxic waste which had caught news editors' attention.

And they had all picked up the story at the same time. That suggested a common source. It wasn't the management at the plant. Nor, apparently, the Fist of the Gaels. So who was it? Who had known? The more Lorimer thought about it, the more relevant the question seemed.

He told himself that it wasn't his concern, his job here was finished. The ministry men, aided by experts from the plant and scientists from at least one university, were doing everything possible to clear up the pollution and stop it reaching the fish farm on Loch Damph. Burton and his team could be left to deal with things; he should go back to London.

But Grantley had sent him up here in the first place to check on what the police were doing to trace the people who had burnt down the company's house. That investigation had now been overshadowed by the attack on the waste plant and Rona Smith's murder, but United still had a valid interest in seeing that it wasn't forgotten. Rona Smith might have started the fire, but there were other people behind her.

The police had taken over a room at the back of the hotel usually used for ceilidhs and meetings to serve as their incident room. Lorimer saw their comings and goings and wondered what progress they were making; since making his statement about finding the body he had had no contact with them. They never came into the bar and went about their work tight-lipped, as if they feared contamination from the islanders more than from the polluted water. Lorimer knew Wallace was amongst them, but apart from a brief nod once when they met in the street he had only seen him from a distance.

The reporters at least were prepared to talk, and soon it was common knowledge on the island that the dead girl's parents had separated while she was a child, her mother had died last year and she had lost touch with her father, who was believed to be working on an oil rig in the Far East. No one knew where; the university had only her mother listed as next-of-kin.

"Didn't she talk about anybody?" Lorimer asked Moira. "Family? Boyfriends?"

"She had a boyfriend," Moira answered. "She was always talking about him. She called him Roy."

Roy: Moira didn't know his surname. It wasn't much to go on, Lorimer thought, crawling along between traffic lights in the usual Princes Street jam.

He was hot; today was one of those rare occasions when Edinburgh was the warmest place in Britain. The sun shone from a cloudless sky on the perspiring tourists thronging the pavements, and glinted back from the windows of the cars around him. Even with the sunroof open, the interior of the Maestro was like a hothouse.

When Rona Smith registered at the Islands Hotel she had given her address as "c/o Edinburgh University." Driving here from Oban, Lorimer had wondered if even the name was her own; maybe when he checked at the registrar's office they would tell him they had no record of a student named Rona Smith.

But they hadn't; Rona Smith existed. Had existed. Clearly they had wondered why he should want to know the address of a student who had died a few days ago, and Lorimer suspected that they thought he might be a reporter. After all, Rona had been murdered. But he had convinced them that he was neither a reporter nor a policeman, and rather reluctantly they had given him it, a house in Ravelston shared by half a dozen students.

The lights changed, and with a feeling of relief Lorimer turned out of Princes Street and headed across the western side of the New Town.

The house had the appearance peculiar to houses occupied by numbers of people who know they won't be there long, a look denoting a lack of interest rather than deliberate neglect. It stood back a few yards from the road, behind a parched lawn and some untidy shrubs, a plain detached Victorian building which once had been the home of some prosperous tradesman. Looking at it from the road, Lorimer was reminded of another house, in which he had lived for two years when he was at university; it was less than a mile from here, but it seemed a world away.

The front door was open a few inches, and he rang the bell and waited. At first there was no answer, and he was about to ring again when a girl came. She was young and plain, with a mop of ginger hair which clashed with her scarlet T-shirt. Below the shirt, her bare feet were thrust into grubby trainers. The trainers weren't laced, as if she had put them on when she heard his ring and not waited to do them up. Holding on to the edge of the door, she eyed him with a blend of enquiry and apprehension which puzzled Lorimer.

"I understand Rona Smith lived here," he said.

The flicker of expression which crossed the girl's face was gone before he could decide whether it was grief or mistrust.

"Yes," she said. She had a marked accent. Probably German, Lorimer thought, although it might as easily have been Dutch or Swiss.

"Did you know her?" he asked. She nodded. "You may be able to help me then."

The girl looked back over her shoulder. "How help you?"

"There are some things I'm trying to find out."

"You are from the police?"

"No."

"The police have been here. They had a warrant and they searched everywhere. Pigs."

"I'm nothing to do with the police."

Again the girl looked over her shoulder. Lorimer tried to see past her into the hall, but the house faced away from the sun and it was too poorly lit for him to make out more than the outlines of a table and the newel post at the foot of the stairs. A door on the left was ajar, and light from the window in the room beyond it made a bright patch on the lino-covered floor. Was there somebody in the room? Somebody the girl didn't want to hear what they said? But she had seemed to be looking up the stairs, and they were in deep shadow.

"Maybe we can talk out here," he suggested.

The girl hesitated, then nodded uncertainly. Pulling the door to behind her, she led the way round the side of the house to another lawn at the back. The grass here was longer and greener than that at the front, and a clothesline had been strung across the nearer end of it from the corner of a shed to a down pipe at the back of the house. A tea-towel, two pairs of women's briefs and a bra hung limply in the warm afternoon air.

"What's your name?" Lorimer asked the girl.

"Heidi Strauss." Clearly, she was still nervous.

"How long had you known Rona Smith?"

"About one year, I think."

"Did you know her well?"

Heidi hesitated. It was as if she were trying to decide which answer was the safe one, Lorimer thought. Which one, "Yes" or "No," someone else would want her to give. And if she gave the wrong one?

"No," she said, "not well. You were a friend of hers?"

"I found her."

"Oh." There was a moment's silence, then Heidi asked, "It is true, she was shot?"

"Yes." Lorimer waited, but she said nothing more. He had the feeling that he had confirmed something she had been trying desperately not to believe. "She had a boyfriend, didn't she? Roy. Do you know him?"

"No. No, I 'ave never met him."

It was obviously a lie. Involuntarily, it seemed, Heidi looked up at the side of the house, then away again quickly. Whatever she had seen, clearly it had made her even more nervous, and Lorimer looked where she had. A man was standing at a window on the first floor watching them. It was difficult to see much because the sun was shining on the glass, but Lorimer had the impression that he was young and good-looking. Then he was gone.

"Is he another student?" Lorimer asked.

Heidi looked startled. "Who?"

"The man at the window."

"I did not see anybody."

Lorimer let it pass. "But you knew of Roy?" he asked. "Rona talked about him?"

"No, never. I did not know the name until you say it."

"Is that Roy watching us?"

"No," Heidi said. "No! Why do you keep asking about this Roy?"

Lorimer didn't believe her. "What do you know about the Fist of the Gaels?"

"Nothing." The answer came too swiftly. "What would I know? I am German, I am not Scottish. I do not know anything about such things."

"You lived in the same house as Rona for a year; she was a member."

"I told you, we were not friends."

"And I told you, I'm nothing to do with the police," Lorimer said. "What are you so frightened of?"

"I am not frightened. Why should I be?"

"I don't know, but you're scared stiff about something."

As if she couldn't stop herself, Heidi looked up at the window again. Lorimer looked too: the man was back.

It was obvious that the girl wanted Lorimer to go, and he doubted if he would get anything more out of her while she was so scared. He allowed her to lead the way back to the front of the house.

As they reached it another girl came out by the front door. Apparently she wanted to speak to Heidi, for she stood a few yards away, watching them and waiting.

"My name's Graham Lorimer," Lorimer said. "I'm staying at the Muirfoot Hotel off Willowbrae Road. If you decide you want to tell me anything, I'll be there for the next day or two. Tell Roy too."

This time the girl didn't bother to deny that she knew him.

FIVE

HUGH HADN'T CHANGED MUCH, Lorimer thought, eyeing the comfortable figure in the easy chair. It was several years since they had met, and if there were a little more white in his hair and another inch or two round his waist, they were hardly noticeable. Even his crumpled alpaca jacket looked suspiciously like the one he had worn a dozen years ago.

Bascomb felt in his pocket and brought out his pipe, followed by a worn leather pouch and a box of Swan Vestas. He was in his middle sixties, but could have been anything from fifty to seventy, a burly man with a good deal of curly grey hair, a small beard and eyes which twinkled behind horn-rimmed glasses. His deep, slightly booming voice was misleading; he was the gentlest of men. At the same time he was shrewd, with a keenly ironic eye for human frailties and pretensions. As one of his students, Lorimer had both liked and respected him.

Bascomb was a bachelor—student gossip had it that in his younger days he had pursued and bedded half the prettiest girls in Edinburgh— and he had occupied this apartment in Morningside for more than thirty years. It was a very ordinary flat in a very conventional house, but after so long it seemed to have absorbed much of his personality.

"If I didn't know better, I'd be flattered you'd bothered to look me up," he remarked, prodding tobacco into the bowl of his pipe with a stubby forefinger. "So what's it all about, young Graham, eh?"

"Information," Lorimer said.

"You astonish me." Bascomb struck a match and held it to the tobacco. "D'you know," he observed between sucks at his pipe, "it's one of the disappointments of my life that while my old students must surely acknowledge my great wisdom, they seldom come to me for advice."

Lorimer grinned and watched, fascinated by the ritual as he had been when he was a student. Plenty of men smoked pipes. Some of them enjoyed doing so, others liked the image they believed it helped create, but he had never met anyone who did so with the same deep inner satisfaction that Hugh Bascomb did. For him, lighting a pipe was an experience to be savoured, as rewarding as listening to a well-loved piece of music, almost sensual. Fragrant grey-blue smoke rose in a column from the bowl.

"Nationalism used to be one of your subjects," he remarked.

"Interests," Bascomb corrected him. "It's never been one of my provinces academically. Except as a by-product."

"Interests," Lorimer acknowledged. "Have you heard of a group that calls itself Dorn nan Gaidheal?"

"The Fist of the Gaels. Of course I've heard of them, they burnt down a house on some island a few weeks ago; now they claim they've damaged a pipe or something at a toxic waste plant."

"They blew the bottom out of a tank."

Bascomb eyed his companion through the veil of smoke. "I don't understand physics," he said. "Never did."

"Do you know anything about them apart from what's been in the papers and on television?" Lorimer asked.

For several seconds the older man seemed absorbed in his pipe. The smoke no longer rose straight, but curled up lazily, wafting away above the two men's heads. "Am I permitted to ask why you're interested in them?" he enquired.

As briefly as he could, Lorimer explained. Bascomb listened in silence. Anyone looking at him might have thought that his thoughts were far away, but Lorimer wasn't deceived.

"I'd heard rumours there might be some of them in Edinburgh," he conceded when Lorimer had finished. "It's not surprising, this is that sort of place. It's one of its great charms, a mixture of the artistic, the intellectual, the idealistic and the hard-nosed commercial."

"There's nothing idealistic about this lot," Lorimer commented. "Not artistic or intellectual either."

"No, there isn't." Bascomb's slightly bantering tone had suddenly become serious.

"Are they important?"

"If it's your house they burn down, or you get in the way of one of their bombs, they are."

"Otherwise?"

Bascomb hesitated. "I'd say not yet, but they may be. Extreme nationalist movements are almost invariably terrorist in nature. The romantic extremist isn't sentimental, he's like any other extremist, completely oblivious to other people's interests. And often the most fanatical nationalists are expatriates; not the first generation but the second and third, even after that. Look at some of the Irish in London and the U.S.A., they love to think and talk of themselves as Irish, but they'd never dream of going to live in Ireland, even if the Irish would have them. And they're not the only ones, the Scots are nearly as bad: all those Burns' nights and Caledonian societies. They're like religious converts, they feel a need to be more passionate than anyone else to prove they're what they want to be."

"You're an island of Englishness," Lorimer observed, smiling. Hugh might be only half serious, but there was a solid element of truth in what he said.

"*Touché.*" Bascomb paused, the upper half of his body almost concealed by smoke. "The world is becoming more and more like those vast international companies, and a lot of people don't like it. They feel they're losing their identity, being submerged, so they'll support a movement that they think will help them to preserve it. Almost any movement; we get all these splinter groups, some of them composed of cranks, some of them of dangerous opportunists. There's a great danger in the romantic ideal of splitting the world up into tiny states, there'll come a time when some Big Brother with too much ambition starts wanting to take them over."

Lorimer remembered that his companion was an old-fashioned Liberal and had been an enthusiast for a united Europe when few people in Britain were. If he had his way, the world would eventually consist of one federated state, but he was far too sensible to believe it was a practical possibility. "What about the Fist of the Gaels?" he enquired.

"There are always anti-government and anti-London feelings in Scotland," Bascomb replied. "You know that. Just as there are in other parts of England. This government has exacerbated them, they've increased nationalist sentiment and given it a sort of logic. There are people who are ready to trade on that. Some of them want to stir up trouble in the hope that eventually Westminster will become fed up and cut Scotland off."

"And the Fist of the Gaels are part of it?"

"I don't know. I imagine they're like the rest, a few romantics and idealists, a few misfits—and a few hard-headed terrorists who control the whole thing."

"They seem to have money."

"Do they?" Bascomb looked interested.

"Who's Roy?" Lorimer asked.

"Roy?"

"You know, don't you?"

The older man regarded Lorimer curiously through the haze of smoke. "You've changed," he observed. "You never beat about the bush, now you've the confidence to go with it."

"We weren't talking about me," Lorimer said, smiling. He suspected that Hugh was attempting to sidetrack him, and that wasn't like him. He must have a reason.

"Roy McIndoe," Bascomb said after a lengthy pause. "He claims he's a writer, but I don't know what he's ever written. He has a flat near the Commonwealth Pool: Carlyle Road."

"Is that all?"

"What else do you want to know?"

"Everything."

"Leave him alone, Gray."

"Why?"

"He's dangerous. And he has dangerous friends."

"Could he have killed Rona Smith?"

Bascomb's shoulders moved an inch, sketching a shrug. "Who knows who's capable of killing, given sufficient motive and the right circumstances?"

"That's a cliché," Lorimer objected. "You said he was dangerous."

"A statement's being a cliché doesn't make it any less true." For a moment Bascomb smoked in silence, then he said, "The older I get the more I incline to the belief that some people are born inherently evil, and there is nothing anyone can do about it, except put them away."

"You think McIndoe's like that?"

"Perhaps, I don't know. I was thinking of a man who was with him when he came to my room at Riccerton once."

"McIndoe was one of your students?" That possibility hadn't occurred to Lorimer, and he was startled.

"You didn't know?" Bascomb regarded him with interest. "I took it you did, as you'd come to me about him. Yes, three or four years ago. He dropped out after his first year. I've no idea who the other man was, but I saw them together in a pub a few weeks ago."

"What was he like?" Lorimer asked.

"Young and thick-set, average height. I thought he looked German or Dutch, possibly Scandinavian, but I didn't hear him speak, and I'm probably wrong."

If he wasn't, Lorimer thought, it was unlikely that McIndoe's companion on those occasions had anything to do with the Fist of the Gaels. "May I borrow that telephone directory?" he asked.

The book was on the table by Bascomb's elbow and he handed it over. "You're not thinking of going to see him, are you?" he enquired.

"I don't know," Lorimer admitted, not entirely truthfully.

Slightly to his surprise, there was a number listed for "McIndoe R., 35 Carlyle Road," and he handed the directory back.

"I've given you my advice," Bascomb told him. "Leave well alone. It isn't only his friends, there's something wrong in him."

"Yes, thanks."

"Whether he killed that girl you found or not, people like him are dangerous, Gray. They don't live by our rules, they make theirs up to suit themselves—when they have any. And they don't like outsiders taking an interest in them. People with guilty consciences rarely do."

"I'll remember," Lorimer promised.

They went down the stairs together.

"Don't let it be so long before you come next time," Bascomb said.

"I won't."

They shook hands and Lorimer walked out into the sunny street. It had been a long shot that Hugh might be able to tell him who Roy was, but it had come off.

It was only a ten-minute drive to Carlyle Road, an old street of tall red-brown tenements. If it was McIndoe he had seen at the window of the house in Ravelston, the chances were that he was still there, or had been frightened away by his visit to some other bolt-hole, but he had to try to see him. Parking by the kerb outside Number 35, he entered the narrow hall. A young woman was lifting a baby out of a pushchair.

"Can you tell me where Mr. McIndoe's apartment is?" Lorimer asked her.

"Number 3, first floor." She had answered without looking up, all her attention focussed on the baby, who was crying bad-temperedly.

The stairs were covered with worn linoleum and the banisters looked as if one good push would send them tumbling into the hall. Lorimer found a door with a cheap metal "3" screwed to it at a slight angle and tapped on it. There was no answer, and he tapped again.

The result was the same. Then the next door opened and an old woman with a scarf only partly concealing the rollers in her hair stuck her head out. There was something faintly obscene about the shiny pink and blue plastic tubes nestling in her thin white hair.

"Are you the polis?" she enquired suspiciously.

"No," Lorimer assured her.

"Och well, if you're looking for that Roy McIndoe, you'll not find him there. He's not been here for days. The polis came asking for him yesterday."

"I'll try again later then," Lorimer said. "Thanks."

He went back down the stairs. In the hall the young woman was nursing the baby and crooning to it. It had stopped crying.

"He's no' there, is he?" she said.

"Mr. Lorimer?"

Lorimer turned. The girl was about twenty and slightly built, with thin features, a rather pointed nose and auburn hair. He was sure he had seen her before, very recently, and couldn't remember where. The failure irked him like a small pain. She had been dressed differently then, he thought; now she was wearing a white nylon blouson open over a blue sweat-shirt and baggy fawn trousers. The shirt had a slogan in black across the front, but it was three quarters hidden by the jacket, and Lorimer couldn't read the words.

"I'm Sue Johnstone," she said. "I saw you at the house this afternoon. You were asking about Rona, weren't you?"

Lorimer remembered her now. She had come out to speak to Heidi and waited for him to leave. "What makes you think that?" he asked.

"I heard Heidi talking to Roy after you'd gone. She has the room next to mine, and Roy was mad. He didn't keep his voice down."

Lorimer looked round. The hotel was small and catered mostly for sales reps and junior managers in Edinburgh on business. At this time in the evening most of them were out sampling the city's nightlife, and

the bar was deserted save for an elderly man sitting by himself in a
corner. "Will you have something to drink?" he asked the girl.

"I'd like a vodka and tonic, if that's all right."

Lorimer bought it and a half of heavy for himself, and they took the
drinks over to a table as far from the bar and the man in the corner as
possible.

"Who is Heidi?" Lorimer asked.

Sue shrugged. "Just one of the students. She's got a thing for Roy, but
he couldn't care less."

"And Roy was Rona's boyfriend."

"Yes. At least . . ." Sue stopped, and the shadow in her eyes deep-
ened.

"At least what?" Lorimer prompted her.

"I always had the feeling he couldn't really care less about Rona, he
was just using her. And since she was killed—it was terrible what happened, but he doesn't seem upset or anything." The girl hesitated again.
"Heidi told him you found her."

"Yes." Roy wouldn't be distressed if he had killed Rona, Lorimer
thought. But he was going too fast, there was no evidence that McIndoe
was the murderer. "Who is he, apart from being her boyfriend and a
student who dropped out?" he asked.

"I don't know much about him, except what Rona said. He edits a
rock magazine or something."

"And now he's living at the house?"

"Sort of, he moved in with Heidi at the beginning of this week." Sue
paused. "I'm sorry for her, he isn't interested in her, he's stringing her
along like he did Rona. I don't think he cares about anybody except
himself, he just uses them. Heidi's okay."

"She's scared," Lorimer said.

"Yes."

"What of?"

"I don't know." Sue avoided his eye.

You're lying, Lorimer thought. So far you've been telling the truth,
but now we're getting on to dangerous ground, and you're afraid too.
Afraid for yourself, because of what you know, or for Heidi, who probably knows more.

"Roy's a member of the Fist of the Gaels," he said, watching the girl's
face to see how she reacted. "You know that, don't you?"

She looked down at her glass. "Yes," she muttered.

"And so was Rona."

"Yes."

"Are you?"

"No." Sue shook her head and looked up to face him squarely. "I've no time for that sort of thing. Rona was really keen, she was lonely and she was a romantic and Roy filled her head with all sorts of ideas. She would have done almost anything he said."

"Almost anything? Hell," Lorimer said warmly, "she blew up a house when there might have been a family asleep in it."

"She knew the house was empty." Sue's distress was clear. "I don't say what she did was right, but she would never have burnt down that house if she hadn't known nobody would be hurt."

"So it's okay to destroy a family's home and everything they possess, as long as you don't burn them too?"

"No, of course not; I said it wasn't. But to Rona it had to be done."

"She blew a hole in a tank at the toxic waste plant on Liavaig too. It might have killed hundreds of people. What more do you want?"

"She didn't do that."

"What makes you think she didn't?" Lorimer was angry. "The Fist of the Gaels say they did it. She was a member, she'd been to Iniscaig spying out the land just before, she was there at the right time, and when I found her she was wearing a wet suit. You don't go scuba diving at night on your own."

Sue faced him. She was frowning, and for the first time she seemed unsure whether she could trust him. "Who are you?" she asked. "Why are you so interested in what happened? Are you from the police or something?"

"I work for United," Lorimer told her. "It was our manager's house she burnt down on Iniscaig, and I was sent up there to see what was going on. When she let all that poison out into the sea and it looked like affecting our fish farm I had to go back. I left there this morning."

"She didn't have anything to do with damaging the tank," Sue insisted stubbornly. "I know she didn't, she saw how dangerous it was. Not to her, to the environment and the people up there; she was always worrying about the environment and what we were doing to it: tropical rain forests, endangered species, seals. Besides . . ."

"Besides what?" Lorimer asked.

"I heard her arguing with Roy about it. She told him she wouldn't do whatever it was he wanted her to. They didn't know I was there, and I thought it was something to do with sex." Sue looked very solemn. "Now I think it was sabotaging that tank."

If that were true, Lorimer thought, it might explain why Rona Smith was murdered: to prevent her revealing anything about the plan and Roy's part in it to the police or anyone else. And Dorn nan Gaidheal was a more violent, murderous organisation than he had suspected.

"Can you remember what they said?" he asked.

Sue's brow puckered. "I didn't hear the start of it; I wasn't trying to listen and Roy was talking quietly, but Rona sounded upset. She said, 'We can't, not that.' He said something else and she repeated, 'We can't. I don't want to have anything to do with it. I don't want to know.' Then he told her, 'We haven't any bloody choice, we've got to.' I heard him go down the stairs, and when Rona came down later I could see she'd been crying."

"When did you see her the last time?"

"On the Saturday morning; she came into the kitchen when I was getting my breakfast and said she was going away for the weekend. She didn't say where to, and I didn't ask her. I took it for granted she was going with Roy, but when I went out just afterwards I saw her getting into a car. Roy has a real banger, an old Post Office Telephones van, but this was big and expensive-looking: a BMW, something like that. There was just one person in it, and I only saw his back, but it wasn't Roy."

Lorimer remembered what Hugh Bascomb had told him about McIndoe's friend. "Did they see you?" he enquired.

"I don't think so, I was only just coming out of the gate and the car was parked a little way down the road. Anyhow they were looking the other way.

There were such things as rear-view mirrors, Lorimer thought. But Sue was probably right, and, if they had noticed her, there was no reason why that should alarm the BMW's driver.

She had finished her drink, but she declined another.

"How much do you know about the Fist of the Gaels?" Lorimer asked her.

"Nothing, except that Roy's a member—I think he's one of the leaders—and so was Rona. I'd never even heard of them, but one day she was furious over something the government had done; she was always getting furious about something. I said there wasn't much anybody could do, and it wasn't any good getting worked up about it. She called me spineless and said it was people like me who didn't care who were responsible for everything that was wrong in Scotland, and there were some people who meant to do something about it. A group, I think she said. She didn't say what it was called, or that she was a member, but I guessed she was." Sue paused. "I didn't take it very seriously then, but now I suppose it is serious."

"Ay," Lorimer agreed sombrely, "it's serious. Heidi said the police had been to the house and searched it; where was Roy?"

"Out. Heidi was the only one there, and she wouldn't say anything about him."

"Has anyone else been to see him?"

"There was a man came this afternoon, soon after you'd gone. He was quite young." Sue hadn't taken much notice of him, and she tried to remember. "He had a foreign accent, German it sounded like, and I thought he'd come to see Heidi. But he asked if Roy was there."

"He called him Roy? Not McIndoe or Mr. McIndoe?"

"I think he said Roy McIndoe."

"Could he have been the man in the BMW?"

"He could have been, I suppose." Clearly Sue hadn't considered the possibility. She paused and regarded Lorimer solemnly. "You think Rona was killed because she belonged to the Fist of the Gaels, don't you?"

Lorimer nodded. But it was beginning to look as if there was a lot more to it than that, he thought. "Does anybody know you've come here?"

"No." The girl looked self-conscious. "It seemed a bit silly, but I thought it would be better if I didn't tell anybody."

"Ay, it could be," Lorimer agreed lightly. "Are you going back to Ravelston just now?"

"No, I'm meeting a friend at the union."

"I'll drive you there."

"Och, there's no need," Sue protested. "I can get a bus easy."

She didn't appear to understand that it was her safety Lorimer was concerned about, not saving her legs: if McIndoe or his friends had killed Rona to prevent her talking, they were unlikely to hesitate before using violence again. Lorimer doubted if they had followed Sue here, but they knew he was asking questions and he was disinclined to take any chances. At the same time, he didn't want his concern to communicate itself to her; perhaps he was imagining too much, seeing dangers round every corner when none existed. But he had learnt that it was better, much better, to be safe than sorry. Sometimes you weren't around later to be sorry.

"That's okay," he said cheerfully. "I was going that way anyhow."

"I wish Roy wasn't at the house," Sue confessed when Lorimer was negotiating the evening traffic near the foot of Calton Hill. "There's something about him . . . Och, I don't know, he makes my flesh creep."

"He's just a Sunday-afternoon nationalist," Lorimer said. "All hot air and wind." He wished he believed it.

After he had dropped Sue he drove back to the hotel. Cars were parked along both sides of the road except for a short space near the front of the hotel which was blocked off with yellow cones. He drove round the next corner, reversed the Maestro into a gap between two other cars and started walking back. The rest of the evening stretched ahead of him. It was pathetic, he thought, here he was back in his home town after years away and he didn't feel like going out or ringing any of his old friends to see if they would join him for a dram somewhere; the shadow of Rona Smith and Dorn nan Gaidheal laid across the evening like a cloud.

The cones had gone, and an old brown Cortina was parked where they had been. Three men were sitting inside, as if they were waiting for a fourth to come out of the hotel and join them.

Lorimer came abreast of the Cortina. As he did so the rear door was flung open, blocking his way. Sensing danger, he stepped sideways. At the same moment a hand reached out from the back of the car, grasping his jacket, and the front door opened behind his back, trapping him. Cursing his lack of vigilance, he struggled to free himself. But he had been caught off balance and the arm holding him was like a steel bar. Slowly, inexorably, he was dragged towards the car.

Shouting was useless, they were thirty or forty yards from the entrance to the hotel and there was no one in sight. Lorimer braced his arms on the car's roof and his right foot against the sill. A man got out of the front passenger's seat, lashed out with a heavily shod foot at his right leg and pushed him violently in the small of his back. Pain shot through the leg and Lorimer's grip on the Cortina's roof slackened. The hand inside the car pulled harder. At the same time the man outside pressed down hard on Lorimer's shoulders. For as long as he could he withstood the pressure; then it became intolerable and he collapsed awkwardly into the back of the car.

Ungentle hands pushed him down on to the floor. He tried to struggle, but the space was too restricted. He was aware of a man getting in on the other side of the car and a hand fumbling in his right-hand jacket pocket. There was a slight jingle, the man got out again and the car started forward. A sickly smelling pad was pressed against his nose and mouth. He fought against it, but the fumes were filling his head, and within seconds he slid into unconsciousness.

His first sensations when he woke were of a head which felt as if it were stuffed with foul-smelling cotton wool and a feeling of nausea. Also he was extremely thirsty. He had had a few hangovers in his time, but never one like this. What the hell had he done last night? But it was night now, he had been asleep and something had woken him. Dimly he was aware of a tapping just beside his right ear. It was absurd how much effort it required just to turn a few degrees to see who it was, he thought. A man's face crowned by a peaked cap with a checkered band peered in at him.

What was a face doing there? Lorimer wondered muzzily. Come to that, where was he? This wasn't his bed. It wasn't a bed at all, he was sitting behind the wheel of a car. No, sitting was the wrong word, he was half lying on his back, restrained from falling sideways by his seat-belt. It wasn't even his Rover, the upholstery was a different colour. And there was a strong smell of whisky.

The tapping became more insistent and he made himself concentrate. If only his head was clearer and he wasn't so damned thirsty.

The head wearing the cap receded. Thank God its owner, whoever he was, had gone away and he could go back to sleep, Lorimer thought. The next moment the door was pulled open and only his seat-belt prevented his falling out of the car.

"Christ!" a Scots voice said. After a moment it asked more formally, "Are you all right, sir?"

What sort of damn silly question was that? Lorimer asked himself. Even a bloody fool could see he was far from all right. "No, I'm not," he said with feeling.

"Would you mind getting out of the car, sir?" The voice was polite, devoid of any expression, and in an odd way it seemed to come from a long way off.

Lorimer tried, but it took him a few moments to find the release for the seat-belt. Moreover, finding it was one thing, undoing it was a different matter; he failed miserably.

The policeman waited. Lorimer was vaguely aware that he had been joined by a colleague who was walking slowly round the car, studying it as if he had never seen one before. His brain was clearing slowly, although his head still ached and he wanted to be sick. He tried again to get out, and this time he succeeded.

"God!" he groaned.

The policeman regarded him with features as blank as his tone had been. "Have you been drinking, sir?" he asked.

Lorimer realised that the stench of whisky came from him. There was some on his lips and he licked them. Apparently it had dribbled down his chin on to his jacket, but there wasn't anything he could do about that. With difficulty, because either the car or the ground seemed to be tilted upwards at a crazy angle, by holding on to the door he managed to stand upright.

"I had a half of heavy at lunch time and a pint this evening," he replied. It was strange, he could remember that.

The second policeman had completed his survey and joined his colleague. Now, leaning past Lorimer, he reached into the car, felt between the front seats and produced a whisky bottle, two-thirds empty. "Is this yours, sir?" he enquired.

"No."

"It's in your car. It is your car, sir?"

"It's one I hired." Lorimer rubbed one hand across his eyes.

It was several seconds before he could remember where he kept the papers and his driving licence. When he produced them the policemen studied them without comment, returned them and asked him to take a breath test. When they saw the result they looked at each other.

"We'll have to ask you to come with us, sir," the first one said.

Lorimer thought that if he hadn't been so muzzy, he would have been angry. So perhaps it was as well that his head still felt full of cotton wool; arguing with the two policemen wouldn't have achieved anything, except even more trouble.

"I was drugged," he said. "They bundled me into their car, held me down and stuck a pad over my face." Even to him it didn't sound very plausible.

Apparently the policemen thought the same. One of them held open the rear door of their car.

"One thing," Lorimer said. "Where are we?"

"Longniddry golf course," the second policeman informed him. "You were in a bunker by the sixth green."

Lorimer couldn't believe it. He wanted to laugh, but he suspected that the policeman wouldn't appreciate the joke, and perhaps it wasn't really all that funny.

They had to stop on the way to the police station in order that he could get out to be sick. By the time they arrived he felt considerably better, his head was clearing and his temper was rising.

A sergeant took down his personal details. A little later a doctor came, gave him a blood test, took a sample and departed. When he had gone Lorimer was taken to a cell, the door clanged shut, and he was left alone.

He slept deeply and uneasily and was woken by an unfriendly voice telling him to get up and come with him. This time there was no nausea and, apart from the terrible thirst, he felt more like his normal self, although the stench of his jacket revolted him.

The constable led him to a small room with a single barred window, a table and three upright wooden chairs. A man in plain clothes seated on one of the chairs gestured to Lorimer to take the one on the other side of the table, and the constable posted himself just inside the door. In case he tried to make a bolt for it, Lorimer supposed. They must be joking.

"I'm Detective Inspector Harries, Mr. Lorimer," the plain-clothes man informed him. "Would you mind telling me what you were doing between nine and ten-thirty tonight?"

"What time did your fellows find me?"

"Just after ten-thirty."

"At nine I was in the—" Lorimer stopped. He had been going to say that he was in the bar of the Muirfoot Hotel, but that would only help to confirm what they already believed. "The Muirfoot Hotel," he said.

"Were you alone?"

"I was then, except for the barman and an old boy in the corner. About ten past a girl came to see me."

"What was her name?"

"Sue." Lorimer tried to remember Sue's surname. "Sue Johnstone."

"How long were you with her?"

"About three quarters of an hour, I suppose."

"In the hotel all the time?"

"Until I took her to the students' union. She said she was meeting a friend there."

"What time did you leave her?"

"I don't know exactly. About five to ten."

"And you were in the bar all the time?"

"Yes. Look," Lorimer said, "what is all this? If you're suggesting we went to my room, we didn't."

Harries ignored the question. "And when you left the hotel you drove straight to the union?" he enquired.

"Yes."

"Do you know Miss Johnstone well?"

"I'd never met her before last night."

"Oh?" The inspector's eyebrows rose.

"She came to tell me something."

"About what?"

"Some information I wanted."

"Very well, we'll leave that for the moment." Harries sat back on his chair. "What did you do after you took the young lady to the union?"

"Drove back to the hotel. There was a space by the kerb outside, but it was coned off, and I parked round the corner. When I walked back the cones had gone and there was a car parked in the space: an old brown Cortina with three men in it. When I was level with them they grabbed me and pulled me inside. One of them took my keys and got out, then the car drove off. They shoved a pad soaked with chloroform or something over my face, I passed out, and that's all I knew until your men found me."

It didn't sound any more likely now than it had done last night, Lorimer thought, and he half expected the inspector to tell him he had seen that film too.

But he didn't. Instead he said, "Yesterday afternoon you went to a house in Ravelston and asked questions about a girl named Rona Smith and a man named Roy McIndoe. Later you went to McIndoe's flat in Newington looking for him. When Miss Johnstone came to see you you still seemed very interested in him. Why, Mr. Lorimer?"

"Why not? It's not a crime."

"Maybe not," Harries conceded. "But I'd think again, if I were you."

"Why?" Lorimer demanded again.

The inspector's expression was inscrutable. "Because about ten past ten last night Mr. McIndoe was murdered," he said.

SIX

LORIMER STARED AT HIM. "How?" he demanded.

"He was shot."

"Through the back of the head with a .38?"

Harries' tone didn't change. "Are you telling me or asking?"

"Asking."

"He may have been. But perhaps you'd know all about that."

"How could I?" It seemed to Lorimer that events were running out of his control, sweeping him along with them. He had had the feeling before, and he didn't like it. "Where was he killed?" he asked.

Harries gave him a curious look. "Cockenzie. A man out walking his dog heard a shot. He didn't think anything of it at the time, he thought it was a car backfiring maybe, but he saw two men getting into a car on the road there where it runs along beside the sea. A few minutes later his dog found McIndoe's body on the beach." The inspector paused. "You say that at ten past ten you were drugged and unconscious in your car, being driven to Longniddry?"

"Yes." He had to cling to that, Lorimer told himself. It was about the only hard fact he had on his side. "Two of them must have taken McIndoe out to Cockenzie in the Maestro and shot him while the other one drove me to Longniddry. They met up there, moved me into the Maestro and went off in the Cortina. If your men found me at half past, and I was as drunk as they say I was, I couldn't have shot anybody twenty minutes before."

"But you weren't drunk, were you?" Harries observed reasonably.

Oh God! Lorimer thought. It seemed there was no way he could win. He had begun to think that a charge of being drunk in charge of a car was preferable to one of murder; now, it seemed, he hadn't even that choice. He wished he hadn't been clever about the gun just now.

"Whisky had been poured into your mouth and down your shirt, but you hadn't swallowed any of it," Harries went on. "Did you pour it yourself, Mr. Lorimer?"

"Why should I?" But he knew why: to make it look as if he had been too drunk to murder Roy. Cockenzie was only two or three miles from the turning where the lane which crossed Longniddry golf course left the coast road; there would have been plenty of time for him to kill Roy, dump his car in the bunker and pour whisky over himself before pretending to be in a drunken sleep.

But why had the murderers staged this elaborate charade? And why pick on him? To put him out of the way, he thought. Perhaps for a very long time. The corollary, that they must see him as a threat, did nothing to improve his morale.

He had been drugged to ensure that he had no alibi for the time of McIndoe's murder. "If my car was in a bunker at Longniddry, how did your men find me?" he asked. "It was pretty dark by then."

There was no humour in Harries' smile. "You forgot to turn your headlights off," he replied. "They were pointing up to the sky like a couple of searchlights."

"I didn't."

"Ay, so you say."

His abductors had had to ensure that he was found within a reasonable time. Preferably while he was still woozy from the chloroform. Otherwise he might simply have walked away, returned to the hotel and called the police to report that his car had been stolen.

Harries could see no reason why he should tell Lorimer that the doctor had found indications of chloroform when he carried out his tests, and he had a question of his own. "Why were you so interested in McIndoe?" he demanded.

"I believed he was behind the blowing up of a house that belongs to the company I work for."

"The house on Iniscaig."

"Yes."

"We know he was the leader of a group calling itself the Fist of the Gaels; we've talked to Miss Strauss and Miss Johnstone. Miss Johnstone confirms that she went to see you at the Muirfoot Hotel and that you left her outside the union just before ten o'clock."

"So I couldn't have shot McIndoe at Cockenzie at ten past."

"I wouldn't say that." Harries' tone wasn't encouraging. "It may not have been ten past exactly when the old gentleman heard the shot. He's not all that certain, and it could have been maybe ten minutes later. If you left Miss Johnstone at ten to ten, say, you could have done it; it's a fast road now, and there would not have been all that much traffic on it at that time of the evening."

Lorimer felt defeated. Every time he came up with something that seemed to prove he couldn't have killed McIndoe, the inspector showed he could.

"I suppose you know about Rona Smith too?" he asked.

"Ay, we do."

"So what happens now?"

Harries stood up. "We'll take your statement, then you can go."

Lorimer couldn't believe it, he must still be more woozy than he had thought.

"There's somebody here wants to talk to you first," the inspector added. With a brief nod he walked out, followed by the constable.

Lorimer wondered who wanted to see him. It couldn't be the girl Heidi or Sue Johnstone, there was no reason why either of them should come, even if they knew he was here, and he couldn't think offhand of anyone else.

Then Jenkins walked in.

"Hallo, Gray," he said.

Lorimer stared at him. Jenkins worked for a branch of one of the intelligence services, which one Lorimer had never been sure, and the two men had first met two or three years ago when the Welshman and a colleague had searched his flat during the Hizbollah business. Lorimer had become involved, and since then he had once asked Jenkins for information he couldn't obtain anywhere else, but they had never met socially, and not at all for more than a year. What the hell was Jenkins doing here now?

"What's all this about, Owen?" he demanded. "Why are you here?"

Jenkins closed the door. "Sit down," he said, taking the chair Harries had vacated. His leathery features wrinkled in disgust. "You smell awful."

"I feel awful," Lorimer told him warmly. He was almost used to the smell of the whisky by now, but he hadn't had a chance to wash or shave yet. Moreover, although the cell had been clean enough, it had left him feeling dirty. As if merely being in it had soiled him. Taking off his jacket, he tossed it into a corner; it would have to be cleaned anyway. "If that makes you feel better," he said. "What's going on?"

"First, what took you up to Iniscaig twice in a month?"

"The Fist of the Gaels burnt down our manager's house."

"That was the first time, why did you go back?"

"Our factory there buys most of the catches from the local boat, and it has a big fish farm on Loch Damph. When those maniacs blew a hole in the tank at the toxic waste plant on Liavaig it killed a lot of shellfish."

There was a risk that some of our stock might be contaminated and the
tides would carry the pollution up to the loch."

"And you found Rona Smith's body." Lorimer nodded. "Is that why
you came to Edinburgh?"

"Yes, why did you?"

Jenkins didn't answer. Looking at him, Lorimer thought, not for the
first time, that no one meeting Owen casually would imagine that he
was involved in intelligence. He was a shortish man in his early forties,
dark and wiry, with shrewd eyes and a weather-beaten look. And although he hadn't lived in Wales for many years, his speech still held
traces of a Welsh lilt.

It occurred to Lorimer that he had no idea where he was. Until now
that hadn't seemed to matter, it was the least of his problems, but it
would be as well to know. He asked Jenkins.

"The main police station in Edinburgh," the Welshman told him. He
had a detached, objective way of looking at people, and he regarded
Lorimer thoughtfully. "You make a habit of involving yourself in things
people like you have no business meddling in," he observed.

"United pay me to sort out problems," Lorimer retorted.

"Not to go haring off on your own after terrorists." Jenkins' tone had
sharpened; he meant it.

"Terrorists? You mean the Fist of the Gaels?"

Again Jenkins didn't answer at once. Lorimer guessed that he was
calculating how much to tell him, weighing the debt he and his bosses—
not to mention a lot of other people in government and out, both in
Britain and the U.S.A.—owed him against his professional obsession
with secrecy. Jenkins was a modern man, shrewd, clever and tough, and
there was nothing of the old school tie about him, but in one thing at
least he was old-fashioned: you wouldn't find him writing his memoirs,
or going on television to talk about his department after he had retired.
Lorimer respected that. At the same time, Jenkins had trusted him in
the past and he hadn't let him down.

"It isn't only what's happened up here," the Welshman said at last.
"That's small stuff. During the last month there've been an explosion of
methane gas at a toxic waste dump in Staffordshire, a minor leak at a
nuclear generating station in Cambridgeshire, serious pollution of the
Avon with industrial spillage and another leukaemia scare near a nuclear power plant in Norfolk. Plus your two incidents."

Lorimer was startled. "Too many too close together?" he suggested.

"It could be coincidence."

"Or a conspiracy? Is that what you're saying?"

"I'm not saying anything," Jenkins said.

"You wouldn't be here if you didn't think it was."

"All right, it could be."

Lorimer recalled how little had appeared in the papers about Rona Smith's death. Almost nothing, and that not true. He hadn't really believed before that Whitehall had used its authority to block the story; now he wondered. They had to be careful these days, after all the furore about government interference in the press and television and the new Official Secrets Act, but no doubt it could still be done. There were always ways if you had the power.

"And if it is, the Fist of the Gael are part of it?" he asked. This time Jenkins did say nothing. "Was McIndoe the leader?"

"Possibly. They may not have a leader; small groups like them don't always, they act like a committee."

"They have pretty impressive resources for a tiny group," Lorimer commented. "The bomb that blew up the Burtons' house wasn't the sort of thing any fifth-former could make."

"No."

"Which is one reason why you're interested in them." Jenkins' expression didn't change. "So there are other people behind them. Did they kill McIndoe?"

"If those were two questions, the answer to them both is, 'We don't know.'"

"Nor why?"

"No."

"He was rebellious—and he knew too much?" Lorimer suggested. Roy McIndoe and Rona Smith had been killed in the same way, possibly with the same gun. Perhaps McIndoe hadn't shot the girl after all.

"It's possible," Jenkins agreed. "What are you going to do now?"

"Go back to the Muirfoot, have a clean-up and get some breakfast, then catch a plane back to London."

"That's the best thing you can do." The Welshman stood up. "You needn't worry about the police here, once they have your statement they won't be interested in you any longer."

Lorimer hoped he was right.

In the doorway Jenkins paused. "I wouldn't wear that jacket on the plane if I were you," he said. The door closed behind him.

The Maestro was parked behind the police station, sand still clinging in patches to the walls of its tyres. The windows had been closed all night, and when Lorimer opened the driver's door the stench of stale whisky was like a physical blow. He drove to the hotel, had a shave and a bath, changed his clothes and went down to breakfast. By ten o'clock he had paid his bill and was heading west out of the city towards Glasgow.

He knew he was turning his back on Iniscaig. The circumstances of his return had been very different from any he had imagined when he had thought about going back there one day. The island was as beautiful as he had remembered it, but it was a place, inhabited by people with prejudices and fears like any others, not the Shangri-la he had dreamed up in his imagination. And Moira Cameron was a woman with her own life and her own memories, not the pretty eighteen-year-old he had fancied all those years ago. Perhaps it was a good thing he had gone back; doing so had purged him of his fantasies, and fantasies, like dreams, only cluttered up your life.

At the airport he returned the Maestro, apologising for the smell. He had had the driver's window open and the fan on all the way there, but the odour still lingered.

"A friend of mine spilt half a bottle of whisky," he explained.

The pretty receptionist smiled. "Och, what a waste!" she said sympathetically.

Lorimer paid his bill and caught the next flight to Heathrow. It was Sunday afternoon, he could go straight to his flat and relax. He needed to sit down quietly and think about the events of the past three days. So much had happened so quickly that he had had little time to consider what was behind it all, but one thing was clear—the attempt to frame him for McIndoe's murder meant two things: one, the murderers knew too much about his movements for comfort, and two, once they knew they had failed they might act again.

The next morning Lorimer went to United House as usual. There was a triple load of papers to check on Mondays, and it took him some time to go through them. When he had finished he started writing his report. He was still working on it when his phone rang and the chairman told him to come in.

"He has Mr. Forsyth with him," Helen Wilkins said as he passed.

Grantley was seated at his big desk, United's newest director on a chair at an angle to it. The sun, shining in through the tall windows, lit Forsyth's face. A lock of his hair had fallen forward, and he pushed it back in a gesture so often repeated that it was almost unconscious.

"Sit down, Gray," the chairman said. "How did you get on?"

"Not too badly. There were one or two problems, but I don't think they'll affect United."

Grantley knew his man too well to let that pass. When Lorimer spoke of problems he didn't mean there were no television sets in the hotel bedrooms. "What happened?" he demanded.

"It was a girl called Rona Smith who blew up the house; she was a student at Edinburgh and she'd stayed on the island just before. Her body was washed up on the beach near the factory on Thursday; she'd been shot through the back of the head."

The two men gazed at him.

"I saw something in the *Times* about a girl being washed up there," Forsyth said. "It didn't say she'd been shot. And there wasn't anything about her being a member of any group."

"No," Lorimer agreed.

Grantley was frowning. "Didn't the police know about her?"

Lorimer had asked himself the same question. They must have enquired about anybody who had visited the island recently and checked on them. Maybe they had known about Rona Smith; the odds were Wallace wouldn't have told him if they had. There were too many angles to this business. Too many prohibitions. Did they account for Jenkins' being in Edinburgh? "I don't know," he said.

"You think she was involved in the sabotage at the plant on Liavaig too?" Forsyth asked.

"Not actively. I talked to somebody who heard her arguing with another of the group that they shouldn't go ahead with it." Lorimer paused. "He was murdered near Edinburgh on Saturday night, shot through the back of the head like her."

"Good God!" Grantley looked shaken.

Briefly Lorimer related what had happened that night, omitting any mention of Jenkins and what he had told him. The Welshman was his private contact, and the fewer people who knew about him the better. Grantley did, but he wouldn't say anything.

"I see what you meant by some problems," Forsyth said drily when he finished.

The chairman smiled ironically. "Gray's given a new meaning to the term 'trouble-shooter,'" he commented. "He's more like a trouble-diviner."

Forsyth laughed. "So it looks as if they were both murdered by another member of the group," he said, serious again. "They sound fanatical enough. What's the position now?"

"It's up to the police," Lorimer told him. "They're satisfied I didn't have anything to do with what happened to McIndoe and the girl, and as far as I'm concerned that's that."

"It's something, anyway," Grantley conceded. "Burton says that the worst of the trouble there seems to be over, but he's getting supplies from Mallaig and Ullapool to see them through until the local fishing picks up again."

"This business will have hit the island boats pretty hard," Forsyth said. "It'll take a while for things to get back to normal."

The chairman grunted. He wasn't unsympathetic, but it wasn't his or United's responsibility to alleviate the fishermen's plight. No doubt the waste disposal company would compensate them in time. "All right, Gray," he said. "Thanks."

Lorimer returned to his own room.

Ten minutes later Forsyth stuck his head round the door. "I wondered if you'd care to come round for dinner one evening," he said. "I'd like to hear more about Iniscaig, we've a place up there."

Lorimer was surprised, both by the invitation and because he hadn't known that Forsyth had such direct connections with Iniscaig. At the same time he didn't want to go to dinner; Forsyth seemed pleasant enough, but he was a director, and in Lorimer's book there was a word for people who hobnobbed socially with their bosses. Moreover he couldn't see why Forsyth should invite him merely to talk about a part of the country he apparently knew well already.

"How about Thursday evening, if you've nothing better to do?" Forsyth suggested. "Are you married? If you—"

"We're separated."

"There'll be just the three of us then. Seven-thirty all right? It's 23, Fairhaven Gardens, off Campden Hill."

Lorimer knew he was cornered. "Thank you," he said.

"We'll look forward to seeing you then. 'Bye."

Forsyth went out, and Lorimer resumed writing his report. He finished it before lunch, and for the rest of the day concentrated on the work which had accumulated while he was in Scotland.

He reached home in time to switch on for the Channel Four News at seven. The main story, about political developments in France, was followed by another long report on environmental issues. Channel Four wearing its heart on its sleeve, he had once commented to Rosalind, who had worked for Independent Television News before moving to Barbican. She hadn't been amused.

This evening, remembering what Jenkins had told him, he watched more attentively than he might otherwise have done. He heard nothing new, and when the next item was a report about the by-election for the European Parliament in that part of London, campaigning for which had just started, he switched off and went out for a meal. When—if— the European Economic Community became a united Europe, it would be different; in the meantime he found it hard to work up much interest in an election for a parliament which still lacked real power and whose activities received scant attention in the media.

Some of the windows along the street displayed posters supporting one or other of the candidates. The area was a Conservative stronghold, yet many of them were in the green and white of the Nature Party, a small, fairly way-out movement which took up every environmental issue going. Times were changing.

Lorimer didn't linger over his meal and went straight home afterwards. When he walked into his flat the phone was ringing.

It was Rosalind. "When did you get back?" she asked.

Lorimer kicked the door shut. "Yesterday evening."

"How was your trip?"

She sounded too interested. Nowadays any overt show of interest or affection from her aroused Lorimer's suspicions. "Okay," he said.

"There's something I want to talk to you about. Will you come to the Nature Party's election meeting tomorrow evening?"

"Me?" Lorimer was startled. "You must be out of your lovely little mind, you know what I think about politicians."

"It could be interesting," Rosalind said matter-of-factly. "You've never heard Edward Horwill, have you?"

Lorimer recalled reading that Horwill had taken over as the party's leader after the election a few months ago. "No," he admitted.

"He isn't like the others."

The way Rosalind said it stirred Lorimer's curiosity. "Do you know him?" he asked.

"As a matter of fact, I do." Her tone was too light, too carefully casual.

Know your enemies, Lorimer told himself. But he had no intention of going to any party's meeting. Then he remembered his conversation with Jenkins and decided it might be worth hearing what capital the Nature Party made out of the recent "accidents." It was hardly likely they would ignore such ammunition when it was handed to them, on a plate. "All right," he agreed.

"Oh good!" Clearly Rosalind was both surprised and pleased.

The meeting was being held at a hall not far from Southwold Terrace; they arranged that she would come to his flat at seven, and Lorimer hung up. He had an uneasy suspicion that Edward Horwill was the new man in Rosalind's life. But if so, why did she want him to go with her to hear him speak? She had never wanted him to meet her men friends before. Horwill must be different. And she had said there was something she wanted to discuss with him. Was it a divorce? Lorimer liked that thought even less, but he still couldn't see why Rosalind had wanted him to accompany her to the meeting. Maybe she was keen to show off Horwill, for him to be impressed. If so, she was going to be disappointed.

The hall was old and more than a little dingy. When Rosalind and Lorimer arrived five minutes before the meeting was due to start Lorimer was surprised to find the main body already fairly full, and, to judge from the shuffling of feet overhead, the balcony was filling up fast. He said so to Rosalind, and she smiled. A shade smugly, Lorimer thought.

"You get so immersed in your own little world you don't see what's going on round you," she told him.

The unjust jibe stung Lorimer. "The Nature Party's a nine day wonder," he said. He would have preferred to sit near the back, but Rosalind had ignored his pleas and led him resolutely to the front where he perched uncomfortably on a flimsy chair at the end of a row.

"You think so?" Clearly Rosalind didn't, and she was confident that she was right.

A steward was patrolling the aisle on their side of the hall. He was young, probably a year or two younger than Lorimer, and about six feet tall, with rather long, curly fair hair. He was wearing a tan leather jacket over a sports shirt open at the neck and denim trousers. There was nothing unusual about his appearance, you saw a hundred men like him walking along the streets any day, but it seemed to Lorimer that he had seen him somewhere before. He tried to remember where.

He was still doing so when the platform party appeared from the wings and settled itself, and the chairman rose to introduce Horwill. Lorimer hadn't known what to expect, but he wasn't prepared for the youngish, dark and smoothly handsome man who stood up, smiled and thanked the chairman. In his grey suit, his striped tie carefully knotted, the party's new leader looked like a yuppie who had made it. As a Conservative candidate he would have been conventional; as the leader of the Nature Party he was startling.

He spoke with the fervour Lorimer had expected, but it was a fervour based on hard practicalities. Horwill was no dreamy idealist. For him, it seemed, his party's policies were the only ones possible if the world wasn't to destroy itself. He was against nuclear weapons and for a strong, united Europe. Most of all he was against the world's blind refusal to stop destroying itself.

"Have we learnt nothing from Chernobyl?" he demanded. "In terms of what might have happened, what may still happen, Chernobyl was a minor incident, yet hundreds of people have died, thousands will die and tens of thousands have been made homeless as a result of it. Even now sheep in parts of Scotland and Wales and the North of England can't be moved because they're contaminated by the fall-out. And another Chernobyl could happen here tomorrow, a Chernobyl far worse, far more devastating than the first one. We know now it happened at Windscale in the fifties and was hushed up by the government of the day. People were deliberately misled then, as they are misled now. If we go on putting our faith in nuclear energy, building new power stations, those monstrous temples to ignorance and folly, it will happen again. Only in the last few days we have had reports that the rate of leukaemia amongst children in an area near one of our nuclear power stations is ten times the national average. The U.S.A. has stopped building them; will we never learn?

"But nuclear energy isn't the only major threat to our future. Perhaps toxic waste is an even greater danger. No sane person will condone the act of a group of fanatics who blew a hole in a tank at that disposal plant in Scotland, releasing highly toxic waste into the sea and killing thousands of fish. And not only killing those fish; three miles away was one of the biggest fish farms in Britain, supplying a major cannery. The company which owns them is highly reputable, and I am confident it will have ensured that none of their stock was contaminated. At least" —Horwill paused for a moment—"we must hope so. But you can see how close disaster was. To any intelligent being it must be almost inconceivable that the government, any government, should allow a toxic waste disposal plant to be built there. But it was done. And what happened at Liavaig is a warning to us all. It's not how it happened that matters, but that it could."

There was an outburst of applause, and Horwill took a sip from a glass of water on the table in front of him. He had all the politicians' tricks, Lorimer thought bitterly. He was a smooth, conceited bastard, an opportunist politician climbing on to a fashionable bandwagon, and, if he was interested in the causes he espoused, they came behind his own interests. A long way behind.

"At last," Horwill continued, "the powers-that-be in other countries are listening to the scientists who have been warning for years about dangers to the atmosphere: a year or two ago an American official came out and stated publicly that it was ninety-nine percent certain that the Greenhouse Effect was responsible for the worst drought for decades in the greatest grain-producing area in the world.

"Natural disasters we may be able to do little or nothing to prevent; does that mean we should reduce our chances of survival by courting unnatural ones? The Nature Party isn't the insignificant little group of cranks our opponents would have you believe; all over the world thinking people know we are right. Our opponents say we are reactionaries, that we look back to an idealised world which never existed. I tell you, we are not reactionaries, we are in the vanguard of a great, a world-wide movement. For years now the Green Party in Germany has had members in their parliament and has been a real force in national politics— do we have to lag behind?"

When Horwill eventually sat down the applause was spontaneous and enthusiastic. It lasted for several minutes, and Lorimer saw that Rosalind's eyes were shining.

"Well?" she demanded.

"He's good," he conceded grudgingly.

"That's all you can say?"

"Okay, a lot of what he said's right." There was no point in telling her what he really thought of Horwill, she would put it down to spite or jealousy.

"You admit that?"

"Of course I do. Any intelligent person would."

"The trouble," Rosalind observed bitterly, "is that so few people are intelligent. What are you going to do now?"

"Eat?" Lorimer suggested.

Rosalind hesitated. But on the platform Horwill was surrounded by enthusiastic supporters. "Yes, all right," she agreed.

They joined one of the lines of people moving slowly towards the doors. The fair-haired steward was on duty in the foyer. Lorimer chanced to look that way, and for a moment their eyes met, but the steward showed no sign of recognition.

"Are you coming, Gray?" Rosalind said with a touch of impatience. Lorimer realised that he was blocking the way. "Yes," he said.

He had remembered now where he had seen the steward before; the man had come with Jenkins to search his flat that night more than two years ago. Jenkins had called him Clive. What the hell was he doing here?

"People are worried, Gray." Rosalind frowned earnestly.

They had come to a little Spanish restaurant near the hall, and now she leaned forward, her chin resting on her clasped hands. She had always looked particularly lovely when she was being serious about something, Lorimer thought. And when she was happy, her eyes shining. God, how he wanted her! He ached with longing. Lust and love, where did one end and the other begin? He should have seen her to the Tube station and said good-bye, he must be a masochist to bring her here.

"They're beginning to see what our way of life is doing to the world," she went on, apparently oblivious of his suffering. "You saw how many people were there tonight; a year ago there wouldn't have been a dozen. And I'll take a bet with you that ninety percent of them have always voted Tory or Democrat until now."

"People have to be concerned about something," Lorimer told her, making himself think about what she was saying because it was easier than thinking about the way she looked and how close she was. "If it isn't cancer, it's heart disease. And if it isn't either of them, it's nuclear war or acid rain."

"You're saying we shouldn't care?"

"No, of course I'm not." Too late Lorimer reminded himself that Rosalind had always been able to make him rise to her bait when they had an argument. She was too intelligent, that was the trouble. But he couldn't stand feather-brained women. "It's just that you attract all the nuts."

"All right," Rosalind said, "how many people did you expect would be there tonight? Be honest."

"Ten or fifteen."

"There you are."

"For heaven's sake, it's a by-election—for the European Parliament, not Westminster. It doesn't mean anything."

"And the European election in May? When the green parties did better than they'd ever done before, not only on the Continent but here as well? Did that mean nothing?"

"It was a protest against the other parties. When the next general election comes people will go back to voting the way they've always done." They might be worried, but not many put environmental matters ahead of issues like defence, education and unemployment; they were the icing on the cake. It was all a question of personal priorities, like choosing whether to buy a new carpet or go on holiday when you couldn't afford both. The trouble was no party's policies provided for all your priorities, you had to compromise.

"You said you wanted to talk about something," Lorimer reminded Rosalind. He *was* a masochist, he thought. Why otherwise should he bring that up now, when she hadn't mentioned it?

For the first time that evening she looked unsure of herself. "Not now, Gray," she said. "I'd rather leave it to another time."

"Okay." It might be only postponing the evil day; it was still a relief. "Your trip went all right then?"

"Not bad."

Like Grantley, Rosalind knew Lorimer too well to let that pass. "What happened?" she asked.

Just in time Lorimer remembered that, although his wife might be a television producer now, she was still by instinct and training a journalist. "Have you heard anything about a stop being put on any story during the last few days?" he asked her.

"A stop?"

"A D-notice, or whatever they use now. Some sort of official ban."

"I haven't heard of one. I wouldn't necessarily, though. Why?"

Lorimer hesitated. But Jenkins hadn't told him to say nothing, and Rosalind might be able to help. "The girl who blew up United's house on Iniscaig was a member of Dorn nan Gaidheal," he said. "Her body was washed up there on Thursday. I found her. She'd been shot through the back of the head."

"Oh no!" Living in a world where she saw images of violence all the time, both at work and on television at home, Rosalind was still appalled by it.

"She was wearing a wet suit, and the pathologist said she'd probably been killed the previous Sunday. That was the night they blew the hole in the tank on Liavaig."

Rosalind frowned. "What are you getting at, Gray?"

"I don't know. Nothing maybe. But there were three reporters still on the island, and I wonder why the story that got into the press didn't mention that she belonged to the group, or that she'd been shot. Her boyfriend, Roy McIndoe, was one of the Fist too. He was murdered on Saturday evening, shot the same way as she was, and there hasn't been anything about his connection with them either."

"You mean, there's been an official cover-up?"

"I don't know," Lorimer said again. Jenkins had talked about other incidents, which might or might not have been the work of the Fist of the Gaels, although it seemed unlikely, but that didn't explain the apparent embargo on news about the two murders.

"Do you want me to see what I can find out?" Rosalind asked.

"If you can," Lorimer said. "Please."

SEVEN

GREAT OAKS from little acorns grow. Similarly, shattering consequences may result from the most trivial remarks.

"Come and meet my wife," Forsyth said.

Lorimer followed him across the hall.

Good-looking men often marry plain women, as if subconsciously they shrink from the competition a pretty wife would provide. Forsyth was either very sure of himself, or he didn't care; the woman who came towards them as they entered the drawing room was exquisitely beautiful. A little above average height, she was slender, although there was nothing in the least boyish about her figure, with fine grey eyes under delicate, rather straight brows, and almost silver blonde hair. She was wearing a simple dark red dress with a pearl necklace and pearl stud earrings.

"Darling, this is Graham Lorimer," Forsyth said.

She held out a slender, capable hand. "Hallo, Graham. Robin's told me about you; I'm so glad you could come." Her eyes smiled at him and there was no trace of graciousness in her manner. Her voice, a rich, slightly husky contralto, was another surprise; Lorimer hadn't known Forsyth's wife was American.

"What will you have to drink, Gray?" Forsyth asked.

"Whisky, please."

"You, darling?"

"My usual."

Her husband walked over to a table by one wall and busied himself with bottles, decanters and glasses, and Hilary turned back to Lorimer.

"Robin says you've been up to Iniscaig," she remarked. "Isn't it beautiful? We both love it, Iniscaig Lodge is our real home. We'd spend longer there if it weren't for Robin's work; he's so busy here and in Edinburgh we never seem to get a chance to go away."

Lorimer had seen the Lodge, a Victorian Scots-baronial house nestling between the mountains in Glen Fhada, many times, but he had had no idea that the Forsyths owned it. And when he invited him to dinner this evening Forsyth had only said vaguely, "We have a place up there." Lorimer had assumed he meant somewhere on the mainland.

Hilary's wonderful eyes clouded. "You had a horrible experience while you were there, he said."

Lorimer wondered which experience she meant.

"Finding that poor girl washed up like that."

"Yes, it wasn't very pleasant. Mrs. Forsyth—"

"For God's sake!" Her smile wasn't brilliant—that would suggest something too obvious, too superficial—rather it was warm and genuinely amused. "You make me feel about seventy! I'm Hilary."

"And I'm Robin," Forsyth said over his shoulder. He came back with their drinks. "What did you think of the meeting the other evening?"

Lorimer was startled, he had had no idea that his host had been there. He wasn't a supporter of the Nature Party, surely; had Hilary dragged him along? He knew Forsyth was watching him, waiting to hear what he said, and he wondered why he should have this feeling that his answer mattered. After all, it was only social chat. "I thought he spoke well," he said carefully.

Hilary's laughter was devoid of malice. "Is that all? My God, you Scots! You're as cautious as Robin."

Forsyth ignored the jibe. "Yes, he did," he agreed. "He's a damned fine speaker."

He had spoken thoughtfully, and Lorimer gained the impression that there was more behind the words than was immediately apparent. It was as if Forsyth, too, had reservations about Edward Horwill.

"You men don't trust him because he's so attractive," Hilary protested. She was looking at Lorimer, but her words were directed at her husband. "You think there must be something wrong about a man who's as gorgeous as that."

" 'Such men are dangerous,' " Lorimer quoted, and immediately felt foolish.

"To other men," Hilary said, her eyes full of mischief and speaking to Lorimer now. "Personally, I thought he was wonderful. Everything he said was just so true."

Lorimer was torn between pleasure at the suggestion of intimacy in the way she was looking at him and a wish that she wouldn't. Why did some women possess an aura of sexuality which had nothing to do with their actions?

"Do you know anything about Horwill?" Forsyth asked, apparently oblivious of the effect his wife was having. Perhaps he was too used to it to notice.

Lorimer dragged his thoughts back. "Not much," he admitted.

Rosalind had told him that the Nature Party's new leader was the chairman of a company producing advanced computer software. He was wealthy, lived in Hampstead and was deeply committed to the party's cause. She had met him when he had appeared on a recent "Mirror on the Week" programme.

"And?" Lorimer had asked. He wondered if it was significant that she hadn't mentioned Horwill's personal qualities; if she had said he was charming or clever, he would have known things weren't serious. As it was . . .

"And what?" Rosalind had bridled slightly.

"You want him."

"Do you have to be so bloody basic?" She had toyed with the food on her plate. "Very well, I like him."

"And?" Lorimer had asked again. He dreaded her answer, but he had to know.

"I'm not sure," Rosalind confessed reluctantly. "We've been out a couple of times; he and his wife are getting divorced. I don't know."

He didn't want to talk about Horwill, Lorimer thought now, sipping his drink and trying not to look at Hilary Forsyth too often. He wanted to forget all about him and have Rosalind forget him too. Because this time it was serious, he knew that.

"You think he and his crowd are right?" Forsyth enquired.

"I think they have a point."

"Oh yes, they have, several points. Very valid ones. That's how they succeed in appealing to so many intelligent people."

"One should listen to all sides," Hilary observed with a hint of irony. "Even if one disagrees with them. That's the civilised way, I guess."

"But you don't, do you, darling?" Forsyth said. Somewhere swords clashed.

Hilary smiled at Lorimer. "I agree with Gray."

Her husband's thoughts had moved on. "The trouble is, they twist everything to justify their arguments," he said. "We've got to have progress, or we'll end up in another Dark Ages. And it's regrettable, but there are bound to be accidents; there always have been, and there always will be. You don't accept all Horwill said, do you?"

It sounded like a challenge, Lorimer thought. Everybody seemed to be challenging him lately. "No," he answered. "Not all of it."

"The price for what people call progress may be too high," Hilary protested.

Forsyth ignored her; he was still watching Lorimer.

"I'm not that interested in politics," Lorimer told him. "I only went because my wife talked me into going with her."

"Was that lovely girl you were with your wife?" Hilary asked.

"Yes." Lorimer was pleased by the compliment to Rosalind, but he knew he was deluding himself if he thought he had any part of it. He had gone to a meeting with a beautiful woman, that was all; it made no difference to anything. Seeing the look on his host's face, he explained, "We're still friends, we see each other sometimes. She knows Horwill, and she wanted me to hear him."

"Oh, I see," Forsyth said. Lorimer wondered why he sounded so thoughtful.

Soon after that they went in to dinner. It was a pleasant meal, the food and wine very good and the atmosphere relaxed. Forsyth wanted to know all that Lorimer could tell him about the situation on Iniscaig: how serious the pollution was, its effect on the island's fishermen as well as the salmon farm and the cannery, and what was being done to clear it up.

"Have the police any idea who's behind Dorn nan Gaidheal and who murdered those two?" he asked.

"I don't know," Lorimer admitted. "They weren't saying anything." Most of what he did know he had told Grantley in Forsyth's presence the other day; part of the rest he intended keeping to himself.

Forsyth frowned. "What's secret about it?"

Lorimer didn't know that either; Rosalind hadn't been able to find out anything.

Hilary sensed that he didn't want to talk about Iniscaig any more and changed the subject by asking if he had seen a new film which had opened in the West End a few days before to a barrage of advance publicity. After that no one mentioned Iniscaig or the Fist of the Gaels. Lorimer realised that he was talking more than usual, and he suspected that the Forsyths, perhaps from different motives, were deliberately drawing him out. He didn't mind. On the contrary, he was curious: he couldn't see why his host should be interested in his opinions.

Hilary contributed her share to the conversation. Lorimer hadn't doubted that she was intelligent; now he found that she possessed a sense of humour too, and she clearly enjoyed provoking him with extravagant assertions she expected him to challenge. At times her husband seemed content to be an observer, listening to the two of them and taking no part in the talk. Then he would join in again, easily and fluently, revealing his knowledge of a wide range of subjects but never flaunting it. Lorimer had a feeling that a steely quality underlaid his easy charm, and he was glad that Forsyth wasn't an enemy.

Agreeable though the evening was, he wondered why he was there. He knew he was being assessed. So much was obvious—more than once he saw an appraising look in Forsyth's eye—but why?

He walked home feeling restless and vaguely ill at ease. Too much was happening which he didn't understand, but which seemed to involve him. Too many apparently unconnected things. Originally he had believed that the men who abducted him in Edinburgh hadn't intended him to be found until the effects of the chloroform had worn off; now he thought it more likely that they had wanted him still to be unsteady on his feet, with a brain like soggy paper. The police would discover that, however much whisky he appeared to have drunk, there was very little alcohol in his blood, they would learn of his visit to the house in Ravelston that afternoon and his interest in McIndoe and assume that he had faked his drunkenness to provide him with an alibi for the time of the murder. At the least they would concentrate their inquiries on him for a time, and perhaps time was all the murderers needed.

Time to get away? Out of the country, perhaps? Hugh Bascomb had believed that the man he had seen twice with McIndoe was Dutch or German and, according to Sue Johnstone, the man who went to the house in Ravelston looking for McIndoe on the afternoon he was killed had spoken with a German accent. Bascomb had said something else too—that he had had an impression of inherent evil. And Hugh wasn't given to flights of fancy.

So much Lorimer could understand, and presumably Jenkins' appearance on the scene had been as fortuitous as he claimed, but what had Clive been doing at Tuesday's meeting? Lorimer suspected that Hilary's comment about listening to all sides was only half the truth, and she and Forsyth had had a more concrete motive for going to hear Horwill.

Even at past eleven-thirty traffic was streaming along Cromwell Road. Lorimer crossed at the lights, turned left, then almost immediately right into a street of uniform Victorian houses. He wondered if Jenkins was correct, and the string of incidents which had started with the burning down of the Burtons' house were more than coincidence. He couldn't believe it. Because, if so, it meant that there was a conspiracy to cause damage to the environment on a massive scale, and that didn't make sense.

Anyway there was a snag to such a theory—the burning down of the house didn't fit it. It was the sort of act which was becoming almost routine for extremist groups like the Fist of the Gaels, designed to hurt the "enemy" and attract publicity for the cause, but it had nothing to do with the environment.

The sabotage of the toxic waste tank was a different matter, it fitted only too well. But it too differed from the other incidents in one important respect: while they, contrived or not, appeared to be accidents, the Fist of the Gaels had claimed responsibility for the attack on Liavaig almost immediately. Perhaps they had had to, because it would have been impossible to make the damage to the tank look like an accident. But whatever their reasons, their claim had ensured that responsibility for it was placed fairly and squarely on a small group of Scottish extremists. No one else was considered.

The Fist had done it, but had they been acting alone? The group was new, unknown even to the police until they blew up the Burtons' house; had that act been intended, not as a blow against United or the "English" government, but to establish their credentials and give them a recognisable identity? So that when the real operation was mounted at Liavaig no one would question their claim that they were responsible.

According to Sue Johnstone, Rona Smith had protested, "We can't, not that," and McIndoe had told her, "We haven't any choice, we've got to." Not "You've got to," but "We." That suggested that not only Rona, but he too, and probably the whole group were under pressure from outside. Lorimer knew he might be jumping to conclusions, but he was satisfied that Rona and McIndoe had been talking about attacking the tank at Liavaig; the Fist had admitted responsibility for no other act since then.

Moira Cameron had maintained that Rona was too sensible and too concerned about the environment to be a party to the sabotage; it looked very much as if she had stuck to her principles, and paid with her life for doing so. Perhaps she had threatened to go to the police.

And McIndoe? Why had he been killed? After his talk to Sue Johnstone, Lorimer had believed that McIndoe had murdered Rona; now he was less sure. It seemed more likely that the same person had shot them both. Had McIndoe known too much about the girl's death and other matters? The police had been looking for him; had someone felt he couldn't be trusted to keep his mouth shut when they found him?

One thing was certain; if anybody was backing the Fist of the Gaels, they were even more ruthless than the group they were using.

The next morning as usual Lorimer bought a paper on his way to work. There was a good deal about the by-election, and he scanned it briefly. The latest opinion poll showed support for the Conservatives down by six percent and for the other main parties by almost as much. The only gain had been made by the Nature Party, up by nine percent. If the trend continued, the paper's political correspondent wrote, the unthinkable would happen and the Conservatives would lose the seat. The editorial considered the reasons for the phenomenon, which was manifesting itself in other countries in Western Europe as well as Britain. Not least, it suggested, was the dynamic new leadership of the parties.

Rosalind would be pleased, Lorimer thought. The notion gave him no satisfaction, and he turned to the sports pages. But he didn't read what was there; he kept thinking about Hilary Forsyth. He had met plenty of attractive women in his time, some of them lovely, but only one with her combination of beauty, warmth and intelligence. And Rosalind was no longer available.

The train stopped at Victoria. He went up the escalator to the street and walked along to United House, making a conscious effort not to think about anything to do with last night. Whoever was behind the Fist of the Gaels—if anybody was—and whatever was going on, it was no concern of his. Jenkins was in the picture, and the Welshman was an experienced, intelligent officer. An expert. Leave it to him.

It was no good. If he was right, it was his concern, and he couldn't just opt out.

Nor did he want to. His feelings owed nothing to altruism or public spirit: they had attacked him and used him, and he was damned if he would just sit back and do nothing about it. But what could he do?

In the foyer of United House people were hurrying towards the row of lifts.

" 'Morning, sir," Dobbs said. "Lovely day again."

Lorimer realised that he hadn't even noticed that the sun was shining and it was warm. He was becoming obsessed. "Lovely," he agreed.

The usual pile of newspapers was on his desk where one of the porters had put it, ready for him to go through. He sat down, picked up the top one and scanned the front page.

A few minutes later he heard Helen Wilkins go into her room and close the door. It was a day just like any other, and he hoped devoutly that it would stay that way.

The only references to United or any of its subsidiaries in the papers were notes on the City pages of two of them reporting a prominent brokers' recommendation of the shares as a "hold." City comment didn't come within Lorimer's ambit, and he ignored them.

At a quarter past ten he dialled the Forsyths' number. A woman's voice that was nothing like Hilary's answered and told him Mrs. Forsyth was out. Lorimer asked her if she would tell her that he had called to thank her for such a good evening last night. The woman promised she would and he replaced the phone feeling more disappointed than he had any right to do.

Grantley was addressing a BIM conference in Oxford, and Lorimer was free to get on with his other work. He had had his coffee and was concentrating on a report from a manager in Singapore when there was a tap on his door and Hughes, the porter who looked after the fourteenth floor, put his head round it and told him that there was a lady to see him.

Lorimer couldn't remember the last time anyone had been to see him here.

The porter stepped back and Hilary Forsyth walked into the room looking elegant and beautiful in a grey and white dress and a lightweight white coat, her blonde hair immaculate. With her came a hint of some subtle perfume.

"Hallo, Gray," she said.

Hughes withdrew, closing the door softly behind him, and Lorimer stood up, hoping the little surge of pleasure and excitement he couldn't quite suppress didn't show. Hilary must have come to see her husband

and looked in to have a word with him while she was here. But surely she knew that Forsyth only came to United House on Thursdays for board meetings, and wouldn't be here today?

"Hallo," he said. "Will you sit down?"

She did so gracefully, folding her long legs. "You look surprised."

"I am," Lorimer admitted. "I tried to ring you a little while ago to thank you for last night."

"Did you? I hope you enjoyed yourself, I did." Hilary paused. "I thought, if you weren't doing anything, we might have lunch."

Lorimer felt slightly stunned: directors' wives didn't often walk into p.a.'s' offices and suggest lunch together. Hilary might be no older than he was and an American, but they didn't do it in America either.

"You aren't, are you?" she asked.

"No."

"That's great. I have to get some things at Harrods, what do you say we meet in the Trafalgar Bar at a quarter past twelve? Can you make it then?"

Lorimer was free to come and go more or less as he liked, and the prospect of spending an hour or two with Hilary was more than just pleasant. Nevertheless he was uneasy; he was pretty sure that Robin Forsyth wouldn't be joining them. If she had been twenty years older, or if her manner last night had been cooler and more remote, it would have been different, but she wasn't, it hadn't and she was very desirable.

Hell, he thought, where was the harm in it? She was suggesting lunch, not an afternoon in some sordid hotel. Maybe having lunch with a director's wife at her invitation counted as duty; after all, duty didn't have to be unpleasant.

"Robin's gone to Edinburgh," Hilary said, as if reading his thoughts. "He's on the boards of two of those investment trusts, and they have their offices in Charlotte Square."

Lorimer didn't need telling that the solid Victorian buildings round the square housed some of the shrewdest financial brains in the world; Forsyth was a member of a peculiarly distinguished club. "Oh," he said.

"That's all right then?" Hilary asked. "Twelve-fifteen at Harrods? I want to ask your advice about something."

"Yes," Lorimer agreed. It would make a change from the staff dining room or a pint and a ploughman's in the pub round the corner.

"Good." Hilary unfolded her legs and stood up.

As they passed the end of the side corridor on the way to the lift

Lorimer saw Philip Rayment coming towards them. If Rayment only knew, he thought. He smiled at the idea.

"You look cheerful," Hilary said.

"Shouldn't I?"

"Why not? I guess it's a compliment."

Lorimer saw no need to explain that she was only indirectly the cause of his good humour, and pressed the button for the lift.

There weren't many people in the Trafalgar Bar at ten past twelve. Lorimer found a table and ordered a gin and tonic.

Hilary arrived only a few minutes late. "You don't have to rush back, do you, Gray?" she asked when the waiter had come and she had ordered a glass of dry white wine.

"No."

"So we can just relax and enjoy ourselves. Great."

Time seemed to flow gently rather than rush by. They had another drink, and it was nearly one o'clock before they went in to lunch. Lorimer's initial uneasiness had faded. He was enjoying himself, and he wondered how much of his enjoyment was due to his feeling that they were breaking the rules.

Amongst the suburban housewives and tourists in the restaurant Hilary stood out, cool, elegant and poised. She had asked for a table by a window and—inevitably, it seemed to Lorimer—they had been shown to the last one still unoccupied.

"You said you wanted to ask me about something," he reminded her when they returned from the carvery.

Hilary's plate was piled high. There was nothing wrong with her appetite, he thought.

"Oh that. It can wait." She watched while Lorimer poured wine into her glass. "I guess you think I hi-jacked you into having lunch with me, don't you?"

"No."

"I wanted to see you again." She said it simply, as if she meant it.

"I came to dinner last night," Lorimer pointed out.

"That was eighteen hours ago." She faced him squarely across the table. "You aren't blind, you know why."

"Look—" Lorimer began.

"I said I wanted to see you again. What the hell's wrong with our having lunch together?" The people at the nearest tables had gone and Hilary had spoken quietly; no one could have heard her. "I'm not suggesting we go to bed. If you think it isn't right because I'm married and my husband is one of your bosses . . . That's what you mean, isn't it?"

"Something like that," Lorimer admitted.

"It's garbage. We're adult people, not slaves. Anyway, Robin couldn't care less."

Lorimer couldn't believe he had heard her right.

Hilary toyed with her fork, ignoring the food on her plate. "He has other interests." She saw Lorimer's expression. "You don't believe it? There's a girl in Edinburgh."

"I'm sorry." It sounded damned silly, Lorimer thought. Inadequate. But he didn't know what else to say.

"You don't believe me, do you?" Hilary looked down at her plate, avoiding his eye. "Well, it's true. I wish to God it wasn't. Now let's talk about something else."

When eventually the time came for them to go she insisted on paying the bill.

Lorimer protested, but short of creating a scene in front of several hundred people, he didn't see what he could do.

"It was my idea," Hilary said. She smiled. "You can pay next time."

Lorimer told himself she didn't mean it, it was just something people said, and wished she had.

While they waited for the lift she told him, "I have to get something for my niece in the book department, so I'll get off there. I've enjoyed our lunch, Gray."

"So have I," Lorimer said.

The lift came at that moment, and they were swept into it by the people waiting behind them. Lorimer saw Hilary smiling at him between two heads, then the lift stopped at the second floor and she got out, mouthing a silent "Good-bye."

He was nearly back at United House before he remembered that she hadn't mentioned whatever it was she had intended to ask him. But perhaps there hadn't been anything; she had wanted a shoulder to cry on and he had provided it.

It was better than nothing, he supposed. But not much.

EIGHT

LORIMER DIDN'T EXPECT to see Hilary Forsyth again. If by chance he did, it would be when she was accompanying her husband at some group function. She was a dream and, like most dreams, she was unattainable. She wasn't only the wife of one of United's directors, she was rich in her own right; her father had made a fortune in Texan oil and augmented it by deals in property and television stations while the economy of the Lone Star State was still booming. Even if she hadn't been married, nothing could have come of their seeing each other, they inhabited different worlds.

Maybe she was indulging in her own fantasies. If what she had told him about Forsyth was true, that was understandable, and asking him to have lunch with her had been a game, perhaps to prove to herself that she was still attractive to men. As if she could have had any doubts about that. Whatever her motive had been, her talk of another time had meant nothing, and they both knew it.

Lorimer turned his thoughts to other things. In Edinburgh, when he had suggested to Jenkins that there were people behind the Fist of the Gaels, backing them, the Welshman had ignored the bait. Possibly he didn't know, but Lorimer doubted that. Jenkins was as devious in his way as Grantley. Which was saying a lot.

What was his real interest in the group? Was it what he claimed, that there had been too many "incidents" for them all to be coincidences, or was there more to it? Something he wasn't prepared, or able, to divulge even to Lorimer, whom he had been ready to trust in the past?

To hell with the whole business, Lorimer thought. He had done what he had gone to Iniscaig to do, his report would be on the Old Man's desk tomorrow morning and he had enough work on his desk to keep him busy for the next week. He couldn't care less if anybody was backing McIndoe's group.

Even at the time he didn't believe it.

On his way home, he bought a *Standard* at Victoria. There was more about the by-election, but he ignored it. To hell with Horwill too.

If it had been a few weeks later in the year, he would have had tomorrow's match to think about. Travelling, the game itself and a few drinks with the rest of the lads in the evening would have occupied most of Saturday. But pre-season training didn't start for another five weeks, and being away last weekend he hadn't made any plans for this one.

Other people were going home along Southwold Terrace. Lorimer turned into Number 15, climbed the stairs to the second floor and felt in his pocket for his keys.

A leaflet had been pushed under his door. He stooped to pick it up, saw the legend "THE NATURE PARTY—THE SAFEGUARD FOR YOUR FUTURE" and took it into the living room.

The man standing by the window turned. "Hallo, Gray," Jenkins said.

Lorimer tossed his briefcase on to the settee. "Och no!" he exclaimed disgustedly. "What the hell are you doing here?"

"I came to see you."

"How did you get in?"

"You gave me a key, don't you remember?" Jenkins came into the middle of the room.

"No," Lorimer said. He was damned sure he had never given Owen a key and he was angry, not so much with Jenkins for using some dubious method to get into his flat as with the implications of his being here. He didn't want anything more to do with whatever interested the Welshman and his bosses, Wycliffe and the others. He wanted to get himself a meal, then go to see a film or something. Preferably a comedy. Certainly not a thriller. "The only people I give keys to don't wear trousers," he said. "Not your sort, anyway."

"Nor kilts." Jenkins grinned.

Lorimer wasn't in the mood. "I don't want to know," he said. "As far as I'm concerned, it's finished."

"That's the easy thing to think, isn't it, boy?" Jenkins sat uninvited on an easy chair and Lorimer saw that he was in earnest. The time for badinage was over. "You're an awkward sod, Gray. When I tell you to forget it and leave things to other people, you insist on getting involved: when I want to involve you, you don't want to know. It's that Scotch blood of yours."

The flat had been shut up all day and the room was hot and airless. Lorimer took off his jacket, draped it over a dining chair and opened the window. The sounds of traffic wafted in from the main road two streets away. It was serious, he thought. Jenkins' letting himself in to wait for him instead of arranging to meet him somewhere was evidence of that.

"Okay," he said, sitting on the end of the settee facing the other man. "What's it all about?"

The Welshman hesitated before he spoke, and when he did it was hardly an answer. "Strictly within these four walls," he said. "Very strictly."

"You know that by now," Lorimer told him.

Jenkins nodded. "You were at the Nature Party's election meeting on Tuesday, what did you think of Edward Horwill?"

Lorimer wondered how many more people were going to ask him that. First there had been Rosalind, then Forsyth, now Jenkins. Also he was surprised: what was Jenkins' interest in Horwill? "I thought he was impressive as a speaker," he answered carefully. "A bit smooth."

"Would your judgement be coloured by his friendship with your wife?"

"No, it wouldn't." Lorimer felt his anger returning.

"All right. His party's doing well in the election."

"I can read that in the papers."

Jenkins ignored the sarcasm. "The Green, the Nature, the Ecology parties, call them what you like, they're the fastest growing political movement in the world," he said. "They're successful for two reasons: one, people are tired of the old parties, they want something more than their scrapping and dogmas; two, they appeal to the basic fears of a prosperous, articulate generation with all its nostalgia and its inherent conservatism. With a small *c*. We're a generation of worriers, we worry about the food we eat, the water we drink and the air we breathe. When people are near starvation all they care about is having something to put in their bellies, they don't mind if the bread's brown or white. A man in a desert doesn't worry about the water at an oasis having fluoride in it. We're too well off, and we're neurotic. Death isn't inevitable, it's an obscenity."

Jenkins paused for a moment. "We want all the benefits of exploiting the world, but we're afraid of the consequences. We've unleashed a monster, and we're scared that the people we've put in charge can't control it. Whether anyone can. Harness all those fears—and the reactions to them—and think what power you'd have."

Lorimer was impressed in spite of himself. He had never heard Jenkins speak like this before, never heard anything to suggest that he might have social and political views of his own.

The Welshman smiled grimly. "Speaking hypothetically," he said.

"You're saying they're not genuine concerns?" Lorimer asked.

"No. It's the fact they're genuine that makes the whole thing possible."

Lorimer saw then. Perhaps he had been dense not to see before, but his mind hadn't been working on those lines. "That's why Clive was at the meeting," he said.

"Clive?" Jenkins' tone was all innocence.

"He came here with you before, three years ago. He searched the place, remember?"

"And found your girlfriend wrapped in a quilt." The Welshman smiled. "He thought you recognised him."

"It's all right, I haven't said anything."

"I didn't think you would."

Lorimer supposed that that was a compliment. "Are you saying that the Nature Party is behind the Fist of the Gaels and groups like them, and they've caused those 'incidents' to scare people into voting for them?" he asked incredulously.

"Not all the incidents," Jenkins conceded. "One or two were genuine accidents—the leak at the nuclear power station was—but Horwill and his friends planned some of them. They were responsible for the industrial waste getting into the Avon and the explosion at the dump in the Midlands. And they got hold of some out-of-date figures for leukaemia amongst children in part of Norfolk and started a scare. The experts say it was one of those flukes that happen every now and then and can't be explained; I'm not an expert, I don't know. Have you noticed anything about all those incidents?"

"No," Lorimer said. "What?"

"They've all occurred in mainly middle-class constituencies held by the government or one of the Democrat parties by small minorities. It's the Tory and Democrat voters who'll be most influenced by that sort of campaign."

Lorimer frowned. "I don't believe it," he said. "They're a respectable party."

"They were," Jenkins corrected him. "Until Horwill and the people behind him got rid of the old leadership and took over. The rank and file don't know what's going on. And all the new leaders are interested in is power."

"Power? They'll never get more than one or two MP's at the most," Lorimer objected.

"That's what people said in Germany, now the Greens have more than twenty seats in the *Bundestag*. Do you read the City pages?"

"Sometimes."

"The major companies have appointed a lot of new directors lately."

"They're always doing that. What about it?"

"Nearly a third of them are members of the Nature Party or have links with it."

Lorimer gazed at Jenkins. "Are you saying—" he began.

"I'm not saying anything," Jenkins replied. "Except that it's a surprising proportion for such a small party—and one with policies which are basically anti-big business."

"It's the sort of movement that attracts bright people," Lorimer told him. "We've a new non-executive director at United. He doesn't agree with all Horwill says, but he went to his meeting."

"Forsyth, I know. You needn't worry that he's one of them. Just the opposite." The Welshman permitted himself a half-smile.

Lorimer wondered if he meant that Forsyth was one of his kind. Was that why Robin had asked him to dinner? To sound him out about his presence at Horwill's meeting and discover his political views? By making it a social occasion with his wife there he had sought to conceal his interest. All that talk about Scotland and books and the rest of it had been a smoke-screen. But he had failed.

A less palatable thought occurred to Lorimer: was that why Hilary had invited him to lunch today? It was naive to mind, but he did. Anyway, they hadn't mentioned politics.

"Does he know I know you?" he asked.

"No."

"So why are you here?"

"He wasn't sure about you. You seemed very interested in McIndoe's lot and you could have had some ulterior motive for going back to Iniscaig. He thought you should be checked out."

Lorimer stared at his companion. "Christ!" he breathed.

Jenkins grinned. "I said I'd have it done. Why did you go to the meeting, Gray? You've always said you haven't any time for party politics."

"Rosalind was keen for me to hear Horwill. Is that all?"

"Not quite."

"What's the rest of it?"

"It would help if you'd get close to him."

"Me?" Lorimer might not often be surprised by anything Jenkins said; he was startled now. And he didn't like what he was proposing for two reasons. First, he might dislike Horwill, but he had no illusions about what Jenkins was asking him to do, and that sort of undercover work smelt too much like treachery. Second, he knew the Welshman meant him to use Rosalind. If this had been a real emergency, he might have felt differently, but he wasn't satisfied that it was. "No," he said.

"I thought that's what you'd say." Jenkins didn't seem unduly concerned.

"So you're not disappointed."

"I didn't say that."

Lorimer wondered why he should feel that he had to justify himself. It angered him a little. "It's like the dirty tricks MI5 used to get up to," he said. "The Nature Party's a legitimate organisation, and you want me to spy on the leader because you think he may be doing something criminal and he's a friend of my wife's. I'm not a policeman, get Special Branch to do your dirty work."

"All I'm asking you to do is get to know Edward Horwill," Jenkins said. "It could be important." He wasn't joking now.

"I'm damned if—" Lorimer began.

"Think about it. And if you've still got any qualms, remember what somebody did to Rona Smith and McIndoe. You made yourself too evident in Edinburgh, Gray. These people aren't amateurs, they're powerful—and they're ruthless. I'd be careful, if I were you."

"They've no reason to worry about me," Lorimer protested. "I did what I went to do, now I've finished and anything else is up to the police and you cloak-and-dagger people. All I want's a bit of peace and quiet."

"Good." Jenkins stood up and walked to the door. "I hope you get it —and Mrs. Lorimer doesn't become involved."

Lorimer glared at him. "Blast you, Owen," he said bitterly.

When Jenkins had gone he went into the kitchen, cut two thick slices of new bread, added butter and a substantial wedge of Stilton, and poured himself a can of beer. It was nearly seven o'clock, and taking the food back to the living room he switched on the news.

He was just in time to catch one of the series of government commercials urging business people to prepare for the coming of the free European market in 1992. He had seen others featuring prominent figures like Richard Branson, and paid little attention; they weren't directed at him. But this time he was jolted into taking notice, for the face on the screen and the voice were Robin Forsyth's. He appeared for only a few seconds, but he was quite impressive, Lorimer thought. Straightforward and without any irritating mannerisms.

The news included a report on the by-election. It reminded Lorimer of the leaflet he had found on his doormat and laid down on the table when he saw Jenkins. He picked it up. On one side, under the Nature Party's slogan was a picture of Peter Dillon, their candidate; on the other, in large black print was the simple message:

CHERNOBYL

THREE MILE ISLAND

FURLEIGH HEAD ???

Furleigh Head was the nuclear power station where the leak of low grade waste had occurred.

Lorimer slept badly that night. He was a long time dropping off, and when at last he did he woke again about two. After that it seemed to him that he laid awake for hours remembering what Jenkins had said about Rosalind's becoming involved. His meaning had been only too clear: she could be in danger. Owen had been lying. He knew how he felt about Rosalind, and he had used his knowledge to put pressure on him, to scare him into doing what he wanted. He didn't really believe she was in danger. He couldn't, it was inconceivable that anybody should see Rosalind as a threat. Inconceivable or not, the uneasiness remained.

Lorimer told himself that fears were always exaggerated in the night. When morning came he would see things differently.

It didn't help. If Jenkins was right, and Lorimer no longer seriously doubted that he was, Horwill and his associates couldn't be judged like normal men; they were playing for high stakes and they were ruthless. Already they were responsible for at least two murders. Now they would be on their guard, ready to see danger anywhere. Horwill might remember telling Rosalind something. Even her working for an investigative programme like "Mirror on the Week" might be sufficient for her to be considered dangerous.

Jenkins believed that the new leaders of the Nature Party were behind several of the recent "incidents" and manipulating the public unease they had caused to further their own aims. What Lorimer couldn't see was how they could realistically hope to gain the sort of power they must crave. Men like them wouldn't be content with winning the odd seat in by-elections, very likely to lose them again when people's fears faded and they reverted to their normal voting patterns. What were they after?

It hardly mattered. What did was the chance, however slight, that Rosalind could be in danger. Jenkins, the clever bastard, had known he wouldn't turn his back on that.

At last Lorimer fell asleep again.

By morning some of the night's fears had faded; Lorimer had almost forgotten them. But he hadn't forgotten the only one that counted, that Rosalind might be in danger. That refused to be banished.

When he had dressed he walked round to the newsagent's in Gloucester Road and bought an *Independent.* He was about to turn away when he noticed a copy of the *Financial Times* at the end of the display of papers laid out on the counter, and on an impulse he bought that too.

Back at his flat, he put on a kettle for coffee, cut two slices of bread and dropped them in the toaster. While he waited for them to do he turned to the *FT*'s list of new company appointments. None of the names meant anything to him, and he was about to toss the paper aside when a short paragraph caught his eye, bringing him up short. Edward Horwill, leader of the Nature Party, had been elected to the boards of two large public companies.

Lorimer stared at the report, then read it through a second time. His toast popped up, but he didn't notice it: the companies were Morgans and Excelsior, and Robin Forsyth was the chairman of both. He frowned. Then, glancing at his watch, he went through to his living room and made a phone call.

Mark Preston, the producer of "Mirror on the Week," lived in Islington. Thirty years ago the street had been a slum; now the houses fetched staggering prices and the old inhabitants had been edged out by media people and exchange dealers. Lorimer found the last space along the kerb between the BMW's and Porsches, parked and walked back.

Before moving to Barbican, Preston had worked with Rosalind at ITN and the two men had met occasionally in the days before Rosalind and Lorimer separated. While they were on good terms, they had remained acquaintances rather than friends, and it was more than a year now since they had seen each other.

"Come ye in," the producer greeted his caller. He yawned expansively. Preston was six feet three, lanky, and affected an air of languor which deceived no one who knew him. This morning however he looked below his best.

He lived with an actress, and Lorimer caught a tantalising hint of her perfume as he followed him into a large, airy room which with the kitchen occupied most of the ground floor.

"How's Diane?" he enquired.

"Fine. She's out shopping." Preston flopped on to an easy chair and waved a hand vaguely in the direction of another. Lorimer sat. "What's all this about, for Christ's sake? I didn't get in until nearly four this morning and this is a weekend. It's nothing personal, but I don't feel like seeing anybody."

"I need some information," Lorimer told him.

"At this hour on a Saturday?"

"You're not a Jew."

"I'm a worker, I need rest."

"You can have it when I've gone. It's important, Mark—and it's very confidential."

Preston was by instinct and training a journalist, and his interest was aroused. "All right," he said wearily. "What is it?"

"First, who was the leader of the Nature Party before Horwill?"

"Arnold Kennedy. You could have found that out without bothering me."

"Who's he?"

"God, what a thing it is to be young! He was a lecturer at Keele or Essex, one of those provincial universities they used to call red brick. He was Labour in those days, he stood at a couple of elections, and he was one of the leaders on the Aldermaston Ban the Bomb marches with Canon Collins and Michael Foot and the rest of them. Then he got fed up with Labour, or they got fed up with him, and he started the Nature Party. That was about six years ago."

"He's still alive?"

"He was two days ago."

"So why did he stop being the leader?"

Preston shrugged his cashmere shoulders. "Differences over policy. That's what they'll tell you, anyway."

"Meaning he wasn't militant enough?"

"Partly. I expect he was like a lot of elderly revolutionaries, he'd come to prefer comfort to combat. And there've been stories about his living surprisingly well considering his legitimate income. Strictly rumour, of course—and don't you quote me. He ran everything, including the party funds."

"Then Horwill took over," Lorimer said. "What do you know about him?"

"Not a lot. He started as an estate agent, made some money in property deals and used it to get control of an up-and-coming computer company. Since he took it over it's bought three other firms, diversified and increased its turnover tenfold. He's shrewd, capable, rather impressive in an unpleasant sort of way. An eighties man *par excellence*. He's certainly made the hell of a difference to the party."

"Yes." Lorimer paused. "What do you know about Euro-frauds, Mark?"

The producer's expression changed and he regarded his visitor with the single minded interest of a female weasel eyeing a rabbit. "Are the two subjects connected?"

"Not as far as I know."

"You never were a good liar, Gray." Preston settled himself more comfortably, like a man preparing to ride his pet hobby-horse. "The official estimate is that frauds account for at least ten percent of the EEC's whole budget. Most of them are in agriculture: subsidies claimed for olives grown on trees that were never planted and exports of non-existent oranges, that sort of thing. Who's going to check on the number of orange trees on a farm? There aren't the men.

"The EEC's imposed a big levy on beef imported from countries outside the Community, so high quality meat is bought in places like South America and documents are forged that describe it as offal. No levy's paid, and the meat's sold at top prices. Then there's the 'carousel.' All EEC farmers get the same price for their produce, and when cattle, say, are moved across the border from a member country where they're comparatively cheap, like Northern Ireland, to one where they're more expensive, like Eire, the dealer is supposed to pay an MCA, another sort of levy. So they're smuggled across at night. It's easy enough with so many back roads and the police on both sides busy with other things. Later they're sold back openly to the North, and the dealer claims the MCA. They reckon carousels cost the EEC fifteen million last year."

"Strewth!" Lorimer exclaimed.

"There are plenty of other fiddles, cheese, maize, you name it. Some of them are controlled by the Mafia and some of the proceeds go to finance terrorism. Now they're so big nobody's got the resources to stamp them out."

"How do you know all this?" Lorimer asked, impressed.

"We're an erudite lot at Barbican, didn't Rosalind tell you?" Preston grinned. "As a matter of fact, we did a lot of research for a programme on Euro-frauds a year or two ago, but the BBC beat us to it. What's all this about, Gray?"

"Just an idea," Lorimer told him. "One other thing."

"What's that?"

"I think there was more to Kennedy's being kicked out than people know. It could be quite a story. If he was prepared to come on your show and talk about it, would you be interested?"

Preston looked thoughtful. "We might," he said. "Yes, we very well might."

If, Lorimer told himself. It was the hell of a big if.

NINE

NOWADAYS Arnold Kennedy had fewer visitors than when he was the leader of the Nature Party, and when Lorimer rang and asked if he could come to see him his first thought was to wonder what it was about. His second was whether he could make anything from his call.

To the public at large the old campaigner seemed a benevolent figure, his thinning mane of white hair blowing in the wind and his eyes peering out over his half-glasses, but those who knew him better saw a different man. Still ambitious at seventy-one, his bitter resentment of what he saw as concerted efforts by his enemies to keep him from high office amounted almost to paranoia. He was caustic, intolerant, mean and on occasions malicious, and when Edward Horwill's friends had suggested that the party needed younger, more dynamic leadership, there were plenty of people only too glad to see the old man go.

"When do you want to come?" he demanded in his rather high-pitched, imperious voice.

"Would this afternoon be all right?" Lorimer asked.

"I'm very busy." Kennedy might believe it, but it was manifestly untrue: one of his troubles was that he had too little to occupy his days. "Oh, very well, if that's the only time you can manage. Three o'clock." Three, he thought, was too late for him to share his after-lunch brandy and too early for him to be obliged to offer tea. "Don't be late," he added.

The old politician lived in Highgate in a tall, narrow Victorian house in a quiet road leading down one side of the hill. Most of the houses, once the homes of affluent middle-class families with several servants, had been divided up into flats occupied by their even more affluent successors.

Kennedy couldn't abide other people in his house, but his commercial instincts had persuaded him to let the top floor to a lecturer at the LSE. He moved about the rest, alone except for the woman who came in every day to attend to the housework and get his meals, like a wispy, bad-tempered ghost.

As Lorimer parked his Rover, a grey Jaguar drove past slowly. The driver pulled into a gap fifty yards up the road and switched off the ignition. Apparently he was waiting for somebody to come out of one of the houses, for he adjusted the car's rear-view mirror and settled himself lower in the driving seat.

Kennedy's tiny patch of front garden was almost completely filled by a stunted laburnum which, having struggled hard for many years, was now prepared to die slowly and quietly, if without much dignity. Avoiding its sparse foliage, Lorimer rang the bell. It was answered by Kennedy's daily help who showed him to a small book-lined room which smelt faintly of mothballs. Kennedy was seated in an easy chair at one side of the fireplace, a tiny figure in a dark green corduroy jacket and a striped shirt with a pink bow-tie. He looked frail, but his appearance was misleading; his slight frame was still wiry and he moved easily enough.

"Sit down, sit down," he said impatiently, not standing up himself or holding out a hand for Lorimer to shake. "Well, what's it all about?"

Lorimer had no intention of being hustled. Kennedy's manner irritated him, and while he wanted something from the old man, he wasn't prepared to flatter him to get it. "You were the leader of the Nature Party until last year," he said coolly, sitting on a chair on the other side of the hearthrug.

"I founded it," Kennedy corrected him tetchily. "I *was* the party until a lot of new people joined and started wanting changes. Young people." He scowled: young people questioned established practices and he bitterly resented anyone questioning his *diktats*.

"Like Edward Horwill?" Lorimer suggested.

"You know him?"

"Of him."

"I should think that's enough." Kennedy paused, and a cunning look came into his eyes. "Why did you say you wanted to see me?"

"I didn't, you didn't ask." Lorimer grinned. "I'm writing an article about the by-election and I'm looking for background information about the party." He wished he knew more about how journalists worked; Arnold Kennedy was probably used to their ways and would see through his pretence.

His concern was unnecessary. The old politician's vanity and resentment made him only too ready to talk. "Horwill!" he snorted. "The man's a charlatan. What does he know about politics? He's an opportunist, climbing on the bandwagon now he sees the party's successful."

"How did he get elected then?" Lorimer asked.

"He packed the meeting with his friends. Half of them weren't even members. If I'd known what was going on, I could have called on twenty times as many who'd have supported me." There was a bombastic note in the old man's voice. "It was dishonest, but no doubt that was how he was used to doing things in business."

Lorimer gathered that business, like youth, was contemptible. "Why didn't you do anything about it?" he enquired. "You could have demanded another meeting, or gone to court."

An evasive look came into the old man's eyes. "It would have been bad for the party," he said. "It was better to let things be."

"Even if you knew the new leader was dishonest?"

"Yes, yes. In the circumstances."

"Well, he seems to be giving the party a dynamic image," Lorimer suggested.

Kennedy glared at him. "Dynamic! Gimmickry! Only a fool would be deceived by what he's doing. He and his friends. If I told you . . ." He stopped abruptly.

Lorimer waited, but the old man didn't continue, and after a moment he repeated encouragingly, "If you told me . . . ?"

Clearly Kennedy wanted to forget whatever he had been going to say. "Underhand methods," he muttered vaguely, his thin white hands moving restlessly on the arms of his chair.

"It's more than that," Lorimer said.

Kennedy looked at him, then away. "I don't know what you mean," he said.

"You do. That's why you're afraid. You'd give a lot to get even with Horwill, but you daren't, he's got some hold over you." He was shooting an arrow in the air, Lorimer thought, and, like Bassanio, he didn't know what it would strike or where it would land. It might hit him, but that was a chance he had to take. And there was at least a possibility that he was right. Why else would a vain old man like Arnold Kennedy stand aside and let Horwill and his friends take over without a struggle the party he regarded as his own?

"What you're saying is slander." Kennedy's voice rose, but it was made querulous by uncertainty.

"There's nobody else here," Lorimer said.

For several seconds the old man didn't speak, then he said, "You don't know anything. You're making wild accusations, hoping I'll tell you something you can use."

"The French call it direct action," Lorimer told him. "The other name's murder."

Kennedy looked as if he had run into a brick wall hard. His eyes were wide with shock. "What do you mean?" he demanded.

"How much do you know about the Fist of the Gaels?"

"Nothing."

"And Rona Smith and Roy McIndoe?"

"Nothing. I've never heard of any of them."

He could be telling the truth, Lorimer thought. On the other hand, he probably wasn't. Not entirely. "The Fist of the Gaels is an extremist group," he said roughly. "Rona Smith belonged to it. She was a student; she burnt down a house in the Hebrides in their first operation. When she wouldn't blow up a storage tank at a toxic waste processing plant they murdered her. McIndoe was one of the group's leaders; somebody murdered him too."

"Who did? I don't know anything about it." The old man's voice faltered, and Lorimer could see the fear in his eyes. Nothing, he thought, was as pitiable and embarrassing as the fear of the old.

"What's the link between the Nature Party and the Fist of the Gaels?" he demanded.

Kennedy stared at him. Not much traffic came along the road outside during the day, and for several seconds it was very quiet in the stuffy little room. The faint odour of mothballs was making Lorimer feel sick. Then the old man said in a surprisingly firm tone, "It's no use asking me. I told you, I don't know anything about any of it."

This time Lorimer believed him. Unlikeable and probably dishonest as Kennedy was, there was no reason to suppose he had any connection with the Fist of the Gaels or the murders. Once he had been ousted from the leadership of the party he was an outsider, he would know nothing of its secret activities. Unless he had stumbled on something. If he had, that would explain his fear.

"Would you be prepared to be interviewed for a television programme?" he asked.

The old politician looked wary. "What about?"

"How you were manoeuvred out as chairman. It would be a chance to expose Horwill, and once you'd done it you'd have him and his friends off your back for good. They wouldn't dare take any action against you, and you'd become the leader again." It probably wasn't true, and Lorimer knew he was taking a risk, but he was counting on the old man's vanity being stronger than his fear.

"You're working for the Tory press," Kennedy accused him angrily. "That's why you're here."

"I couldn't care less about politics," Lorimer told him. "The only person I'm working for is me."

They stared at each other, and Kennedy looked away first.

"I don't know," he muttered.

Lorimer could almost see his conceit and his desire to reinstate himself struggling with his fear. "You wouldn't have to answer any questions you didn't want to," he said.

The old man's vanity won. "Very well," he agreed. Sententiously he added, "The public should know the truth."

"Good." Lorimer was conscious of a wonderful feeling of relief. It wasn't why he had wanted Kennedy to agree so badly, but when the old man had said his piece Rosalind would have to see Horwill in his true colours, and she would be saved from any involvement with a crook. Possibly a murderer. People didn't like having their illusions shattered, and Rosalind was proud; it might take her a long time to forgive him. That was something Lorimer didn't want to think about. "Somebody will be in touch about the arrangements," he said, standing up.

The daily woman let him out. He crossed the road, climbed into his Rover and started the engine.

Farther up the hill the grey Jaguar was still parked by the kerb. As Lorimer drove past it a man in the passenger's seat got out, stood for a moment looking up and down the road, then walked back down the hill. Lorimer caught only a glimpse of him, but something about the way he carried himself seemed familiar.

Back at his flat Lorimer rang Mark Preston.

"Kennedy says he'll do it," he reported. "According to him, the meeting when he was voted out was rigged, half the people there weren't even members. I'd say the rumours you've heard are right, he fiddled the books, and they gave him the choice of accepting his defeat or his sins finding him out."

"He always was a sanctimonious bastard," Preston observed cheerfully. "Is he prepared to say how Horwill fixed the vote?"

"More, I'd say. He's bitter, give him the chance and he'll talk."

"Okay. We won't be able to do anything until after the election though. And even then the people upstairs may block it."

"Fair enough," Lorimer agreed. He had been prepared for that. "Does Rosalind know about any of this?"

"No. I'd rather she didn't find out I've had anything to do with it."

"I can understand that," Preston said drily. "May I ask what your motives are? Apart from a desire to help a struggling television producer?"

"Personal."

"Oh, I see. Rosalind and—" Preston stopped. "Yes, of course."

"No," Lorimer said. "Something else." But he didn't suppose Preston believed him. "Is she there?"

"Somewhere about, I think. Hang on and I'll put you through."

Lorimer waited.

"You asked me to give you a ring when I got back from Iniscaig," he reminded Rosalind when she came on the line.

"Did I?" she said, her tone hardly encouraging. "I can't imagine why."

"You said we should get together for a meal, remember?"

"Vaguely. Anyway, we did: we had dinner after Edward's meeting."

"That doesn't count."

There was a moment's silence. "What's all this in aid of?" Rosalind demanded suspiciously. "I also remember your making a snide remark about Barbican not paying you."

"I take it back."

"That's magnanimous of you! All right, when and where?"

"How about this evening?"

"This evening?" Rosalind sounded shocked. "I can't, I'm doing something."

"Seeing Horwill?" Lorimer had tried to speak casually, as if he couldn't care less, but he knew he had failed miserably.

"No!" Rosalind told him. "And it's no concern of yours what I do and who I see."

"Sorry. How about Fred's at eight?"

Fred's was their name for a fairly expensive restaurant in Chelsea where they had sometimes celebrated special occasions in the old days.

"That's not fair," Rosalind said accusingly. "You must have a guilty conscience—or you want something. Probably both." She hesitated. "I suppose I could get out of what I'm doing."

"Would you rather go somewhere else?"

"No, Fred's would be fine. I haven't been there for ages."

Nor had Lorimer. It was silly, but somehow going there without Rosalind would have seemed like a betrayal. "I'll pick you up at seven-thirty," he said. " 'Bye."

" 'Bye," Rosalind said.

The phone clicked and she stared at the handset she was holding. What the hell did she think she was doing? It was all over between Gray and her. Dead. So why didn't she bury it and walk away as her friends kept telling her she should? She despised herself for being so indecisive. Now she would have to ring Maggie and say she couldn't make it to her party this evening. And Maggie, being Maggie, would expect an explanation.

"You okay?" Preston enquired, coming into the room.

"No," Rosalind replied bitterly. "Blast you bloody men!"

Lorimer just hoped he would be able to reserve a table at such short notice.

The waiter had taken their order and departed and Rosalind looked round the busy restaurant. "I was afraid it might have changed," she said.

"So was I," Lorimer admitted. She was looking particularly lovely this evening, he thought. Rosalind was one of those women maturity suited, she seemed to be more beautiful and more desirable every time he saw her. And this evening there was something more; it wasn't only the soft lighting and her make-up, there was a glow about her and her eyes were shining. He wished it had been on account of him.

"I'm glad it hasn't," she said. Her manner changed and became businesslike. "All right, what's this evening in aid of, Gray?"

"I don't know what you mean," Lorimer protested innocently. It occurred to him that he was echoing Arnold Kennedy; when people didn't know what to say they resorted to clichés. "Does it have to be in aid of anything?"

"That proves it is," Rosalind told him.

"Your trouble is that you have a suspicious nature," Lorimer said.

"Living with you developed it." Rosalind watched her husband break a roll and spread butter on it thickly. "You should watch what you eat, you're putting on weight."

"It'll soon come off when I start training."

"Yes, of course. Football." Her tone was mildly contemptuous. "So why this evening?"

"I went to see Arnold Kennedy this afternoon."

"Oh?" Rosalind frowned. "Why?"

"I hoped he could tell me something."

"What about?"

"The Fist of the Gaels, for one thing."

"And could he?"

"Not in so many words. He was scared."

"What of?"

"I'm not sure. Exposure. Retribution."

One waiter brought their starters and another the bottle of Soave Lorimer had ordered, and there was a brief hiatus while the formalities were completed.

"What's he like?" Rosalind enquired when both waiters had gone.

"Who?"

"Arnold Kennedy."

"Conceited. Unpleasant. I didn't like him." Lorimer half cut, half pulled off a piece of Parma ham.

"There've been stories that he did very well out of the party while he was the leader," Rosalind said.

"Did Horwill tell you that?"

"Look—"

"It's all right, I've heard them before. I just wondered how authentic they were."

"I knew about them before I met Edward."

"He talked about the party as if it was his private concern."

"He would. As you say, he's conceited."

"Why haven't the new people done anything about it, if he cooked the books?" Lorimer asked. But he didn't need Rosalind to tell him; they were holding the evidence of the old man's fraud over him to ensure his silence. That silence was worth far more than they could hope to recover if they took him to court.

"It would be bad publicity for the party." Rosalind sipped her wine. "Anyway, he may not have cooked them, just claimed more expenses than he was entitled to."

There was a moment's silence.

"How close are you and Horwill?" Lorimer asked.

Rosalind didn't answer. Instead she put down her glass and faced him across the table, a dangerous glint in her eyes. "I don't think that's any business of yours, Gray," she said coldly.

"I'd like to meet him, that's all."

Lorimer had meant it when he told Jenkins he wouldn't have anything to do with his request, and he would have found it difficult to explain why he had changed his mind. Perhaps it was something to do with his call on Arnold Kennedy. And with Rosalind.

"Oh." She looked mildly embarrassed. "I thought . . . Why do you want to meet him?"

"Business."

"Meaning you won't tell me."

"Meaning there isn't anything to tell. It's just a case of making contacts."

"All right," Rosalind agreed. "I'll see what he says."

"You're in love with him, aren't you?"

"That definitely isn't any concern of yours!"

"I don't know," Lorimer said. "It could be."

The telephone was ringing when he got back to his flat, and, wondering who could be calling so late, he went to answer it.

"I've been trying to get hold of you all the evening," Arnold Kennedy said peevishly.

"I've been out," Lorimer told him.

The old man grunted. "I'm ringing to say I've changed my mind, I can't do that television programme."

Lorimer's spirits sank. "Why not?"

"I told you, I've changed my mind. I don't have to justify myself to you."

"What are you frightened of?"

"What do you mean, frightened?" Kennedy blustered. "Nothing."

"I can smell it over the phone," Lorimer told him roughly. "You're scared. Who's got at you, Mr. Kennedy?"

"I don't know what you're talking about. It's just that on consideration I've decided I can't take part in any television programme. It would be bad for the party." The old man put down the phone without saying good-bye.

Lorimer told himself that at least Kennedy's decision would save him trouble with Rosalind. The bad news was that he would have to go back to Mark Preston and tell him the project was off.

That night Professor Johann Feldhuis died in a motor accident near Amsterdam. In the normal course of events his death would have attracted little attention outside his immediate circle; an obscure academic doesn't often become a world figure. But Johann Feldhuis was also the chairman of the Netherlands Nature Party. Politicians rank higher in news value than professors of applied chemistry, and his death was reported briefly all over the world.

On Monday Lorimer's paper contained a short obituary, but what caught his eye first was a paragraph on the front page: the professor, who was alone, had died when his car left the road on a dangerous bend and plunged into a river.

Feldhuis was Dutch. Hugh Bascomb had said that McIndoe's friend was either Dutch or German, and a man with a German or Dutch accent had called at the house in Ravelston to see him on the afternoon he died. Certainly neither of them had been the professor, and surely it was too much to suggest he could have had any connection with them? On the other hand . . . Lorimer pushed the thought aside, it was too improbable and it had nothing to do with him.

He had two telephone calls that morning. The first was from Rosalind: Horwill would be pleased to meet him and suggested he ring to fix a time and place. The second, just after eleven, was from Hilary Forsyth.

"Hallo, Gray," she said. "Robin's away on business. He didn't tell me he was going until yesterday, and I've two tickets for the play at the Apollo tonight. Will you take pity on me?"

Lorimer was startled. Despite all his good intentions and his telling himself that it was highly unlikely they would meet again, he had thought about Hilary far too often for his peace of mind. He wasn't seventeen, it was ridiculous to be affected like this by a woman he had only seen twice. More stupid to become involved. Apart from the other considerations, he didn't play around with married women, whatever their difficulties with their husbands. The fact that Forsyth was one of United's directors was irrelevant.

"It's very good of you," he began awkwardly, "but I—"

"Don't say you've seen it." There was a pause ended by a ripple of laughter. "Oh—h, I see."

"Well—"

"I shall be very offended if you don't come. Please, Gray. The curtain's up at eight, come here and we'll have something to eat first. Is six-thirty all right?"

Lorimer had the feeling he had experienced before, that he was being swept along by events over which he had no control. "Look—" he said.

"Please. I really do want to see the play, and I'm damned if I'll go alone."

She made it seem that he would be churlish to refuse, Lorimer thought. "Thank you," he said.

"You're a real Sir Galahad."

There was another delicious ripple of laughter, and he wondered if she was laughing at him.

"You'll come at six-thirty?" she asked.

"Yes," he promised.

TEN

SHE WAS WAITING FOR HIM, wearing a silk suit Lorimer guessed had cost as much as he earned in a fortnight, and with her hair up. Her hair done that way made her look more sophisticated and remote. Not that there was anything remote in the way she greeted him. All the same, he was uneasy.

Hilary noticed it. "There's something the matter, isn't there?" she said. She had asked him to pour their drinks, a very cold, very dry white wine for her and a gin and tonic for himself, and now they were sipping them before going in to the cold meal laid out in the dining room.

"Does Robin know?" Lorimer asked.

"No, I didn't think about asking you until after he'd left." Hilary was watching him, an amused half-smile touching the corners of her mouth. "Does that hurt your masculine pride?"

"No. I just thought maybe it was his idea, so that you could find out more about me."

"His idea? Why should it be?" Hilary looked bewildered. "And what do you mean, 'find out more about you'?"

"You don't know?"

"No." Her bewilderment was replaced by the beginnings of anger. "And I don't think I like it. I don't ask Robin who I can see—and he surely doesn't tell me who to."

"He's been checking on me," Lorimer said.

"Checking on you? How?"

"My politics, what I think, whether I'm 'reliable.' That's why he asked me to dinner the other evening, didn't you know?" She had to, he thought. At the same time, he hoped very much she hadn't, although that would complicate things even more.

"No, and I don't believe it." Hilary drank a little more of her wine. "Even if you're right, what about it? It's standard practice to find out as much as you can about the bright young people in your corporation."

"I'm not in his corporation," Lorimer said. "He doesn't have anything to do with staff at United."

Hilary's slim shoulders sketched a shrug. "I guess maybe he's got his eye on you then. You should feel flattered: Robin may have his faults, but he's a good judge of people, and if he's checking on you, that's nothing for you to be worried about. Just the opposite."

She might believe that, Lorimer told himself. He didn't.

"I thought you were helping him," he explained, "and that's why you asked me to have lunch with you on Friday and to come tonight."

"Let's get this straight," Hilary said, putting her empty glass down on the table beside her and speaking very distinctly. "I don't know anything about Robin's checking on you. I thought I'd made it plain on Friday why I asked you to have lunch: I wanted to see you again. And that's why I suggested this evening. What we do is between you and me, it has nothing to do with Robin." She looked down at her glass, saw that it was empty and put it down on the table beside her. "He's lost any right he ever had to monopolise me, and if he doesn't care, why the hell should I?"

Nevertheless she did care, Lorimer thought. She had been looking at him, her eyes unwavering; now she looked down for a second before raising them again. "I guess we'd better go and eat, I hate rushing into a theatre at the last minute."

The play, a comedy, had opened three weeks before to enthusiastic reviews, and the house was full. Lorimer soon forgot his doubts in his enjoyment of the play and of Hilary's company. Once during the first act, when their hands touched by accident in the darkness, her fingers pressed his. But when he glanced at her she was gazing straight ahead at the stage, her eyes shining and her lips slightly parted. What did she want? He knew what he did, but it wasn't on, and being here with her in the intimate semi-darkness of the theatre wasn't doing him any good at all. He had been a fool to come.

"Wasn't that wonderful?" she exclaimed when the curtain came down at the end of the act.

"Yes," Lorimer agreed. "Shall we try to get a drink?"

"Sure, let's."

They joined the crowd in the stalls bar. Lorimer bought their drinks and carried them over to Hilary, who was standing by the wall just inside the door. He handed her hers and turned. Facing them, a few feet away, was Philip Rayment.

It was clear that he had seen them. He had seen them together at United House on Friday too, Lorimer thought. He had a sudden mad idea that United's personnel director was spying on them. He knew it was absurd—with any luck Rayment wouldn't know that Hilary was Robin Forsyth's wife—but dislike for the older man welled up inside him.

Then Rayment said, "Good evening, Mrs. Forsyth," and, more coolly, " 'Evening, Graham." With a nod to Lorimer, he turned back to the plump middle-aged woman at his side, and they moved off.

"Who was that?" Hilary enquired, lifting elegant eyebrows.

Lorimer told her.

"I remember, he was at a party Aidan Grantley gave so that Robin and I could meet the other directors. He was so stuffy!" She laughed quietly. Then her laughter stopped abruptly. "It won't matter for you, will it, Gray?"

"No," Lorimer said. He told himself that Rayment had probably assumed that Forsyth was with them and had gone to the bar or the loo. Unless he had been watching them since they came in and knew they were alone. In that case, he would disapprove and, disliking Lorimer as he did, he might try to make trouble.

"Oh God! I hope it doesn't," Hilary said. She looked stricken.

"Don't worry," Lorimer told her.

The second act was as entertaining as the first, and by the time they left the theatre he had almost forgotten Rayment.

Luck was with them, and they got a taxi almost immediately. Lorimer was beginning to suspect that Hilary was one of those people who always got the best tables and found taxis when no one else could.

"You did enjoy it, didn't you?" she asked him, leaning back against the seat. She still seemed cocooned in a sort of euphoria, but she needed him to confirm his enjoyment.

"Very much," he said.

"And wasn't the cast good?" She turned to him, her eyes shining and her lips slightly parted as they had been in the theatre, but this time it wasn't in anticipation of the next laugh. Leaning across, she kissed his cheek, letting her lips linger on his flesh before she drew back a little. "That's for a wonderful evening," she said softly. Taking his arm, she put it through hers and pressed it.

She hardly spoke the rest of the way, and when the taxi reached Fairhaven Gardens she asked, "Will you come in for a drink?"

Lorimer hesitated. He wanted to say "Yes," and what harm would it do?"

"I don't think so," he answered.

"Don't you want to?" Hilary was smiling, but there was a note of appeal in her voice.

"Yes," he said. "You know I do."

"Then come, Gray." Lorimer said nothing. "My God, you make it difficult."

Lorimer wondered if she thought it was easy for him.

Suddenly she put her hands behind his head, pulled it down and kissed him hard on his mouth. "That's for an evening which could have been even better," she said.

The next second she was out of the taxi and going up the short path to the front door.

That night, for the second night running, Lorimer slept badly. More than once he woke, thinking of Hilary. He had believed her when she said Forsyth hadn't asked her to check on him—and not only because he wanted to, or because to do so flattered his vanity. She had asked him to have lunch with her on Friday and go out with her last night because she wanted to see him again. Probably she felt neglected. Betrayed. It was as simple as that.

Only it wasn't simple at all. The fact that Forsyth was one of United's directors was immaterial; he didn't play around with married women, however unfaithful their husbands might be. Relationships couldn't stand still, they either developed or they died. The odd lunch or visit to the theatre might be enjoyable, but it wouldn't satisfy him for long, and to carry on seeing Hilary would inevitably lead to a sordid mess and a lot of grief. Especially for her. Also it would almost certainly mean his having to find another job. Two or three years ago that might not have mattered very much, but circumstances had changed since then. He liked his work, and he couldn't think of anything else he might do that would provide the same enjoyment.

He made himself think about other things, and eventually he drifted off again into an uneasy sleep.

When he woke it was light. He had a headache and felt no more rested than when he came to bed. He tried to remember what he had been thinking about just before he fell asleep. Something Owen Jenkins had said. According to Owen, a suspiciously high proportion of the new directors elected to the boards of major British companies recently were Nature Party members or supporters. That meant either that the party was attracting many of the brightest of the younger executives, which was possible, or it had already infiltrated enough boardrooms to make its influence count.

Jenkins believed there had been too many environmental "incidents" recently for them all to be accidents. The implication was that some of them had been caused deliberately and, as far as Lorimer could see, the only people to gain from them were Horwill's party; they could hardly have been timed better to help its campaign.

It wasn't chance that Horwill and his colleagues had chosen to make their first major bid in a by-election for the European Parliament; such elections usually aroused about as much interest as a match between two middle-of-the-table fourth-division sides on a wet Saturday at the end of the season. Apathy had always been the ally of the extreme Left and Right; this time it looked like the weapon of the Nature Party. It was clear already that the Tories, over-complacent, had been wrong-footed.

Lorimer tried to remember what he knew about the European Parliament. Democratic rule in the Community was shared between the parliament, the EEC Commission and the Council of Ministers of the twelve member countries. The parliament debated major issues and could amend proposals for new laws put forward by the commission. Also, with the Council it fixed the Community's annual budget.

The green parties' members comprised most of the so-called Rainbow Group. A year ago there had been twenty of them. Now there were over forty, mostly Germans and Belgians, but with a sprinkling of Dutch, Irish and Spaniards, and they wielded a power out of all relation to their numbers.

Lorimer was wide awake now. Was that what it was all about? According to the report of the Dutch professor's death in the paper, the police were satisfied that it was an accident, but could there be a connection between the Nature Party in the Netherlands, Horwill's party and Dorn nan Gaidheal?

The idea seemed ludicrous. Not only was Dorn nan Gaidheal a tiny group, it was by no means established that it had links with Horwill's people, let alone anyone else. On the other hand, if it were a front used by Horwill and his friends to do their dirty work, that would explain why McIndoe had been murdered. Lorimer got out of bed and went through to his living room.

Yesterday's paper was still on the chair, and he turned to the obituaries. Feldhuis's was the third, below those of a retired major-general and a former colonial bishop. As a scientist, the writer said, the professor had never reached the heights of some of his contemporaries; as the leader of the Dutch Nature Party he had always supported a moderate line. His interest in politics had stemmed from his concern about the damage he believed the world was doing to itself, and the only power he sought was the power to influence. While that wasn't enough for some of the more militant elements in his party, he was popular with the rank and file, and his position as leader had seemed secure.

Lorimer turned back to the report on the front page. He thought he remembered the last sentence, and now he read it again. "His likely successor is Cornelis van Rijn, 37, who is expected to take a more aggressive line." He couldn't be right, he told himself. Because if he was, they were faced with a vast international conspiracy.

He needed Jenkins' help, and the Welshman wouldn't be at his office for a couple of hours yet; it still wasn't seven o'clock. Fretting at the enforced wait, Lorimer went to wash and shave. When he had dressed he cooked himself some bacon and eggs along with his usual toast and coffee. It helped pass the time, and he realised that he was hungry.

In the past when he had rung Jenkins' number it had been reluctantly, because he needed Jenkins' assistance; this time was different, Owen had asked for his help.

"I need to know something," he said when he had been put through.

"What?" the Welshman asked.

"Which green parties in Europe have changed leaders in the last two years, who the old leaders were, what happened to them and who the new ones are. How the parties' policies have changed and who's backing them."

Jenkins rarely allowed himself to show surprise, even when he was startled, and he didn't now. All he said was, "It's relevant?"

"It could be."

"Where will you be this morning?"

"United House."

"I'll ring you there about eleven."

Lorimer put down the phone and went to work feeling less restless. He had set the wheels in motion.

There was nothing in the morning's papers that seemed likely to concern United, and when he had scanned them he got on with some routine tasks he had started on Friday.

Jenkins rang just after eleven. "We'd better meet," he said. "The Albert Memorial at one."

"Okay," Lorimer agreed. Last time it had been St. James' Park, he thought. Owen seemed to like London's open spaces; there was less chance of being overheard when no one could come within fifty yards of you without your seeing them.

Putting down the phone, he resumed the work he had been doing before it rang. But almost at once it rang again. This time it was Grantley.

"Come in," he said curtly.

Wondering what was up, Lorimer went. Helen Wilkins gave him her usual smile as he passed; if something was wrong, she didn't know about it.

The chairman was seated at his desk, his heavy features set in an angry frown.

"Sit down," he said brusquely.

Lorimer obeyed. Since he had come to work on the fourteenth floor he had seen the chairman in a variety of moods, but rarely like this. Grantley was angry—and it seemed clear it was with him.

"I've thought you were all sorts of things, but I'd never thought you were a complete fool until now," he said bitterly.

Lorimer waited. He thought he knew now what it was about.

"Some people say it's no business of a company's what its employees get up to out of the firm's time," Grantley continued. "That's sentimental rubbish. If I get roaring drunk and go berserk in Piccadilly Circus, the papers will pick it up and United's image will suffer. If a bank cashier has bank robbers for friends, the bank has a right to be worried and do something about it."

"What am I supposed to have done?" Lorimer made an effort to speak calmly.

"Don't be a bloody fool, Gray." Grantley's anger was more disturbing for being tightly controlled. "You went to the theatre with Robin Forsyth's wife last night. Just the two of you."

"That's a crime?"

"Don't bandy words with me." The chairman's temper flared. He hated this. Moreover he knew that in coming to him with his story Rayment had been motivated by animosity towards him as much as dislike of Lorimer. Lorimer was his man, picked in the face of the personnel director's open disapproval, and Rayment would be delighted if he fell from grace. "Did her husband know you were going?"

"He was away. She had two tickets and she didn't want to waste them."

"Why you?"

"I don't know. She'd probably tried other people, and they couldn't go." Lorimer paused. "I suppose Philip Rayment told you."

"He says you were behaving like people who knew each other well."

"What the hell does that mean? We'd been there about five minutes, and I'd spent four of them queueing up to get our drinks." Lorimer wondered what Rayment would have reported if he had seen Hilary kissing him in the taxi.

"How well do you know each other?"

"Mr. Forsyth asked me to dinner the other night; he wanted to ask me about Iniscaig. I met her then."

"Last night wasn't the first time you'd been seen together."

If he hadn't been so angry, he would have felt like laughing, Lorimer thought. "She came here on Friday and asked me to meet her for lunch," he said. "There was something she wanted to ask me about. Philip Rayment came out of his room when I was showing her to the lift. That was all. We had lunch at Harrods with about two hundred people chaperoning us."

"Lunch on Friday, the theatre on Monday," Grantley commented more quietly. "What the hell do you think Forsyth's going to say when he hears? Somebody's bound to tell him."

Somebody like Rayment, Lorimer thought. "If Philip's interested," he said roughly, "I took her home in a taxi last night, and I didn't even get out when we got there."

"I don't give a damn what you did," Grantley told him. "That's between the three of you. All I'm telling you is stop seeing her. You know as well as I do it can't cause anything but trouble, and I'm damned if I'm going to have a good set-up here ruined by a bloody stupid relationship between you and a director's wife."

"There isn't a relationship," Lorimer said, controlling his anger.

"You'd better make sure it stays that way then. Philip won't say anything." Extracting Rayment's promise had given Grantley an opportunity to vent his distaste, and he had left Philip in no doubt about how he felt. "Don't put me in a position where I have to get rid of you, that's all."

The warning couldn't have been clearer.

Jenkins was waiting when Lorimer arrived. A group of Japanese tourists, video cameras at the ready, were standing by the memorial, listening to their guide, and he had walked a little way off. In deference to the heat, he was wearing a slightly shabby light-weight jacket and an open-necked shirt.

"You look better than the last time I saw you," he observed judicially when Lorimer joined him.

"I feel better," Lorimer said.

"Smell better too." Jenkins grinned. "We'll go this way."

He started walking northwards, away from the road, and Lorimer fell into step beside him. For a comparatively small man the Welshman could cover the ground surprisingly fast when he wanted to, but now he walked slowly, as if time wasn't a consideration.

"You got the information?" Lorimer asked.

Jenkins nodded. Reaching into an inside pocket of his jacket, he produced three sheets of computer paper and handed them to his companion. Lorimer unfolded them. They were covered with neatly tabulated lists of names and organisations. First were six national parties, those of Germany, France, Holland, Denmark, Belgium and the United Kingdom. Besides Feldhuis, two of their leaders, the German and the Belgian, had died and a fourth had been involved in a scandal and resigned, furiously protesting his innocence. The fifth had also resigned, ostensibly over policy differences. In five of the six cases—the Dutch party had not yet elected a successor to Feldhuis—the new leader was both younger and markedly more militant than his predecessor.

So much Lorimer had expected, and, although the number of parties involved was a surprise, it was the list of leading supporters and financial backers which made him whistle silently to himself. There were one or two names against each party, and they included the chairmen and chief executives of some of the biggest companies in Europe.

"Destroy it," Jenkins said. "That stuff's classified. So what's it all about, Gray?"

"The future." The Welshman's features were so devoid of expression that anyone who didn't know him well might have thought he wasn't interested, but Lorimer wasn't deceived. "Starting with 1992 when all the trade barriers within the EEC come down. When that happens there'll be a single market of three hundred and thirty million people, far bigger than the U.S.A. and vastly more efficient than the Soviet Union or China."

"And powerful."

"Very. But that's only the start of it, whether you like it not, we're moving towards a united Europe. You know as well as I do that some people are already dreaming of a single federated state like the U.S.A. They want to do away with frontiers and have a single central bank and a single currency, even a single police force. We're in the position the Americans were two hundred years ago, arguing about the power of a central government versus states' rights. So far the European Parliament hasn't counted for much, it's a debating chamber without real teeth, but after 1992 it's going to matter more and more; Delours said over a year ago that within ten years it will be taking eighty percent of important decisions affecting the Community countries. That's one reason why the French fought so hard to keep it in Strasbourg."

"Go on," Jenkins said.

"Even one of the British commissioners has said that the move to political and economic unity is unstoppable. Our politicians get their knickers in a twist talking about the Commission imposing its rules for sausages and ice cream on us. They're the sort of topics MP's like, things that catch the headlines and work people up. But they're irrelevant. Complaining about them is like trying to stop a thunderstorm by catching half a dozen raindrops."

"You're all for it then?" Jenkins enquired, his tone noncommittal.

"What I think's got nothing to do with it. In twenty-five years, maybe less, the U.S.A. will no longer be the dominant economic force in the Western World, and the EEC is still growing, more countries want to join. No wonder some Americans are worried, they can see what will happen if Europe ever goes protectionist and blocks their exports. Just as we used to worry about their doing the same thing. There's already been trouble over subsidies to farmers and aircraft manufacturers."

For several moments neither man spoke. From behind them came the subdued roar of the traffic.

"What's all this got to do with the Nature Party and the Fist of the Gaels?" Jenkins wanted to know.

"It's what's behind it all. Power. A greens party has never counted for much here, but in Germany they have more than twenty seats in the *Bundestag*. And the greens are changing, new leaders have taken over, and they're more militant.

"It's what you were saying the other evening, only you didn't go far enough. They've succeeded in worrying people, and they've got their supporters into positions where they have influence. Horwill and the people behind him aren't interested in Westminster. Not yet. One member there wouldn't mean a thing, even if they could get anybody elected, but Europe's different. And because British people by and large aren't interested, they stand a good chance of winning the by-election by default. People who always vote Tory or Labour wouldn't vote for the Nature Party in a general election, but worry them badly enough and they will this time. Just as a warning to the government."

"Are you saying they burnt down a house on Iniscaig and damaged a waste pipe at the toxic waste plant in order to get an MEP elected?" Jenkins might not believe it, but he knew Lorimer too well to scoff at his ideas.

"There's more to it than that," the Scot told him. "Every other country in the EEC elects its MP's by proportional representation. In another few years we'll fall into line, at least for the European Parliament, and when you have P.R. the small parties really come into their own. They can hold the balance of power, and when they do they use it to get the deals they want. Look what happens in Israel.

"The people on that list are probably all under forty. They're clever and they're ruthless: small horizons don't satisfy them, they're out to control the greatest economy in the world. You may not agree with Delours, and say that when it comes to the crunch countries like Britain and France will never give up their independence—that doesn't matter to the new leaders. They aren't concerned with four years on, or ten, they're thinking twenty years. Thirty. And see how they've taken over. Feldhuis was killed in a motor accident, apparently alone on a country road in the early hours of the morning. The German and the Belgian died from natural causes, one of a heart attack and the other from a stroke, both of them in their middle fifties."

"You don't have to be old to have a coronary or a stroke," Jenkins objected. "It happens all the time."

"And they lived under a lot of pressure," Lorimer agreed. "Nobody was too surprised."

The Welshman stopped and gave his companion a level stare. "Are you suggesting they were murdered?"

"No, just that it's possible; you can induce heart attacks and strokes. The one who was forced to resign because of a scandal swore he was innocent."

"He would, wouldn't he?"

"Of course he would. But there'd never been any talk about him before."

"What about Arnold Kennedy?" Jenkins wanted to know. "You haven't said anything about him."

"He was manoeuvred out, then blackmailed into keeping quiet; there've been stories about his milking the party funds. On Saturday afternoon he said he would go on television and talk about how he was ousted. That night he rang me and said he'd changed his mind. Somebody had put the frighteners on him." Lorimer paused. "They don't have to be the largest group in the parliament, just to have enough members to affect the way votes go. With that and their people in important places they'll be in a position to say whether company mergers go ahead or are blocked, how trade is regulated, where social fund hand-outs go and which major projects get supported. They aim to carve up a quarter of the world's trade between them. And it doesn't stop at trade, they'll be able to influence defence policy. Nuclear policy.

"It's the biggest cartel in history, Owen. Bigger than the Mafia. Horwill and his cronies are only a front, the men behind them are the real power. To them what they're after is worth a few murders and a bit of arson. And if they don't bring it off, they still have their connections and the power they give them. They can't lose."

For several seconds Jenkins gazed at his companion in silence. Then, "Christ!" he breathed. He rarely swore, and Lorimer recognised his doing so now as a sign that he was shaken.

"You think it's impossible?" Lorimer demanded.

"No, boy." As usual when he was excited or moved, the Welshness in Jenkins' speech became more marked. "No, it's not impossible. But it's frightening—if you're right. You haven't any proof."

"Proof isn't your province, you deal in suspicion and anxieties." Lorimer looked across the grass to where two children were playing. "In

Edinburgh you said there'd been too many 'accidents.' Who's profited from them and used them to make political capital? Somebody was backing Dorn nan Gaidheal, we know that; McIndoe didn't make enough from his magazine to keep a cat in comfort, and there were plenty of other expenses. Whoever it was probably set up some of the other 'accidents' too. All that took money; where did they get it from?"

"Those wealthy supporters?"

"Part of it maybe. But they wouldn't want their backing to be obvious, and even chairmen can't milk their companies too much. There are other ways."

"Such as?"

"Euro-fraud."

"Euro-fraud?" This time Jenkins didn't quite succeed in keeping his surprise out of his voice.

"Two or three years ago it was officially estimated that frauds accounted for at least ten percent of the EEC's total budget. That was more than two billion pounds a year. Now they're talking about up to six billion. Part of it goes to fund terrorist groups and part to the Mafia; who's to say the Nature parties don't get some?"

"You've done your homework," Jenkins commented grimly. "I'll give you that."

"Contacts, that's all you need." Lorimer grinned. "I haven't any proof, but McIndoe had a German or Dutch friend and a man with a German or Dutch accent went to see him the afternoon he was killed."

Jenkins eyed him thoughtfully. Then it was as if he switched himself off suddenly and he said, "I'm going to get a pint and something to eat, are you coming?"

Together they turned and started walking back towards Knightsbridge. The Japanese had moved on and there was no one round the Albert Memorial. Lorimer felt relief easing away his tension. He had had to convince Owen, and he knew now that he had succeeded. It meant that he could leave him to deal with things and get on with his own life.

"Take away the murders and arson, and it's ordinary politics," he said. "All parties manipulate people, trade on their fears and form alliances with other groups. It's what it's all about."

ELEVEN

THAT EVENING, as usual, the District Line train was crowded and Lorimer, standing jammed between a large man with bad breath and a girl with orange hair and a purple dress, couldn't open his *Standard* until he reached home. When he did he looked to see whether there was anything in it about the election. He told himself that if this had been a by-election to return an MP to Westminster, he wouldn't have had to turn to an inside page to find a report of the latest opinion poll— the front page would have been splashed with the news that for the first time the Tories had lost the lead: Dillon was two points ahead. It didn't necessarily mean anything, the polls didn't claim to be that accurate, and, with nine days of polling still to go, in theory there was still plenty of time for the Conservative candidate to regain the lost ground. It didn't alter the fact that a month ago the situation would have been unthinkable.

And there might not be time in practice. The other parties hadn't taken the campaign seriously enough, with the result that now they hadn't a springboard from which to take off. With Labour in disarray the Tories had been complacent, while the Democrats and SDP were preoccupied with their own differences. None of them had considered the Nature Party a threat, and now it might be too late.

Lorimer wondered what Jenkins would do; he hadn't asked him, and the Welshman hadn't said. Over their pints and ploughmans' they had talked of sport and holidays. Jenkins, who had two teenage sons, was taking his family to Cornwall for a fortnight at the end of July. Lorimer hadn't made any plans. Before he met Rosalind he had enjoyed going off by himself; now the prospect of two weeks alone wasn't so appealing and a "singles" holiday was worse. He supposed he could take his car to France and explore out-of-the-way villages as they used to do. They had been working their way along the Pyrannees from west to east and got as far as Luchon when they split up—he might go on from there.

If he did, he thought wryly, he would spend half the time thinking about her.

And Hilary. Yearning for the impossible. To hell with that, he was thirty-four, not seventeen.

He wondered where Rosalind was going this year. Somewhere exotic with Horwill most likely. The thought depressed him still more.

He was seeing Horwill at seven. Now that he had talked to Jenkins the meeting seemed unnecessary, but he could hardly call it off, and at least it wasn't to be a lengthy, embarrassed conversation over a meal. Horwill had made it clear he had no time for that. Sounding boastful rather than apologetic, he had said flatly that he was busy with the election campaign and had to make a speech at Hammersmith that evening, but they might meet at his club first.

The club was near Fleet Street, a watering hole for business people before the rigours of the journey home. It occupied the first floor of a large modern office block, and its panelling and big leather easy chairs fitted uncomfortably into the concrete and glass round them.

Horwill was waiting in the bar. With him was Rosalind.

Lorimer had expected him to be alone, and of all the people he might have brought with him, she was the least welcome. He wondered whose idea it had been that she come, hers or Horwill's.

The politician was shorter than Lorimer—having seen him only on a platform—had realised, and at close quarters the signs of self-indulgence were more apparent; there was a slackness about his jawline and he had the beginnings of a paunch. True, he was reasonably good looking, and Lorimer could understand some women being attracted to him —not Rosalind, though, she was too perceptive—but something about him struck a false note. This evening he was playing the successful politician, a little too effusive and determined to be pleasant. Lorimer could picture him kissing babies in the street. But behind the bonhomie his streak of vanity was clear.

Rosalind, once she had said casually, "Hallo, Gray," hardly spoke.

A waiter came to take their order. When he had gone, Horwill said smoothly, "Naturally it's a pleasure to meet you, Gray, but I'm afraid I'm not very clear why you wanted to see me."

Lorimer suspected that the other man's public-school accent was as false as the rest of his facade, and he had cultivated it as part of the image he wanted to present to the world. "Rosalind took me to your meeting the other night," he said. "I was impressed."

He was aware of Rosalind watching him. She knew he had reservations about Horwill and she was puzzled by his wanting to meet him. It made her suspicious. She knew him too well, Lorimer thought. At the same time, perversely, the knowledge gave him a feeling of satisfaction.

It was something they shared, and Horwill, his perceptions corroded by his egotism, would never understand.

"Were you?" Horwill said, smiling. It was a self-satisfied, slightly condescending smile.

"I agreed with a lot of what you said."

"Of course you did, you're intelligent, Gray. Anyone who is must see we're right."

Patronising sod! Lorimer thought.

For a minute or two they talked trivialities, then Horwill's manner changed. It became suddenly hard, and he said abruptly, "I hear you went to see Arnold Kennedy."

"Yes," Lorimer agreed. "Who told you?"

"He did. He said you tried to persuade him to go on television." Rosalind frowned and looked quickly at Lorimer, but she didn't say anything. "He wasn't happy about it. He said you bullied him into agreeing."

"That wasn't the impression I got," Lorimer said. "He told me he wanted to talk."

The waiter returned with their drinks, and for a minute or two there was an awkward silence.

"What did he want to talk about?" Horwill demanded when the man had gone. There was no mistaking his tenseness now.

"How you manoeuvred him out by packing the meeting with your friends, and some of them weren't even members of the party," Lorimer said.

Horwill had become very still. "He told you that?"

"And other things."

Rosalind looked as if she were going to say something, but if so she changed her mind.

Horwill appeared to be searching for words, and when he spoke his manner had changed again and he had become once more the smooth politician. "Arnold was a very respected man," he said.

"Respected?"

"Yes indeed. But he's an old man now, and he's bitter. When he's defeated on anything he thinks he's been cheated, he won't accept that it's because his ideas haven't kept up with the times. And like all that generation of socialists, he's still suspicious of Europe; he forgets that for most of our history we've been part of it. Do you know much of Europe, Gray?" Despite his reasonable tone, Horwill's eyes were watchful.

"France," Lorimer said. "Italy. And Holland, I have to go to Amsterdam again this week."

"Oh?" Horwill appeared relaxed, but there was an almost unnatural stillness about him. "I don't know it, but they say it's a beautiful city." His smooth veneer dissolved and there was a harsh undertone in his voice as he asked, "Why did you try to get Kennedy to appear on 'Mirror on the Week'?"

Rosalind could remain silent no longer. "You did that?" she demanded furiously of her husband. "Who the hell gave you the right?"

"Mark Preston," Lorimer said.

"You went to Mark?"

"He's the producer."

"What are you playing at, Gray?"

"Nothing. This isn't a game." Lorimer looked at Horwill. "I'd like to know why he said 'Yes,' then changed his mind after you'd been to see him."

"I said he'd spoken to me, not that I'd been to see him." A complacent smirk curled the corners of Horwill's mouth. "I'm the leader of the party now, if he wants to see me, he comes to me."

Lorimer noticed the flicker of surprise which crossed Rosalind's face and was pleased. She might be reluctant to see any fault in the man, but even she must acknowledge his arrogance and vanity now.

"He rang me and asked me for my advice about what he should do in the interests of the party," Horwill continued. "I'm used to dealing with the media, I have a gift for it, and I told him it would be very unwise for him to involve himself in any interview. They'd make him look a fool or a crook."

"You put the frighteners on him," Lorimer said.

For two or three seconds it was very quiet at their end of the bar. Lorimer heard the chink as the steward put a glass he had wiped down on the shelf and it touched the next one.

"What the hell do you mean?" Horwill demanded, his voice rising angrily. The people at the far end of the bar looked round and the steward stopped wiping glasses. Horwill saw them and went on more quietly, "Are you suggesting what I think you are?"

"What do you think I am?" Lorimer asked. Horwill wasn't the only one who was tense, he thought.

The politician brushed the question aside. "I've no intention of becoming involved in a slanging match with you," he said coldly.

"What sort of car do you drive?"

Horwill gave Rosalind a quick sideways glance. Lorimer saw it and guessed he was thinking that if he lied she would know.

"A Jaguar."

"Grey?"

"Yes, as a matter of fact. Why?"

"There was a grey Jag parked near Kennedy's house when I left him on Saturday afternoon. I saw you get out of it." Lorimer pushed his glass a few inches farther on to the table. "I'll tell you why I wanted to see you. I wanted to ask you about your party's links with Dorn nan Gaidheal and what you knew about the murders of Rona Smith and Roy McIndoe. I thought it was just possible—just—you didn't know anything, but it doesn't matter now."

He sensed Rosalind's anger, but Horwill had regained his composure and his manner was as smooth as it had been when Lorimer joined them.

"Rona Smith, did you say?" he asked. "And Roy McIndoe? Who were they?"

"You said something about a man named McIndoe before," Rosalind said accusingly to Lorimer. She frowned. "He was the boyfriend of the girl who burnt down United's house on that island."

"Rona Smith," Lorimer agreed. "She was killed when she wouldn't have anything to do with blowing up the tank at the toxic waste plant. Then McIndoe was shot because he knew too much."

"Who shot them?" Rosalind looked as if she couldn't believe what she was hearing.

Lorimer looked at Horwill. "Ask him," he said. "He knows, but I don't suppose he'll tell you."

He got to his feet and stood looking at Horwill. Horwill said nothing, and after a second or two Lorimer turned and walked out of the bar. The people at the other end of the room eyed him curiously.

As he passed, the porter in the lobby said, "Good evening, sir."

" 'Evening," Lorimer said.

Outside in the street the air was heavy with the odour of exhaust fumes, dust and too many bodies.

Lorimer didn't need anyone to tell him that his confrontation with Horwill had achieved nothing. Less than nothing. Jenkins had wanted him to get close to the other man; instead he had put as wide a gulf between them as he could have done, and he knew no more than he had before. Worse, he had probably antagonised Rosalind for good. If it wasn't bad enough that he had gone behind her back over the television interview with Kennedy, he had as good as accused Horwill in front of her of being involved in two murders. The strange thing was, he didn't regret any of it. It was as if by tackling Horwill face-to-face he had purged himself. Which was nonsense. Pathetic.

Arrived back at his flat, he got himself a scratch meal, watched the BBC news and read. He half hoped that Rosalind might call; even if it was only to tell him what she thought of him, it would be better than cold indifference. But the only time the phone rang it was a wrong number.

Soon after ten he went to bed.

Lorimer hadn't seen Grantley since being summoned to his office; the chairman had been out most of the afternoon and hadn't returned to United House. Now Lorimer wanted his agreement to something, and he wasn't sure how the Old Man would react in view of what had happened that morning.

However, one of Grantley's strengths was his ability to put the past behind him. He would learn from it, but he wouldn't let it cloud his judgement, and he didn't allow his anger to fester. Lorimer might have acted like a fool; Grantley had let him know what he thought of him, and that was the end of the matter. Grantley had made a fool of himself plenty of times when he was young, he still did occasionally, and Lorimer wasn't going to be judged on one slip.

He doubted whether there was much in it, anyway. If anyone had behaved irresponsibly, it was Forsyth's wife as much as Lorimer: she had put him in a position where he couldn't win. A lovely woman, Hilary Forsyth. Grantley admitted to himself that if he had been Lorimer, and she had asked him to use her spare ticket, he would probably have gone without thinking much about the consequences. He wasn't sure he would have stayed in the taxi either.

When Lorimer came into his room he regarded him almost benevolently.

" 'Morning, Gray," he said. "Nice day again. Anything in the papers?"

"No, sir."

"Good."

Lorimer wondered whether to tell the Old Man that he had met Jenkins yesterday. But it wasn't incumbent on him to do so, and at this stage there was nothing to be gained by mentioning it.

"You wanted to see me about something?" the chairman asked.

Lorimer hesitated. He had thought about this a good deal since last night and he still wasn't sure how to put it. "It's to do with the Fist of the Gaels business," he said.

"I thought that was over as far as we were concerned?"

"There's more to it than we knew."

"That affects us?"

"It could." If it affected most of western and southern Europe, Lorimer thought, United could hardly escape. "I'd like to go to Amsterdam," he said.

Grantley regarded him steadily from under his dark, bushy eyebrows. "Why?"

"There's an angle there I'd like to look into."

"All right, go. You don't have to ask me, you know that." The chairman picked up a sheaf of papers. "Amsterdam's a lovely city. Damned expensive now though." He paused and gave Lorimer another level stare. "One thing. You aren't thinking of getting up to any bloody silly tricks, are you?"

Lorimer grinned. "No, sir."

"Good."

Grantley started reading the top paper and Lorimer went to speak to Helen Wilkins.

"Can you get me on the midday flight to Amsterdam tomorrow and book me a room somewhere for a couple of nights?" he asked her.

"I'll try."

"Och, you're wonderful."

"I know." Mrs. Wilkins, who was the older by nine years and happily married, smiled. "They have lovely diamonds in Amsterdam," she remarked wistfully.

"They have cheese too," Lorimer told her.

For the rest of the day he concentrated on routine tasks, and at five forty-five he went home feeling restless and dissatisfied. It was his own fault, he knew, he had made a mess of things last night. And it wasn't the sort of mess you could put right afterwards.

There was somebody in his flat: Rosalind was sitting on the settee wearing a pale green shirt and trousers and looking angry. Clearly she had been there some time and the wait had done nothing to improve her temper. When Lorimer came in she fixed him with a baleful eye.

"How did you get in?" he enquired curiously. Finding people in his flat was becoming a habit.

"I still have a key, remember?" Rosalind's tone wasn't encouraging.

"I'd forgotten."

"You insisted I keep it. I suppose you hoped I would weaken and come back." She stood up, took a key from her bag and laid it on the table with more force than was strictly necessary. "There never was any point in my keeping it, and there's even less now."

Lorimer looked at the key. He didn't feel any disappointment, it was too late for that. He didn't feel anything much; he supposed he had had too long to get used to the idea that it was all over between them. But somehow the key lying there on the table seemed like a symbol.

"What the hell did you think you were doing?" Rosalind demanded.

"Doing?"

"You as good as accused Edward of murder. If I were him, I'd sue you."

"Isn't he going to?"

"No, he just shrugged it off. I can't imagine why."

"I can." Lorimer took off his jacket and draped it over the back of a chair. "He daren't."

"What does that mean?"

"He's afraid of what would come out."

Rosalind struggled to control her anger. "You're so low, Gray. And you're getting worse: you can't bear the thought of my being interested in any other man."

"I can't bear to see you getting mixed up with a man like Horwill," Lorimer said, losing some of his cool. There had been enough truth in the charge to sting him. "You don't know what he is."

"And I suppose you do?" Rosalind paused. "All right, what is he?"

"A thug. A smooth, vain, ruthless, ambitious thug."

"My God!"

"You saw what he was like last night; he's so vain he nearly falls over bowing to himself. Drop him, Ros. Find yourself a decent bloke, not a poncing bloody politician who doesn't care how he gets power as long as he gets it."

"A man like you, I suppose?" Rosalind said bitterly. "You're eaten up with jealousy. You don't know anything, you're making it all up."

"It's not just me, other people know what he's doing."

"And what is that? Exactly?"

Their eyes met.

"I can't tell you," Lorimer said.

"You're contemptible." Rosalind picked up her bag and glared at him, her hands gripping its strap tight. "I used to think you were straightforward at least, now I see how wrong I was." She walked to the door.

Oh God! Lorimer thought. Don't let it end like this. But he knew there was nothing he could do, anything he tried would only make matters worse. And when he could, if that time ever came, it might be too late for Rosalind.

"He's a crook," he said helplessly.

Rosalind didn't look back, and the door closed behind her.

The next morning Lorimer had just drunk his coffee when there was a tap on his door and Robin Forsyth walked in. Lorimer wondered if Hilary had told him about their going to the theatre the other evening. If so, he seemed quite happy about it.

" 'Morning, Gray." He perched on a corner of the desk and pushed back his rebellious lock of hair. "It's the board this morning."

Lorimer nodded. He was remembering what Jenkins had said about United's new director: that he needn't worry about him, he wasn't one of "them." "You've been checking on me," he said. "That's why you asked me to dinner."

"Partly," Forsyth admitted. "Do you mind?"

"Not much." Lorimer decided there was nothing to be gained by pussyfooting round the situation. "You know Edward Horwill," he said.

Forsyth regarded him levelly. "Slightly," he agreed. "Why?"

"I saw he'd been appointed a director of two of your companies."

"Oh, I see. We like to keep a balance politically, not all Tories, and he's a bright chap. Very bright."

"The Nature Party are getting their people on to a lot of boards."

"Are they? I hadn't noticed. But then, I wouldn't know who are their people and who aren't." Forsyth looked mildly curious. "Why are you interested in Horwill?"

"My wife's friendly with him," Lorimer replied easily.

"Oh." Forsyth watched the well-polished toe of his right shoe swing slowly backwards and forwards. "His party's attracting a lot of youngish, energetic people. You saw them at the meeting the other night. I rather suspect it's the wives who become interested first, and they rope in their husbands. Ecological concern is the in thing these days. If you have children, you worry about what the world will be like for them, and if you haven't . . ." He shrugged.

"Horwill's a pushing sod," Lorimer said.

"Probably."

"And a crook."

Forsyth's eyebrows rose. "Have you any reason for saying that?"

"I think he has connections with Dorn nan Gaidheal."

"Really? It doesn't seem very likely. I don't care for the man, he's far too pleased with himself, and between ourselves I was against his coming on the boards, but I was in the minority. I often am." Forsyth's tone changed. "What makes you think he could be tied up with a bunch of Scottish nationalists?"

"It's all one environment," Lorimer said.

Forsyth regarded him thoughtfully. "Yes," he agreed. "Yes, it is. How is the Dorn nan Gaidheal business going?"

"Pretty well finished, as far as we're concerned. The Burtons have a place to live, the pollution's more or less cleared up and the fish farm and the cannery are getting back to normal."

"Good. What are you doing now?"

"Nothing much. I'm going to Amsterdam this afternoon."

"Amsterdam?"

"Just for a day or two. There are some things I want to check there."

"Have a good trip then." Forsyth glanced at his watch. "I'd better get along." At the door he paused and added, "I'll remember what you said about Horwill."

Lorimer wondered whether he meant it. And, if he did, what difference it would make. Probably none. Even if you were the chairman and you had enough support, you couldn't have a director removed merely because you didn't like him, and Horwill had everything going for him just now.

TWELVE

LORIMER LIKED AMSTERDAM. He liked the old city with its gabled houses lining the canals, the hump-backed bridges and the backwaters with their shady corners. There was something soothing about canals. Yet walk a few yards and you were in all the bustle of a modern city. Some of the newer suburbs might be unattractive, but they were no worse than those of other places, and if you were a visitor you didn't have to go to them.

Feldhuis's house, belying his name, was beside one of the canals. Like most of the buildings in the old parts of the city, it was tall and narrow, but unlike them it hadn't yet been converted into offices. A single flight of steps climbed the three or four feet to the front door. Opposite the house across the cobbled street a row of trees, their leaves not yet scorched and dulled by the sun and exhaust fumes, lined the side of the canal. A flat, broad-beamed cruise boat was passing, and Lorimer could see the passengers craning their necks to peer out through its perspex roof. Turning, he climbed the steps and rang the bell.

It was answered by a young woman with dark eyes and raven black hair wearing a simple black dress. She seemed very young to be Feldhuis's widow and she didn't look Dutch, but nor did she look like a servant.

"I'm sorry," Lorimer apologised. "Do you speak English?"

She nodded. "Yes."

"I wonder if I could see Mevrouw Feldhuis?"

"Who are you?" The young woman's manner was businesslike to the point of curtness.

"My name's Graham Lorimer. I think she may be able to help me."

"How? I am Isabella Feldhuis, Mevrouw Feldhuis is my mother. My father died the other day and she is still very distressed. I do not want her to be worried." She spoke English easily, as if she were used to doing so, with only a slight accent.

"It's about Professor Feldhuis," Lorimer told her.

She frowned. "What about him?"

Lorimer looked up and down the quiet road. A Mercedes was parked by the corner a hundred yards away, but he could see no one within earshot and it was ridiculous to think that he might have been followed from London. Nevertheless the doorstep seemed too public a place to talk. "I think what happened to him may not have been an accident," he said.

"You are suggesting that he killed himself?" A new, hostile note had crept into Isabella Feldhuis's voice.

"No."

"That somebody killed him then?"

"I don't know, I think it's possible. May I see Mevrouw Feldhuis?"

The young woman hesitated for a second or two, then she said, "You had better come in. I will find out if she wishes to see you."

She stepped back just far enough to allow Lorimer to walk past her into a small hall from which a staircase rose steeply to the upper floors; space had been as valuable when the house was built three hundred years ago as it was today. While she was standing in the doorway her face had been partly in shadow; now Lorimer could see her more clearly. She was handsome rather than conventionally pretty, with strong features and large, brooding eyes. Something about her, those eyes, perhaps, and her mouth, suggested a passionate nature, controlled at present, but liable to erupt at any moment. It hardly conformed with her father's moderate, slightly dull image, and Lorimer wondered about her mother.

"It is impossible what you say," Isabella told him. "Who would want to kill my father? He was a good man, everybody liked him."

"A lot of good people are murdered every year," Lorimer pointed out. "And I'm not saying he was, just that I think he may have been." There was something so wildly improbable as to verge on the fantastic about his standing here in this cool, quiet hall discussing with Feldhuis's daughter the possibility of her father's having been murdered, he thought. But the whole business was fantastic.

"Why?" she demanded. "Who are you?"

"I work for a big company in Britain. People have been killed there too, a girl student and a man in Edinburgh. I think there may be a connection between what happened to them and to your father."

Isabella frowned. "I do not understand. How can there be? My father had nothing to do with people in Edinburgh." Nevertheless she wondered if what Lorimer said could be true. He seemed sane, and ever since her mother learnt of her husband's death she had insisted that somebody had killed him. Isabella and her brother had dismissed the idea as absurd, blaming the shock of what had happened and the revelation of his deceit for her refusal to accept the truth. They were more worldly wise, more aware of human failings than she was. Now Isabella was no longer sure.

"I will speak to her," she said. "Wait here, please."

She went up the stairs, moving with a sort of awkward grace.

It was two or three minutes before she returned, and Lorimer passed the time studying an old map of the city hanging on one of the walls.

"My mother will see you, Mr. Lorimer," she said when she rejoined him. More quietly she added, "What has happened has been a great shock to her, please be kind."

"I will," Lorimer promised.

He followed her up the stairs to a smallish room on the second floor. The woman who got up from an easy chair to greet him was an older edition of Isabella, but, unlike her daughter, she had no pretensions to good looks or elegance. She was very fat, her greying hair was pulled back into an untidy bun and her black dress looked as if it had been bought in a hurry at a chain store.

"I am Maria Feldhuis," she said in English that was less fluent and more accented than the younger woman's. "Please sit down, Mr. Lorimer. Isabella says you want to talk to me about my husband."

"If you don't mind," Lorimer said.

"No, I do not mind. It is when people say bad things about him I mind. Things I know cannot be true."

"All I know is what I've read in the British papers." Lorimer glanced at her daughter who was standing with her back to the window. As if she were on guard, he thought. Against what? Him? Did she believe he represented some source of danger? "The report said he had been to a meeting of the Nature Party council that evening. He was driving home alone when he lost control of his car on a dangerous bend and it went into a river."

"That is all you have seen?" Isabella demanded, turning and looking at her mother.

"Yes."

"It is not true," Maria Feldhuis said. "He had enemies in the party, they killed him."

"Mother!" Isabella protested in Dutch. "We've been over this time after time. There is no evidence. It was an accident."

The older woman turned on her. "They say he had been drinking," she said angrily. "He hardly drank at all, you know that. And never when he was going to drive."

They gazed at each other, and Lorimer noticed that it was Isabella who looked away first.

"It would help if I could know everything," he said gently.

"How?" Isabella faced him, no longer making any attempt to conceal her hostility. "Who would it help? You?"

"I don't know until you tell me," Lorimer answered.

"You are looking for dirt."

"Isabella!" Maria Feldhuis protested.

"Well, aren't you?"

"No," Lorimer said. "I believe your father may have been murdered, and that if so what happened to him is connected with those murders in Scotland and several cases of sabotage there and in England."

Isabella frowned. "What is this about sabotage?" she demanded impatiently. "I do not know any of it."

"You have heard of United?"

"The British company? Of course."

"I work for them. A few weeks ago a group of extremists who call themselves the Fist of the Gaels burnt down one of our manager's houses. A month later they damaged a tank at a toxic waste disposal plant so that the waste escaped and polluted the sea. Two of the group, a man and a girl, have been murdered since, and a Dutchman or a German is mixed up in it somewhere. I think he shot them." Lorimer paused. "There's something else."

For a moment their eyes met, and the girl's held a challenge. Then all the spirit seemed to go out of her and she turned wearily to her mother. "Why don't you tell him?" she asked her mother. Bitterly she added, "It's hardly a secret."

"No!" The older woman was sitting very straight, and the passion Lorimer thought he had seen in her daughter blazed in her eyes.

"They found his car in the river on Sunday morning," Isabella said. "He had been drowned and there was much alcohol in his blood."

"Isabella!" Maria Feldhuis exclaimed angrily.

Her daughter ignored her. "Where they found him was ten miles out of Amsterdam, in the country; why should he drive out there at one-thirty in the morning? Why did he not take a taxi home as he always did even if he had drunk only a little?"

"There is no doubt he drowned?" Lorimer asked.

"No." Isabella looked down at her hands.

"Nor that he was alone?"

"The police say he was."

Lorimer wondered why he had the impression that there was something else, something that these women hadn't told him. Perhaps it was something in their manner, especially Isabella's, or the sudden tension in the atmosphere. He turned to the mother. "Thank you, Mevrouw Feldhuis," he said. "I'm sorry if I've caused you any distress."

She shook her head and gave him a wan little smile as she offered him her hand.

Isabella led the way back downstairs.

When they reached the hall Lorimer said, "There's more, isn't there?"

"More?"

"Something you haven't told me."

For a moment she eyed him uncertainly, then she appeared to make up her mind about something.

"My mother didn't want me to tell you," she said. "You understand she is not Dutch? She is Chilean and she has a different sort of pride. The police found out that after the meeting my father and two other men went to a night-club called the Emperor's. A young woman joined them there. The other men left about one o'clock, but my father and the woman stayed on a little while longer. When they left they went to her flat." Isabella paused. "Her name is Klaasje Wijnen. She told the police that she had known my father for six months and that night they made love. When he left her he had drunk a lot and she tried to persuade him not to drive, but he insisted he was all right."

"Who is Klaasje Wijnen?" Lorimer asked.

"I don't know. She calls herself an actress, but no one had heard of her until this."

"You don't believe what she says?"

Isabella shrugged. "It is possible. How much does one ever know about one's parents?"

She had schooled herself to face the question, Lorimer thought. At the same time she couldn't really believe that her father had been unfaithful to his wife. Couldn't, or didn't want to.

"What did your mother mean about his having enemies in the party?" he asked.

Isabella looked down, avoiding his eye. "I do not know," she said. "My father and I were very close, but I had not seen him for more than seven months. My mother does not approve of my living with a man who is not my husband. She was brought up in Chile in the old ways, you understand, very strict, and even after all these years she still cannot accept that it is different here and that times have changed. It has made things very difficult, and I do not come home very often. My father understood, he was used to the ways of young people." Isabella stopped, looking distressed. "I should have been here. I will never forgive myself that I did not see him again before . . ."

"I think you do know what she meant," Lorimer said.

Isabella faced him. "My mother says he told her there were people who did not want him to go on being the leader. Militant people who wanted to use the party to change many things." Her eyes bright, she burst out passionately, "It is not only him they murdered, they killed what he believed in."

"According to the report I saw, he was a moderate," Lorimer said. "He wanted to influence people, not fight them."

"That is right. I do not think he was really interested in politics. But he was a scientist, he saw that the world was destroying itself and he felt he must do something."

"Who will take his place now?"

"Cornelis van Rijn. There is no one else. He is one of those with whom my father had trouble. I have met him and I do not like him, he is too—too smooth, as you say. And too ruthless. Also he shows too much that he is ambitious. A lot of people in the party do not like him. They are afraid of what he may do and they will not be happy that he becomes leader."

"What does he do? His work?"

"He is some sort of businessman, not old but successful." Isabella eyed Lorimer more closely. "I do not understand why you are asking all these questions."

That makes two of us, Lorimer thought. He was groping in the dark, in the hope that sooner or later one of his questions would produce an answer which told him something. Perhaps, instead, it would stir a reaction for which he wasn't prepared. That was a risk he had to take.

"There are twelve countries in the EEC," he said. "In six of them the Nature parties have changed leaders in the last few months. Counting your father, three of the old ones died and two of the others were forced to resign. All five of the new people are comparatively young and much more militant than the ones whose places they took."

Isabella frowned. "I do not understand."

"Nor do I. Not yet. Who were the two men who went to the Emperor's Club with your father?"

"Piet van Else and Albert Mul. They are on the council of the party."

"Can you give me their addresses? And Klaasje Wijnen's?"

Isabella eyed Lorimer uncertainly. "You are going to see them?"

"I may. I don't know."

She hesitated for a moment as if she were about to raise some objection, or, perhaps, to warn him, then she crossed to a small table with a telephone on it, picked up a directory and flicked over the pages. Lorimer watched while she scribbled on a small pad, then turned more pages. When she had finished she tore the sheet from the pad and handed it to him. He thanked her and slipped it into his pocket.

"I'm staying at the American Hotel," he said. "If you think of anything, or there's anything I can do . . ."

"Thank you, I will remember." Isabella held out her hand. "Goodbye, Mr. Lorimer."

The sun was still shining, but a few small clouds were blowing up in the west. At the corner the grey Mercedes was still parked by the kerb. Two men were sitting in it. The driver was stocky and so fair as to be almost white-haired, his companion older, dark and slightly built. As Lorimer passed they glanced up without any apparent interest, two men waiting for somebody. He walked to the next stop and caught a tram to Dam Square.

Dam was thronged with its usual crowd of tourists sight-seeing and window shopping. Lorimer dodged them and walked round to the offices of United's Dutch subsidiary. Willem Leiter, the managing director's assistant, was expecting him, and Lorimer was shown straight up to his office. Leiter was young, two stones overweight and mousy-haired, with noticeably large ears and tinted glasses.

"You have been to see Mevrouw Feldhuis?" he asked when the two men had shaken hands and sat down. Something in his tone led Lorimer to think that he didn't approve.

"Yes," he agreed.

"How is she?"

"She seemed okay. Distressed." How could you tell how somebody was when you had never met them before? You had to know how they usually looked and behaved to discern any difference.

"Of course."

"You didn't know Feldhuis, did you?"

Leiter shook his head. "His name only. Why are you here, Mr. Lorimer? What is it about the Feldhuises that interests you?"

"It's just possible that there's a connection between what happened to the professor and something in Britain."

"And it affects United?" Lorimer nodded. "You work for Sir Aidan Grantley, you are his trouble-shooter. Then it must be something important."

"Don't you believe it. It's probably nothing at all." Lorimer saw that the Dutchman didn't believe him. "It's my job to deal with situations before they become problems; usually there's nothing in them. Yesterday we had a question about something one of our staff in Malaysia had done: it was a nonsense, the manager had misunderstood what the guy said. Tomorrow I'll very likely go back to London and forget all about the Feldhuises." Like hell he would, he thought. But none of this was any concern of Leiter's, he was only here to see if he could tell him anything. "Have you ever heard of two men named Mul and van Else?"

"I do not think so."

"They were with the professor at the night-club the night he died."

"Oh, them. I had forgotten their names." Leiter looked uneasy and Lorimer was sure he was lying.

"They are members of the Nature Party's council," he said.

"I know nothing about them, only what I have read in the papers."

"What about Cornelis van Rijn? They say he's certain to be the party's new leader."

"He is good, a strong man. Or so I have heard, I have never met him."

"And Klaasje Wijnen?"

"According to the papers, she is an actress. Lots of women like her call themselves actresses, you know?" Leiter paused, and his uneasiness became more marked. "Mr. Lorimer, why do you want to involve yourself in what happened to the professor? It was a tragedy, but how can it concern United? Nothing can change what happened, and if you ask questions it will only distress his family and his friends. They will not like it, and some of them are powerful people."

Lorimer smiled cheerfully. "I told you, I'll probably go home tomorrow and forget all about it," he said.

Leiter didn't look reassured. "It may make things difficult for us here in Amsterdam. We are a British company."

"British-owned maybe, United N.V. is Dutch; it's registered here and most of the management's Dutch. Anyway, we're all Europeans now."

"If people think we are interfering in Dutch politics, they will not like it."

"We aren't. And they won't know who I work for unless you tell them." Lorimer stood up. "Och, cheer up. It may never happen."

Leiter looked puzzled. "What may never happen?"

"The worst," Lorimer said. "It's a British expression."

"Yes?" The Dutchman shrugged unhappily, as if to say that he had done all he could and it wasn't his fault if he had failed.

At the door Lorimer turned. "I heard van Rijn frightens people," he said.

Klaasje Wijnen's flat was on the third floor of a modern block. The lift was up at the seventh floor and Lorimer climbed the stairs, rang her bell and waited.

The woman who answered his ring was almost uncannily like the picture he had formed of her, about thirty, very blonde, smartly if a little flashily dressed, and attractive in a hard way. It occurred to him that a superficial description of her might have fitted Hilary Forsyth as well, yet there was really little resemblance between the two women. The advantages were all on Hilary's side.

The Dutchwoman looked him up and down, her eyes appraising him. "Miss Wijnen?" he asked. "Do you speak English?"

"A little."

"My name is Kemp." It was the first name that came into Lorimer's mind; even if anyone should follow his trail here, they wouldn't connect "Kemp" with United. "I would like to talk to you."

The woman frowned. "What about?"

"Johann Feldhuis."

"You are from the English press?"

"No."

"I have nothing to say. What happened to him was very sad, and I do not want to talk about it."

There was no sadness in her eyes, Lorimer thought. Nor her voice. She started closing the door, and he pushed his foot into the gap.

"What are you doing?" she demanded angrily. "Go away, or I will call the police."

"I don't think so," Lorimer said. "Let me come in, I only want to talk for a few minutes."

He gave the door a sudden push. Balanced precariously on very high heels, the woman tottered back and nearly fell. Lorimer walked past her across the hall and into the living room. It was expensively furnished, but somehow, despite the magazines and feminine knick-knacks lying about, it looked more like a film set than a room which was lived in.

"Get out!" Klaasje Wijnen told him furiously.

Lorimer closed the door, took her wrist and led her, still protesting angrily, to the big sofa in the middle of the room. He pushed her and she subsided on to it, glaring at him.

"How well did you really know Professor Feldhuis?" he asked.

"We were lovers." Her tone was defiant.

"Did he pay for all this?" Lorimer looked round the room. "And this?" He fingered the valuable-looking bracelet on one of her wrists.

"No! I am respectable. He gave me presents, that is all."

"An unknown actress, and you can afford this place? And those clothes and jewellery?" Lorimer smiled without humour.

The woman tore her wrist free and struggled to get to her feet, scratching at him with her long fingernails. Lorimer shoved her back on to the sofa.

"You do that again, and I'll tie you up," he said harshly.

"Who are you?" she demanded, her eyes blazing with hate. "You are not the police."

"Just answer my questions," Lorimer told her. "Then I'll go."

"I will not tell you anything."

"Very well." One of the other doors was open, and through the gap Lorimer could see the foot of a double bed and a dressing-table. Hauling Klaasje Wijnen to her feet, he dragged her, not too roughly, across the living room and through the open door. If he had read her character correctly, there was one thing she would mind more than almost anything else except damage to her appearance, and he had no intention of resorting to physical violence. Turning her so that she was facing one of the two huge built-in wardrobes, he said, "Open it."

"What—?" she began.

"Open it."

Reluctantly she did so. From the rail hung dozens of coats, dresses, skirts and trousers, with rows of shoes below them. At the end of the rail were a blue fox jacket and two full-length fur coats, one of them mink. Apparently Klaasje Wijnen was so attached to the symbols of her success that she couldn't bear to be parted from them, even in summer. None too carefully, Lorimer dragged the mink coat off its hanger.

"What are you doing?" she demanded, her eyes wide with alarm.

Lorimer pushed her away and she collapsed on to the bed. Taking his penknife from his pocket, he opened it and picked up the coat.

"No!" she shrieked.

"Who pays for all this?"

"He did."

"Feldhuis? On a professor's salary, with a wife and a home to support?"

"It is not your business. I will not tell you."

"Okay." Lorimer shook out the coat so that the back was spread wide. "No!"

They stared at each other. Lorimer put the point of the knife against the soft fur.

"Piet pays for it," Klaasje Wijnen muttered.

"Piet?"

"Piet van Else."

"When did you first meet Johann Feldhuis?"

"That night. Saturday." She almost spat the words out.

"Did van Else pay you to go to the club and bring Feldhuis back here afterwards?"

"No. It was just like I told the police."

"You're lying," Lorimer said. "You were paid to meet the three of them at the club. When the other two left, you were to stay with Feldhuis for a while, make sure he drank more than he was used to, and bring him back here. The others were waiting for you. Who drove him out into the country and put him in the river? Was it you or them?"

"You do not know what you are saying." Klaasje Wijnen was still angry, but now her anger was tinged with fear. It made her look haggard, and her make-up stood out in ugly blotches.

"Feldhuis didn't die by accident," Lorimer said. "He was murdered. You three killed him."

"No! I did not know what was going to happen."

It was possible that she was telling the truth, Lorimer thought. If so, it was no wonder she was scared by what she had found herself mixed up in. "You'll have to prove that," he told her harshly.

"They said they were just going to show people what the professor was really like and that he wasn't fit to be the leader of the party."

"By killing him?"

"That was an accident." There was a note of desperation in the woman's voice now. "They did not mean it to happen, Piet told me so. They were going to make him resign, but he struggled and the car slipped down the bank into the river. Piet and Albert were lucky to get out."

It was possible she believed that, Lorimer thought. Even possible that she didn't know they had been forcing more alcohol down Feldhuis's throat while he struggled. Personally he didn't believe a word of it. He threw the coat on to the bed beside her and closed his knife. "God help you," he said.

"What are you going to do?" Her eyes, wide with fear, stared up at him. "You will not go to the police?"

"Why not?"

"They will not believe you. I shall tell them you hurt me and I told you things which were not true to make you leave."

Until now Lorimer had accepted her for what she was, a woman without morals, avaricious and mercenary, scared at the position in which she found herself. All that had mattered was the information she could give him. Now suddenly he was revolted by her.

He walked out of the flat, crossed the landing and took the lift down to the lobby. Outside in the street the grey Mercedes with two men in it was parked against the opposite kerb. It was very warm, the air humid and oppressive. Angry grey clouds were massing, threatening a storm, and as Lorimer emerged from the building thunder rumbled in the distance.

When he got back to his hotel he rang Isabella Feldhuis. "I thought you'd like to know," he told her, "I've talked to Klaasje Wijnen."

"Oh. What did she say?" Isabella sounded tense, as if his answer meant a great deal to her.

"She admitted she had never seen your father until Saturday night. She was paid to see he drank a lot and get him back to her flat. Van Else and Mul were there, they waited for a while, then put him in his own car and drove him out to where he was found."

"It was them." There was a strange note in Isabella's voice. "Have you been to the police?"

"No."

"Why not?"

"She would deny it. So would they. The police have written off what happened as an accident, they wouldn't want to know. Besides, there's a political angle."

"But they murdered him!"

"She says they told her it was an accident, they only meant to disgrace him so that he would have to resign, but he struggled and the car slid into the river."

"You do not believe that?"

"No. But it's just possible she does. She's scared."

"I would like her to be more scared." Lorimer was startled by the hatred in Isabella's voice. "And the men. I would like them to be very, very frightened. Like my father must have been. I do not want them to get away with what they did."

"I thought your mother would like to know," Lorimer said. The young woman's passion embarrassed him, it was too naked, too revealing, and he half wished he hadn't rung. After all, there was nothing any of them could do about Klaasje Wijnen or the two men now. Perhaps in time Fate would catch up with them, but for the present they were safe.

"Yes, thank you, Mr. Lorimer. She will be very grateful." Isabella's tone had changed again and become businesslike.

"Do you know anybody who owns a grey Mercedes saloon?" Lorimer asked her.

"I do not think so. But there are many, many Mercedes in the Netherlands. Why?"

"I've seen one twice this afternoon."

"You know, I do not live in Amsterdam," Isabella said. "I do not know what cars people have. Are you staying here long?"

"No. I'll have dinner early, then try to see Mul. There are some questions I want to ask him and van Else, and I have a feeling he's more likely to talk. I'll probably go home tomorrow."

"Then I hope you will have a safe journey. Good-bye, Mr. Lorimer." Isabella replaced the phone.

THIRTEEN

ALBERT MUL WAS DIVORCED. He lived, usually alone, in an expensive flat in the suburbs. He also owned a house near the German border, but that was occupied by his ex-wife, their children, a daughter of thirteen and a son of nine, and her four dogs. Mul never visited the house, and he hadn't seen either of his children for more than two years.

Lorimer took the subway from Waterlooplein and walked the rest of the way. The block of flats was halfway along a quiet road. There was no one in the lobby, and he went up in the lift to the third floor. Mul's flat was at the front. He crossed the landing and rang the bell. There was no answer, and he rang again. Still there was no response. It was only then that he noticed that, although the door appeared to be closed, there was a tiny gap between it and the frame. Pushing the door wider, he stepped inside.

The hall was close-carpeted in mauve, with lilac and cream paintwork. The five spiky modern watercolours on the walls were all the same size and had identical metal frames, as if they had been bought in a package with the rest of the decor. Under one of them there was a semi-circular wrought iron table with a glass top. Lorimer wondered if the decor was Mul's choice or some previous occupant's; at least Mul appeared to be able to live with it.

Of the other three doors, two were closed and the farthest one, that to the sitting room, was open a few inches. Lorimer pushed it hard. Nothing happened. No one behind the door grunted, there was no shouted demand to know what the hell he was doing. On the contrary, it was unnaturally quiet. Deathly quiet.

Mul was lying face down on the pale green carpet, his arms outstretched as if he were reaching for something just beyond his grasp. Salvation, perhaps. He was wearing an immaculate grey suit, and, almost in the middle of his back, looking absurdly out of place, there was a tear. It was an inch long and very narrow, a slit rather than a hole, and a little blood had oozed out from it, forming a crust round the edges.

Lorimer squatted on one knee beside him. Mul was dead. He hadn't died very long ago—his body was still warm.

Lorimer looked round. The room was tidy, there were no signs of a struggle, nor of anyone searching it, and he stood up again. He could do no more here. It would have been better if he hadn't come; Mul would tell him nothing now. He would never tell anyone anything again, except, perhaps, the pathologist and, through him, the police.

Unless he had been expecting a visitor this evening, it was unlikely that his body would be found before the morning. All the same, Lorimer told himself, the sooner he got away from here the better. He went out, releasing the catch on the lock and closing the door behind him. The landing was still deserted, and he started down the wide, elegantly curving staircase, his shoes making almost no sound on the marble. At the first floor landing he met a man in a brown suit coming up. The man took no notice of him, and Lorimer continued down to the lobby and out into the road. Apart from a red car in the distance and a man carrying a briefcase a hundred yards away, there was no one in sight.

He walked to the subway station and caught a train back into the city.

The phone rang and Lorimer reached over to pick it up.

"There is a call for you, sir," the operator told him.

Lorimer wondered who could be ringing him: apart from Grantley and Helen Wilkins in London, only Isabella Feldhuis and Leiter knew he was here at the American.

It was Isabella. "You are still there?" she asked.

Lorimer wondered why she sounded surprised, he had told her he wouldn't be leaving until tomorrow at the earliest. "I'm catching a flight in the morning," he said.

"Don't wait until then," she said urgently. "You must go now."

"Why? What's happened?" Isabella couldn't have heard yet that Mul was dead. Nevertheless Lorimer felt suddenly tense.

"You don't know?"

"I don't know anything."

"But I thought . . ." She stopped. "Klaasje Wijnen was found dead in her apartment two hours ago. She had been shot."

Lorimer was shaken. Two of the three people involved in Feldhuis's death had been murdered within the few hours since his arrival in Amsterdam. Who had killed them? Was it van Else, to prevent them talking to the police?

With a shock Lorimer realised that Isabella suspected him. "How do you know?" he demanded.

"The police came here. They are looking for you."

They had been bound to question Feldhuis's widow and his daughter. All the same, they hadn't wasted any time. But why were they looking for him? Isabella or her mother must have told them he had said he might go to see Klaasje Wijnen. He hadn't tried to conceal his visit, he had just walked up to the door and rung the bell; anybody coming from or going to one of the other flats could have seen him. True, he hadn't noticed anyone, but he hadn't been taking that much notice. Nor had he seen anyone on his way out.

"You did not kill her?" Isabella asked.

Lorimer sensed her uncertainty. "No," he said. "She was alive when I left her. Why are the police interested in me?"

Isabella hesitated. "I am sorry, I had to tell them that you had been here and I had given you her address."

Lorimer felt the anger rising inside him. He had tried to provide some consolation for Isabella and her mother by ringing to tell them that the dead woman had admitted her story of having an affair with Feldhuis was untrue, and she had responded by deliberately throwing suspicion for her death on to him.

"Thanks very much," he said bitterly. But he couldn't blame her; she knew nothing about him and any other law-abiding citizen would have done the same.

"I am sorry," Isabella said again unhappily. "I did not know what to do."

"It doesn't matter," Lorimer told her. "Thanks for warning me."

"You will go now?"

"Why? I had no reason to kill her."

"Please, you must," Isabella said. She sounded almost desperate. "I feel very bad that I had to say you asked me for her address."

Lorimer thought. He knew nothing about Netherlands law, but he was pretty sure that the police might insist that he surrender his passport and stay here while they pursued their inquiries. It could take days to satisfy them that he had had nothing to do with Klaasje Wijnen's death. As far as he knew, there had been no witnesses and, except for the murderer, he was probably the last person to see her alive. Moreover, if anyone had seen him come to the flat, they might well have seen him push his way in. They had probably heard him tell her that his name was Kemp too. Kemp was a British name, and it wouldn't take the police long to link it with the Lorimer Isabella Feldhuis had told them about. His concealing his identity would only make things look worse.

There was another thing, something Isabella knew nothing about: by tomorrow morning at the latest Mul's body would be found. He wondered if she had told the police that he had talked about going to see Mul as well as Klaasje Wijnen.

When he left Mul's flat he had met a man on the stairs. The man might remember him. So might the clerks at the subway stations and, very likely, one or two of the passengers on the trains he had caught out to the suburb and back.

"Okay, I'll go," he said. After all, he had intended leaving in a few hours anyway.

"Good." Even over the phone Isabella's relief was clear. "Good-bye, Mr. Lorimer."

"Good-bye," Lorimer said.

By this time the police probably knew he had arrived via Schipol and held a return ticket to Heathrow, he thought, replacing the phone. If he went that way, he would walk right into them. Picking up the phone again, he rang Reception.

A train left Amsterdam Central station at 8:31 to connect with the boat sailing from Hook of Holland at 10:45 for Harwich, they told him. If he caught that, he would arrive in London at nine o'clock tomorrow morning.

Lorimer looked at his watch: it was already seven minutes to eight. Collecting his things, he pushed them into his bag, looked round to make sure he hadn't left anything behind and took the lift down to the lobby.

He had to wait to pay his bill behind an elderly English couple enquiring about restaurants, and he struggled to control his impatience. He had barely enough time to get to the station, buy his tickets and catch the train, and the police might be here at any minute.

Eventually the couple departed and he asked for his bill.

"I've had a call from Head Office," he explained. "They want me to go back to London right away. I'll have to try to get a plane from Schipol."

"Oh yes, sir?" The cashier wasn't interested. All the same, Lorimer hoped he would remember what he had said about Schipol if or when the police questioned him.

Outside in the street it had started to rain, heavy drops you could hear fall on the warm pavement and which dried almost before they landed. It was half dark, the atmosphere still warm and oppressive. Lorimer walked along to the tram stop outside the theatre. It would have been quicker to take a taxi, but that meant going to the rank, and cab drivers' memories were long: an Englishman might be remembered when the police got round to questioning them.

A tram was coming, swaying and rattling round the bend at the bottom of Leidseplein, and Lorimer climbed aboard. He wasn't safe yet. The police were bound to check at the hotel, and if they learnt that he had just left after enquiring about trains to the Hook, they might follow the tram and stop it before it was halfway to the station, or wait for him there, but he felt better for being on the move.

The tram clanged up Leidsestraat. Despite the rain, people were strolling along the street and stopping to gaze in the shop windows. Anonymous crowds, Lorimer thought. They would provide shelter, but with his case he would be conspicuous even amongst them. Anyway, he had no time for that sort of evasive action; it would take him several minutes at least to walk to another stop and catch a different tram. Better stay where he was. They jolted to a stop at Prinsengracht and two young girls got off, chattering gaily. The bell rang and the tram lurched forward again.

Along the gloomy reaches of Nieuwezuds Voorburgwal passengers came and went. Again Lorimer controlled his impatience and tried not to look at his watch; too obvious anxiety might attract attention and be remembered later. And it wasn't much farther now, just round the big bend at the top of the street.

A police car was parked outside the station. Lorimer got off the tram with the other passengers, telling himself it meant nothing. The crew were probably on a routine patrol, looking out for the drunk and disorderly. Nevertheless he looked round for people he could keep between it and himself. A family of four, middle-aged parents and two girls in their early teens, were just behind him. The father was taller than he was and the mother only an inch or so shorter, and when he slowed to let them catch him up they effectively screened him.

Together the little group started across the open space towards the station's main entrance. Just keep going, Lorimer thought. Then the passenger's door of the police car opened and a man in uniform got out. He remained standing beside it, watching the people making their way in and out of the station, a tall, lean young fellow, alert and intelligent looking.

They were almost level with him now. At that moment the younger of the two girls said something in Dutch and the family stopped. Lorimer could hardly stop with them, and he walked on, feeling horribly exposed. The policeman was turning in his direction. For a second their eyes met and Lorimer looked away, trying to make the movement seem casual while he waited for the man to shout and start running towards him. But nothing happened, and when he dared look again the policeman was gazing at a group of youths near the tourist information centre.

It was then Lorimer saw the grey Mercedes. It was parked some distance from the police car, as if the driver were waiting to pick up somebody coming off a train. Lorimer could see him, a heavily built man with close-cropped hair so fair it was almost white. The same man had been in the car he had seen near Feldhuis's house this afternoon. And when he left the block of flats where Klaasje Wijnen lived a grey Mercedes had been parked across the street. Isabella Feldhuis had said there were many, many Mercedes in the Netherlands and Lorimer knew that was true. It was ridiculous to think the ones he had seen were the same. He must be imagining it.

But he knew he wasn't, there was no mistaking that square head with the close-cut, almost white hair. Were the two men associates of Mul and van Else or policemen? Either way, if they were looking for him, he was in trouble.

The family were several yards behind him now, arguing among themselves and showing no signs of coming on, but just ahead a larger group was making for the station entrance, bustling in the way parties do when they are late for a train or an appointment, managing heavy cases awkwardly, the women struggling a little to keep up with the men. They didn't look Dutch, he thought, they were too dark-haired and swarthy. By dint of a little discreet jostling, he insinuated himself into their midst. One of the men gave him an angry look and said something he didn't understand, but they had no time for an argument and he was swept along with them.

There was no sign of a policeman inside the station, but thirty or forty yards from the main entrance, watching it, was a slightly built, dark man wearing a brown anorak. The second occupant of the Mercedes. He didn't look like a policeman, Lorimer thought. He was more like a hit man in some old gangster film. The idea didn't do much to improve his morale.

The man didn't glance at the group as it passed within a few yards of him, and Lorimer breathed a sigh of relief. But he knew that only when he had bought his tickets and was on the train could he begin to relax. Even then he would still have to pass through the passport and customs checks at the Hook of Holland and Harwich. Whatever was happening here in Amsterdam, by the time he reached the Hook the police would have been alerted and be looking out for him.

Buying his ticket seemed to take hours. Lorimer knew that at any moment the dark man might come here searching for him. But the minutes passed and he didn't appear. Perhaps he was waiting just outside the door. Emerging from the ticket office, Lorimer risked a quick glance along the platform. The man was still standing where he had first seen him, watching the entrance. The train for the Hook was standing at the platform. Lorimer waited until the man's back was turned, then, taking advantage of the cover provided by other passengers, he walked over and boarded it. It wasn't very full, and he was able to pick a window seat across the aisle from the platform, sheltering behind the Dutch paper he had bought.

After what seemed an age the train started moving. Lorimer lowered his paper and looked out at the station sliding past. The last thing he saw as the train gathered speed was the dark man gazing straight at him.

It was not specifically a boat train, and it stopped several times. Each time it did so a few people got off and others boarded it. Lorimer tried to concentrate on the paperback novel he had brought with him from home and not think about what would happen when they reached the Hook and he had to leave the security of the train. He had only made things worse by quitting Amsterdam so hurriedly, and travelling this way when he had a plane ticket in his wallet. No innocent man would have done that.

At last, seven minutes late, the train pulled in to the Hook's harbour station. Bracing himself, Lorimer picked up his bag and followed the other passengers into the terminal building. The hall was already crowded with tourists from the line of coaches parked outside, and, watching over the scene with an air of professional indifference, were two policemen.

Lorimer could see no way of avoiding them. Even to try would only make matters worse. He joined a line moving slowly towards the passport check and kept his head down. When they checked his passport it would be all up, they would know he was the man they wanted, and by tomorrow morning he would be back in Amsterdam, locked in a cell.

There were only three people ahead of him now. The first of them, cleared, walked away. Then the second. Only a middle-aged woman, smartly dressed, obviously middle class and respectable, stood between him and discovery. The official took the passport she handed him and glanced at her, then at Lorimer.

"A moment, please," he said to the woman in English.

She frowned. "Why?" she demanded imperiously. "What on earth's the matter?"

"Just a moment," the official repeated, looking at Lorimer. He waved to the two policemen.

One of them detached himself from his colleague and strode over, suddenly all brisk efficiency. The official said something to him in Dutch, and he turned to Lorimer.

"You are together?" he asked flatly and authoritatively.

"No," Lorimer said. He felt as if, by denying it, he was severing the last link between himself and safety.

"No," the woman confirmed. The glance she gave Lorimer suggested that she wouldn't have been seen dead travelling with him.

"Your passport, please."

The policeman held out his hand. With a strong feeling of the inevitability of disaster, Lorimer handed him the blue-covered document. He opened it, glanced at the photograph, then the following pages, and passed it to the official beside him.

"I must ask you to come with me," he said in a tone which made clear the futility of refusing.

This was it, Lorimer thought. He was mildly surprised that he didn't feel more than slightly depressed, and supposed it was because he had had plenty of time to get used to the idea.

"Why?" the woman demanded angrily. Lorimer realised with a shock that the policeman was talking to her. "I'm a British subject, I demand to see—"

"Yes," the policeman agreed. He sounded bored, like a man who had heard it all a hundred times before.

Feeling slightly stunned, Lorimer watched as the woman was led away blustering. The official glanced briefly at his passport, muttered his thanks and turned to the man next in the queue. Still bemused, Lorimer walked up the stairs and across the gangway on to the ship.

He never knew what woke him, whether it was a highly developed sixth sense, or the man's stifled curse as he stumbled against something in the near darkness. Perhaps it was neither, but some noise of which he, waking, was unaware, and which had nothing to do with either of them. Whatever it was, that and the man's hesitation in making sure he had found the right target probably saved his life.

It never took Lorimer more than a second or two to become fully awake, and now he saw somebody stooping over him. He assumed it was a man, but all he could see was a silhouette, distorted by its stooping and the jacket or anorak it was wearing. Then the dim light was reflected from something in the figure's hand, and he decided he had better move. Fast.

A man in a reclining seat is at a disadvantage, almost flat on his back and penned in by the arms. Lorimer was thankful that it was a warm night and he wasn't additionally hampered by a blanket. Drawing his legs up swiftly, he catapulted himself forward.

His seat was on one of the gangways and the move was so violent and unexpected that his would-be assailant was taken by surprise. Caught a violent glancing blow, the man staggered back, stumbled against a seat on the other side of the aisle and nearly fell. But he recovered himself quickly, and by the time Lorimer had gained his feet and turned he was running towards the door at the end of the saloon. A thin man wearing a brown anorak. Another second and he was through the door, and it was swinging to behind him.

Lorimer set off in pursuit. By this time many of the other passengers were awake. One or two complained angrily, or demanded to know what was going on. Lorimer ignored them. Since sunset a strong wind had sprung up. The ship was pitching and rolling and he was almost thrown off his feet as he lurched along the aisle between the rows of seats.

Beyond the door a corridor stretched away towards the other end of the ship. Already Lorimer's quarry was halfway along it. Then the man stopped, tugging at one of the heavy doors which led to the outside deck. The next moment he had disappeared. By the time Lorimer reached the door he was running hard towards the stern.

The night might be warm, but it was dark and the few lights along the deck were barely sufficient for Lorimer to make out the lifeboats suspended from their davits. He caught a glimpse of the fleeing figure, lurching from side to side with the movement of the ship; then, suddenly, it was no longer there.

The sea, lashed by the wind, was a heaving black expanse, the waves edged with angry white foam. Far below Lorimer could see the bow wave, a ghostly race in the darkness.

The man in the anorak had been heading for the darkest part of the deck, amidships and between two of the boats. Somewhere there he had disappeared. Lorimer slowed almost to a halt. When he reached the first of the patches of dark shadow, where the light of the lamp outside the nearest door didn't reach, he stopped, ears strained. The ship's superstructure creaked eerily as the wind buffeted her, and behind all the other sounds he could hear the desultory slap of the sea against the hull and the hiss of the wash.

A slight movement between the boats on his left brought him round, nerves tense. As he turned the man pounced. Just in time Lorimer saw his right hand held high, still clutching the knife, and pivoted to his right, turning his shoulder to meet the attack. He wasn't a more than useful soccer player for nothing, and all his weight was behind the thrust. His assailant, leaping from the top of a deck fitting, couldn't stop himself. Lorimer's shoulder crashed into his midriff, and for a second he seemed to hang in the air. Then, with an agonised gasp he fell to the deck.

Lorimer was off balance and the man was tough. It took him only a moment to recover, and he had kept his grip on his knife. For Lorimer, after that time lost all meaning. They struggled in silence, crashing into fittings and the rail and bouncing off the side of the superstructure as the ship pitched and rolled. Lorimer was the bigger, but the other man was strong and wiry. Moreover he knew more about alley fighting than Lorimer would ever know, and he had his knife. The sweat rolled down Lorimer's face as they rolled backwards and forwards, each of them seeking desperately for a grip the other couldn't break. First he was on top, then his assailant.

The end came so suddenly that afterwards he couldn't recall exactly how it had happened. He only knew that they were by the rail and the other man had scrambled up on to something and was threatening him with the knife. The deck was wet and slippery there by the boats, as well as heaving awkwardly. Lorimer succeeded in grasping his assailant's right wrist and pushed it back, at the same time twisting it, trying to force him to drop the knife. The man grunted with pain. The next moment the ship rolled, his feet slid away from him, and he went backwards over the side, his scream as he fell lost in the howl of the wind.

It seemed to Lorimer that the search lasted for hours. He was aware of the ship turning in a wide arc and a boat being lowered, and he prayed that they would find the dark man still alive, but he didn't delude himself that there was more than a faint glimmer of hope.

Once the officers had gleaned all the information he could give them and left him sitting alone in the main saloon, he had plenty of time for thought. Only two of the lights had been switched on and they cast long, obscure shadows, like the patterns in an avant-garde film of the thirties.

He was shaken. He had never killed a man before, even by accident, and the fact that he hadn't intended to now, that he had acted in self-defence and that the man was responsible for what had happened, made little difference. Through his actions a man had died.

For a second before he jumped him, the light had shone on his assailant's face, and in that brief moment Lorimer had recognised him. It was the second man from the Mercedes. After he saw him on the train in Amsterdam he and his blond colleague must have raced it to the Hook. It wouldn't have been difficult, the train hadn't hurried.

All the same, the lengths they had gone to showed how anxious they were to see him dead. It was a form of flattery Lorimer could have done without.

Somebody in Britain must have tipped them off that he was coming to Holland and they had followed him ever since he arrived. But why try to dispose of him there when they had had plenty of opportunities in London? There were two answers to that: one, the people in Britain hadn't been inclined to foul their own doorstep, or, two, it was what he had done while he was in Amsterdam, his calls on the Feldhuis women and Klaasje Wijnen, which had persuaded them that he knew too much.

The men in the Mercedes—Lorimer had no doubt now that they were working for van Else—had almost certainly killed Klaasje Wijnen to prevent her talking to the police. According to Isabella Feldhuis she had been shot like Rona Smith and McIndoe. But Albert Mul hadn't been shot, he had been stabbed. He was the exception—and Lorimer thought he knew why.

The two men hadn't killed Mul, Isabella had. She had adored her father and was tortured by guilt because she had stayed away from him for the last months of his life. When Lorimer told her what he had learnt from Klaasje Wijnen—that Mul and van Else had murdered him, and that it was unlikely the police would do anything about it—she had taken the law into her own hands. There was a lot of passionate Latin blood in Isabella's veins.

When she rang him at the American she had lied; she hadn't told the police about his going to see van Else's girlfriend, they hadn't even been to question her. Tomorrow—today—they probably would, and then she would tell them, offering him as a sacrificial lamb to deflect suspicion from herself. But first she had given him a chance to get away. So much her conscience had demanded.

Or perhaps she was counting on his fleeing strengthening the case against him; she had been very anxious that he should leave straightaway.

Lorimer knew he had been set up. And although in the end everything would have worked out, his position would have been decidedly awkward until it was. Jenkins wouldn't have helped him; he had gone to Holland off his own bat and the Welshman wouldn't acknowledge a man, not even one of his own, who was acting unofficially in a foreign country, however friendly that country might be. And he wasn't one of Jenkins' own.

One question remained, more urgent than any other: where was the fair-haired Dutchman now?

FOURTEEN

LORIMER was later than usual arriving at United House the next morning, and Grantley had already departed for a meeting in Oxford. So much had happened in the last twenty-four hours that Lorimer was slightly surprised to find only one day's papers waiting for him on his desk; it seemed much longer than that since he was here. He sat down and started scanning the top one.

Soon after ten Jenkins rang. "Meet me in Green Park at twelve-thirty," he said tersely. "The lamp post near the tube station."

Lorimer wondered what was up. It didn't occur to him not to go; for one thing, he wanted information that only Jenkins could give him, for a second, he was curious. It had to be something pretty serious for Owen to ring him here, and his manner had been unusually brusque.

It was another very warm day, and a lot of people were in the park making the most of the sunshine during their lunch hours, strolling on the grass or lounging in the chairs. This time Lorimer was determined to be the first to arrive, and he was five minutes early.

When he joined him Jenkins wasted no time on pleasantries. "What the hell did you think you were doing?" he demanded, starting off along the path leaving Lorimer to follow him. "Shooting off without a word, getting yourself involved in God knows what mess. You damned nearly ruined everything."

Lorimer supposed he meant Amsterdam and wondered how he had heard. But Jenkins had his own sources of information. "Are you talking about Holland?" he asked.

"You haven't been anywhere else, have you? If you have—"

"No," Lorimer said. The Welshman's tone was beginning to irritate him. "I went for the firm. Do I have to get your permission before I go anywhere now?"

"Not as long as you don't interfere in affairs which are no concern of yours." Jenkins' eyes resembled small lumps of Welsh anthracite, dark, bright and very hard. "If you threaten the success of anything we're doing," he said distinctly, "I'll have you put where you won't do any damage for a very long time."

Lorimer was shaken. It was the first time Owen had revealed so clearly the iron fist inside the glove he usually wore, and the implications were chilling. "How?" he demanded.

"You think I couldn't?"

"No."

"Good. Because I could, and if I had to I would. I'd do the same to my wife, if I thought it was necessary." Jenkins looked away across the park. "You'd better be glad that's how it is," he said. "The alternative's a lot worse."

Lorimer said nothing. There didn't seem much he could say.

"God knows what you thought you'd achieve in Amsterdam," Jenkins continued after a moment, "but as a result of your going we're no farther forward, the people in the Dutch party have been put on their guard and three people are dead."

"You don't have to remind me of that," Lorimer said bitterly. He no longer felt any guilt over the dark man's death—he had been fighting for his life and what happened had been an accident he couldn't have prevented—but would Isabella have killed Albert Mul if he hadn't told her of his belief that Mul and van Else had murdered her father? He didn't know, and there was nothing to be gained by self-recriminations now, too much remained to be done. "We know for sure that Feldhuis was killed by his own people," he said. "That's another piece in the pattern."

Jenkins eyed him with something very near dislike. "To you it's nothing but a bloody jigsaw puzzle," he said bitterly.

"To me it's bloody real," Lorimer retorted, his anger rising. "It wasn't a toy knife that joker had. He was trying to kill me—and it was a fluke he didn't. Who was he? Do you know?"

"His name was Klaus Leukens. He had a record."

"And the fair one?"

"Rutger Wolf."

"Appropriate." Jenkins said nothing. "I think it was Wolf who went to the house in Ravelston asking for McIndoe, and who Sue Johnstone saw in the car Rona Smith was getting into the Saturday morning before she was killed. While I was in Edinburgh I talked to a man called Hugh Bascomb, he's a lecturer at Heriot-Watt, and he told me he'd seen McIndoe with a stocky, very fair man twice. He said the man had an aura of evil—and Hugh isn't what you'd call fanciful."

"Did he?" Jenkins sounded less contemptuous than Lorimer had expected.

"Do you know anything about Mul and van Else?" he asked.

"Mul was the head of a chemicals company. It's grown fast recently, and taken over several other firms. Now it's one of the biggest in its line in Holland. Van Else has a big wholesale meat business in Amsterdam."

"Meat?"

"He imports a lot—including a surprising amount of offal from South America. The Dutch are looking into that side of things."

It would take weeks, probably months, for them to obtain sufficient evidence of fraud to charge van Else, Lorimer thought. They didn't have that long.

"Until five years ago nobody had heard of either of them," Jenkins went on. "Now van Else is a prominent man. He's popular, has a lot of influential friends and gives a lot to charities. He makes no secret of the fact that he's one of the Nature Party's principal backers, and he's a close associate of Cornelis van Rijn."

"Who's certain to be the party's new leader," Lorimer said. Jenkins nodded. "Can you arrange for Sue Johnstone and Hugh to see a picture of Wolf?"

"All right."

Thirty yards away a small boy of about six was playing with a plastic ball. It was too big for him to hold easily, and he threw it in the uncontrolled way small children do. It rolled across the path in front of the two men.

Lorimer waited until the boy had retrieved it, smiling shyly up at them, and scuttled back to his mother before he said, "If there was a concerted effort all over the EEC to clamp down on the frauds, it would cut off their funds and save the Community ten percent of its budget."

"If," Jenkins repeated. "The trouble is, the rackets are too big and too widespread. Some countries, Germany and Italy and us, make a show of doing something, but it's nothing like enough."

"Anyway it would take too long," Lorimer agreed. "The Nature parties are a popular movement, they're respectable. If they needed money, the big international companies would support them as a matter of good public relations." The only way they would get anywhere was by exposing what was really happening and who was behind it, he thought. And the only way they could do that was by infiltrating the party. Not at grass roots level; it had to be amongst the higher echelons, the people who knew what was going on.

Was that what Clive was doing and how he had come to be at Horwill's meeting? No wonder he hadn't wanted him to show that he had recognised him.

"How does the cartel work?" he asked. "There must be some sort of co-ordinating body."

"There's a council with representatives from each country. It meets every month or so."

"Where?"

"They take it in turns. Last time it was in France, a chateau near Tours."

"And next month?"

"Iniscaig Lodge."

Lorimer stared at him. "That's Forsyth's place."

"Yes." Jenkins looked away across the park.

Lorimer felt as if somebody had struck him a physical blow. "You told me he was okay," he said bitterly. "I relied on that." He might be angry and resentful, he thought, but he shouldn't be so surprised. He had always suspected that Forsyth had invited him to dinner that evening in order to pump him and discover how much he knew about Dorn nan Gaidheal; now he understood why he had wanted to know.

Forsyth was the cartel's British link. As the power behind Horwill he controlled the Fist's activities. Which meant that, indirectly, at least, he had been responsible for the "incidents" on Iniscaig and Liavaig, as well as some of those in England. He might claim that he had opposed Horwill's appointment to the boards of Morgans and Excelsior—there was only his word for it.

Lorimer tried to remember whether he had ever said anything to Forsyth which would have revealed that he knew about the conspiracy. He was pretty sure he had.

It must have been Forsyth who tipped off the Dutch; Lorimer had told him he was going to Amsterdam when Forsyth came to his office before the board meeting on Thursday morning. A casual question to Helen Wilkins would have added the information that he was staying at the American. Forsyth had rung somebody in Holland, van Else, probably, and he had had him followed. Forsyth was responsible for his nearly being killed last night.

They walked on past the office workers, the shop assistants and the tourists sunning themselves on the grass. A fat middle-aged man in a white sweat shirt with "Good ol' Daddy-o!" in scarlet letters across the chest was taking a photograph of an even fatter woman and a skinny girl. The girl looked sulky. Lorimer hardly noticed the sound of the traffic in Piccadilly a short distance away. He was thinking about Hilary.

"When is the meeting?" he asked.

"The weekend after next," Jenkins replied.

They stopped and looked at each other.

Och hell! Lorimer thought. "Have you time for a pint?" he asked.

"Sorry." Jenkins glanced at his watch. "I have to meet a man in the Burlington Arcade at one."

Lorimer didn't say "Another time then." There was no point, he might not see Owen again for months. Perhaps never.

They parted without shaking hands, and Jenkins walked off towards the Ritz. Lorimer returned to Victoria feeling unsettled and out of sorts with the world.

It was only later he remembered that he hadn't asked Jenkins how he knew about the meeting on Iniscaig. Not that it made any difference, Owen probably wouldn't have told him if he had; the information must have come from Clive.

If van Else and his friends had wanted to kill him on the ship, Lorimer reckoned, there was no reason to think they would be any more kindly disposed towards him now that he was back in London. Less, probably. If they didn't know already what had happened last night, they soon would, and if Wolf was in London, he would have no difficulty finding him. All it would take would be a word from Forsyth.

Lorimer didn't relish the notion of a gun being pushed against his head, or a knife thrust into his back, but there was nothing to be gained by worrying about dangers which might not exist, and as the days passed he thought less and less about them. He had no reason to believe that Wolf was here. It was more likely that since the death of Klaasje Wijnen he had been lying low in Holland.

Despite his good intentions, Lorimer thought a lot about Hilary. Forsyth had forfeited any claim to her loyalty; he was a crook, a swindler on a huge scale who connived at murder. Was it possible she knew about, or at least suspected, that side of his life, and that was the real reason for her distress?

Just before eleven on Monday morning she phoned. "Can we meet somewhere?" she asked.

Lorimer hesitated. At that moment he wanted to see her again more than anything, but he knew that, whatever Forsyth was doing, there could be no future in their meeting. It would only make things worse. Quite apart from the fact that he would be risking his job.

She sensed his uncertainty. "I must see you," she said. "Please, Gray."

It was the first time she had pleaded with him, and Lorimer wondered if she had discovered what Forsyth was doing.

"When?" he asked.

"Any time. I could come to your flat this evening."

"All right. I'll be home by six-thirty."

"I'll see you there then. 'Bye, Gray."

" 'Bye," Lorimer said.

He left United House at five forty-five. At twenty-five to seven the doorbell rang, but when he answered it it was two young women who looked like students.

"We're canvassing for Peter Dillon, the Nature Party candidate in the by-election," the taller of them informed him. "Can he count on your vote?" There was a hopeful note in her voice.

It was a shame to disappoint her, Lorimer thought. All over the EEC thousands of well-meaning people like her and her companion were being manipulated and deceived by Forsyth and van Else and their kind. They believed earnestly, even passionately, in their cause. He believed in it too, with certain reservations. For once Horwill had been speaking the truth when he said anybody with intelligence must agree it was right. It was the men perverting it who were wrong, and people like these girls were going to feel pretty sick when the truth came out.

"No," he said. "I'm sorry."

"Oh? Why not?" the second girl asked. She wasn't as pretty as the other one and her tone was more aggressive.

"This planet's not worth saving," Lorimer told her. "The sooner it blows up the better."

They looked shocked.

"But if—" the first girl began.

"Sorry," Lorimer said. "I have to go. Good-bye just now."

As he closed the door he heard the shorter girl mutter audibly, "Bloody uncouth Scotsman." You should get together with Rayment, he thought.

The next time the bell rang it was Hilary. As soon as the door was closed she lifted her head to his and kissed him.

"You don't know how I've been longing to do that," she said when she moved away. She saw his expression. "What is it, Gray? What's the matter?"

Lorimer told himself he couldn't explain. He was painfully conscious of the conflict inside him. It had taken all his self-control not to respond when she kissed him, now half of him wanted her to know about Forsyth while the other half dreaded her finding out. "Nothing," he lied.

Hilary studied his face for a moment, then, with a sigh he barely heard, she turned away and looked round the room. "It's nice," she said in a neutral voice.

"It's okay. I don't need much space now; half the time I'm away."

"This is where you lived with your wife?"

"Yes." Lorimer didn't want to talk about Rosalind. "You said you must see me," he said. "Has something happened?"

Hilary shook her head. "No."

Lorimer went to the cupboard, brought out his only bottle of Glen Morangie and poured two generous measures. He did it as much to avoid sitting there listening to Hilary as because he needed the whisky. Listening was no good, it only made him feel more futile.

I'm a normal man, he thought. All I want is to take you through that door there into bed and make love to you. To look after you, to share everything with you, the good and the bad. That would be the best way of solving your difficulty and mine. But it's not on, you know it and I know it. So take your problem, whatever it is, to somebody who can help you, and leave me in peace.

Perhaps later, when justice or the law or whatever you called it had caught up with Forsyth, things would change. But he knew he was deluding himself, the gulf between their ways of life was too wide, and he didn't want to cross it, even if he could.

Hilary was avoiding his eye. "There's something I have to tell you," she said.

"It won't make any difference."

She looked up then. "How do you know?"

"It can't."

For a moment she gazed at him, her lovely features expressionless, then she said, "Okay, I get the message. Jesus, what a mess I've made of things!"

"What was it you were going to tell me?" Lorimer asked. This evening was the second time she had told him there was something, then drawn back.

"Nothing." With a sudden flash of emotion she exclaimed bitterly, "Christ! What is it about you British men?"

"It's not British men," Lorimer told her. "I want to make love to you more than I've wanted anything for a long time. But you just want to use me to hit back at Robin, and I don't like being used. Especially like that."

"No," Hilary said desperately. "You're wrong, Gray." Their eyes met and she sighed, more audibly this time. "It's no good, is it? I guess I'd better go."

Lorimer didn't try to dissuade her. When she reached the door he asked, "Is Robin going to be at home the weekend after next?"

Hilary looked surprised. "No," she answered. "We're both going up to Iniscaig, he has some business people coming for the weekend. Why?"

"Nothing," Lorimer told her. "I just wondered."

She hesitated a moment longer. "What I told you about him wasn't true. He hasn't a girl in Edinburgh."

She went out and the door closed behind her.

The next day the papers reported that the latest public opinion poll put the Nature Party six points ahead of the Conservatives in the election campaign, with the other parties trailing a long way behind.

Lorimer had just finished his coffee when Jenkins rang to say that Sue Johnstone and Bascomb had identified Wolf as the man they had seen at the house in Ravelston and on two occasions with McIndoe.

With a feeling that the pieces were coming together, Lorimer went to do some research. By the end of the day he knew that Forsyth had been born in 1953, the only son of a wealthy Scottish businessman. He had been educated at Winchester, Trinity College, Cambridge, and the Harvard Business School. In May, 1983, he had married Hilary Anne Templeton, the elder daughter of Colonel and Mrs. Templeton of Halesworth, Connecticut. There were no children.

On Thursday morning he was in his room at United House when the door opened and Forsyth strolled in looking as calm and in control of his world as ever. Lorimer, glancing up, thought how much he hated him. He could see now an arrogance he hadn't noticed before. Forsyth's easy, friendly facade concealed not only a personality so ruthless that it would allow nothing to stand in the way of his obtaining what he wanted, but an ego so monstrous that it saw no wrong in that. Seeing him in the light of his new knowledge, everything about the man struck him as false. Even the boyish-seeming gesture pushing back the rebellious lock of hair.

His dislike welled up in him, sour as gall, and he wished that the other man hadn't come. He knew too much about him, his presence was an embarrassment as well as being unwanted.

"Hallo," Forsyth said cheerfully. "Are you busy?"

"Not particularly." Lorimer told himself that he couldn't afford to relax for a second, he had to pay attention to every word Forsyth said. His life might depend on it.

"How was Amsterdam?"

"Okay."

Forsyth walked over to the window and looked down at the small area fifteen storeys below enclosed by the towering buildings. Two men were standing in the middle of the area talking. From this vantage point they looked too small to be human beings.

"Did you see the people you wanted to?" he asked.

"Some of them."

One of the men nodded and they parted and walked off in opposite directions, leaving the area deserted. A piece of litter, a crumpled sheet of paper or a battered carton, it was too far away to tell which, blew across the flagstones and came to rest against a wall. Forsyth turned and Lorimer saw that he was smiling. As if he knew why Lorimer wasn't giving him straight answers. They were like two card players, neither of them revealing anything about the hand he held.

Then the smile faded and Forsyth said, "I'm having a few people to stay at Iniscaig the weekend after next, can you come?"

Lorimer was startled. There could be only one reason for Forsyth's inviting him to the Lodge: it didn't involve his buying a return ticket. "Me?" he said. "Why me?"

The tension in the little room seemed to increase. Forsyth was looking at Lorimer, but he appeared not to see him. As if he were looking past him at something Lorimer couldn't see.

"They're prominent businessmen, most of them are fairly young and they come from all over the EEC. It would be good experience for you to meet them." His eyes focussed on Lorimer again. "I'll be honest, there's another thing. I want somebody else from this country there; you're the right generation, you've travelled a bit and you speak French."

Lorimer could imagine what sort of experience the other man had in mind.

"Will you come?" Forsyth asked.

Lorimer made up his mind. "Thank you," he said. "I'd like to." It seemed odd to thank a man for an invitation to walk into almost certain danger, possibly death, but he couldn't turn it down. He didn't really want to.

"Hilary will be there to see we're well looked after," Forsyth said. "Apart from her, it'll be a stag affair. It won't be purely social, the idea is to exchange thoughts and ideas and there'll be two or three meetings, but they're private and I'm afraid you won't be able to sit in on them. We'll get together for drinks before dinner on Friday week. Hilary will go up the day before, and I'm flying up in Morgans' chopper on Friday afternoon. Why don't you come with me?"

Lorimer could think of several reasons why he shouldn't, like not wanting to be thrown out of the chopper when it was a thousand feet over the sea, but offhand he couldn't think of a convincing excuse for declining the offer. Anyway, it was hardly likely that Forsyth would try to get rid of him while they were in the air; it might look dramatic in films and on television, but it wasn't very practicable, and there were too many risks involved. Far more likely that he would wait until they were at Iniscaig.

"Thanks very much," he said.

"Good." Forsyth made no attempt to conceal his satisfaction. "I'll be in touch about times and so on."

The door closed behind him.

Until the end of April, Lorimer reflected, he hadn't been back to Iniscaig for thirteen years; now he was going to make his third trip in a few weeks. He wondered if this time would be the last.

Polling day in the by-election was the following Thursday. On Tuesday the Nature Party's headquarters released what it claimed was a leaked Department of the Environment paper proposing that a new toxic waste disposal plant be sited in Surrey. Surrey's being on London's doorstep and pretty solidly Conservative, the leak was calculated to do the maximum damage to the Tory candidate's chances.

The violence of the government's reaction served only to convince people that the paper was genuine, and few believed the minister's assertion that the paper was merely a study document, and that it was extremely unlikely that any plant would be allowed in Surrey. The prime minister was reported to be "furious" and determined to discover the source of the leak. But the damage had been done; the next day Peter Dillon was elected to the European Parliament by a majority of three thousand, seven hundred votes.

FIFTEEN

IN THE COUNTRY, that Friday dawned hazy and still and the Met people forecast another hot day. In London, where there was no haze save the exhaust fumes of the traffic, people went to work cheered by the prospect of a fine weekend.

Forsyth had rung on Wednesday to say that the helicopter would be taking off from an airfield near St. Albans at two and he would pick up Lorimer at United House at one-fifteen.

Hilary hadn't called. Lorimer supposed that she knew he was going to Iniscaig, but didn't want to talk to him after what he had said the last time they met. In one way that was a relief. At the same time, perversely, his not hearing from her seemed like a rejection. He didn't want her any less because she was unattainable. He might tell himself that longing for the unattainable was pointless, even contemptible, that Forsyth was a criminal and, in spirit at least, a murderer, he had no claim to consideration; it made no difference.

Rosalind hadn't phoned since her furious departure from his flat the evening after his meeting with Horwill. Perhaps she never would again. He had made a mess of things all round, he thought, and now he was paying for it.

While he drank his coffee he looked out of his window at the small square that was all he could see of the sky. It was a pale blue, so pale it was almost white. Up there thousands of people were flying off to holidays in Spain or the Mediterranean, looking forward to a fortnight lying on crowded beaches while they lapped up the sun, and to hell with the consequences. How many people did you know who had got skin cancer from sunbathing?

He would be up there too before long, but he wouldn't be flying off on holiday. The apprehension he felt was short of fear—it was always hard to accept that you were facing death and the odds were stacked against you—it was like the feeling he had had as a small boy when he had to go to the dentist and knew there was a filling to be done.

At ten past twelve he cleared his desk, locked it and went to lunch. He was thankful that Forsyth hadn't suggested they eat together—flying up with him and spending the next two days in his company would be bad enough.

The round of beef sandwiches and pint of bitter he had at the pub round the corner didn't taste as good as usual. Lorimer hadn't realised before that apprehension could affect your taste buds as well as your appetite, and the knowledge depressed him a little, like a symptom of some malaise.

He was back in his office by five past one. Nine minutes later Dobbs rang to say that Mr. Forsyth's car had come for him. Grantley and Helen Wilkins had gone to lunch. Lorimer picked up his case and took the lift down to the lobby where the commissionaire was talking to a uniformed chauffeur. Outside, in defiance of the double yellow lines, a sleek black Daimler waited by the kerb.

Forsyth was in the back. His greeting was as friendly as ever, but it was soon evident that he too was preoccupied, and the journey through north London and out into the Hertfordshire countryside passed mostly in silence. Lorimer sat back and looked out at the streets of shops, dreary even in the sunshine, and the women trudging along, weighed down by shopping bags and children. The car was luxuriously comfortable, but he couldn't relax. He sensed that Forsyth too was tense, and wished he knew why. However he looked at it, it didn't seem a hopeful sign.

They passed within a mile or two of Fletcham Albion's ground, and he wondered whether he would be playing there next season. He hadn't many more years' soccer left. He was slower these days. The difference was marginal, and probably few of the spectators noticed anything, but he was aware of it, and so must be the manager and the other players. With a strangely detached feeling he reflected that if the worst came to the worst this weekend, his speed and fitness wouldn't matter anyway.

If he had known more what to expect, he might have been able to devise some sort of plan. But he was completely in the dark. All he knew was that he was going into a house full of enemies, men who saw him as a threat to their conspiracy and proposed to remove that threat.

The car turned off the main road on to a narrow lane, breasted a rise and after half a mile turned in through an unpretentious gateway. The airfield was small, used mainly by a club and a few private owners, and within five minutes of their arrival Forsyth and Lorimer were strapped in Morgans' helicopter and taking off. They were seated side-by-side behind the pilot and Lorimer wondered if, after all, Forsyth planned to get rid of him while they were in the air. He supposed it would be physically possible if the pilot were involved and Forsyth knocked him out somehow first.

They flew quite low, but height, like time, was relative, and you didn't stand a lot of chance if you fell even five hundred feet on to hard ground. Or perhaps they would land in some lonely field in the Borders and . . .

He told himself he was imagining things: Forsyth wouldn't take a chance like that. Even if the pilot were implicated, too many people knew they were flying up together. Grantley and Jenkins for two. Anyway, it would be far simpler to kill him and dispose of his body on Iniscaig.

The time passed slowly. The helicopter was too noisy for conversation and Lorimer tried, without a great deal of success, to identify the places they flew over. Three or four times Forsyth touched his arm and pointed downwards to indicate something on the ground below them, but for the most part each man was busy with his own thoughts.

Somewhere over the Cheviots Forsyth opened a small hamper and produced a thermos and two cups. "Tea?" he mouthed.

Lorimer thought how easy it would have been for the other man to slip something into the flask, and shook his head.

Smiling as if he could read his thoughts, Forsyth poured himself a cup, dropped a slice of lemon into it and drank. Lorimer felt slightly foolish.

They landed once at another small airfield he couldn't identify to refuel, and it was nearly seven o'clock when he looked out and recognised Oban below them. Moments later they were flying over blue water with the islands, green, brown and grey in the evening light, stretching away to the horizon. Below them now was Mull, and there in the middle distance was Iniscaig. Half a minute more and Lorimer could make out the waste plant on Liavaig and United's factory beside Loch Damph. Forsyth pointed and he saw Iniscaig Lodge, its grey stone blending harmoniously into its surroundings. From this altitude the drive up from the road showed clearly, a narrow ribbon running up the glen parallel with the little burn.

There were climbers out on Bheinn Fhada. Lorimer could see them, a dozen tiny figures dotted about the steep slopes, and he wondered if he had looked as vulnerable, as helpless as they did, spread-eagled against the rock. Presumably he had. But their vulnerability was relative too, they knew what they were doing and they were well equipped; he would be in more danger and more helpless in the apparent safety of the Lodge.

The helicopter was losing height, approaching the Lodge up the glen, the jagged peaks of the two mountains towering above it on either side. There was an open space in front of the house and a line of cars, Rollses, Jaguars and Mercedeses, was parked along one side; dipping, the pilot landed neatly thirty yards from the nearest of them.

Lorimer unbuckled his seatbelt and waited for his companion to get out. But Forsyth waved him to go first. You couldn't keep at a level of tension indefinitely and, despite himself, Lorimer had begun to relax on the flight. Now he was conscious of his nerves on edge again. With the sun behind it and the single turret at its left-hand corner, the stark

Victorian house might have been the demon's castle in a children's story. It was easy to imagine dark deeds being committed within those sombre walls. And more, no doubt, would be planned this weekend. Lorimer gazed at them as if they held some dreadful fascination.

Then Hilary came out wearing a white blouse and a kilt of Gordon tartan, and the air of gloom evaporated.

"Hallo, Gray," she said, holding out her hand. The sun shone on her pale gold hair, but despite her smile her eyes were dull, and he wondered if she hadn't been sleeping well. "I was so glad when Robin said you could come. Did you have a good flight?"

"Great," Lorimer told her.

She turned to Forsyth, said, "Hallo, darling," and kissed him.

Lorimer didn't quite succeed in crushing a pang of envy.

"Have they all arrived?" Forsyth enquired.

"Yes." Lorimer saw Hilary's quick frown before she turned back to him. "Come in, and I'll show you your room, Gray," she said.

She led him across a big hall, its walls embellished with stags' heads and dark Victorian paintings, and up a wide staircase to a gallery with several rooms leading off it, then up a second, narrower staircase to a landing. Halfway along she opened a door and he followed her into a smallish room at the back of the house. The furniture was as dark and Victorian as the pictures in the hall, and Lorimer guessed that a hundred years ago the rooms on this floor had been occupied by less important guests and, perhaps, successive governesses. Times hadn't changed much, except that now a p.a. had replaced the governess.

"I'm sorry you have to be up here," Hilary told him apologetically. "It's quite a big party, and I guess most of them expect the best rooms. Robin says it's important we don't offend anyone, most of them are the heads of corporations Morgans deal with."

"That's all right." Lorimer couldn't have cared less. He walked over to the window and looked out on to the bare slopes of Bheinn Beag.

Hilary had closed the door when they came in, and now when he turned she was standing watching him.

"You're scared," he said.

"No. Why should I be?"

She was lying, he could see the fear in her eyes. "You tell me," he said.

"I have to see to some things." Hilary started moving towards the door.

Lorimer held her arm. "How much do you know about this party?" he asked her.

She frowned again, and he noticed the slight hesitation before she answered, "Only what I've told you. Why? What do you mean? Is something wrong?"

"Do you think it is?"

"No." Her eyes searched his face, but his expression told her nothing and she went on, "Very well, if you won't tell me . . ."

Turning, she walked out of the room.

The party assembled in the hall for drinks before dinner. Lorimer had decided that his most sensible course was to keep as low a profile as possible. It shouldn't be difficult, he reckoned. Not many of the guests were likely to be interested in him. All he had to do was keep his eyes and ears open and watch Forsyth and van Else, assuming the Dutchman was here. Simple.

In theory.

Following his own precepts, he timed his arrival in the hall for when he calculated most of the other guests would already be drinking and talking amongst themselves and wouldn't take any notice of a stranger joining them.

From the gallery he had a bird's eye view of the hall. Nearly thirty men were gathered there, all youngish, as Forsyth had said, and all immaculately tailored: the massed ranks of the Nature parties' financial backers, the real power behind the biggest cartel in the world. Lorimer wondered how much money those men represented. Futile to think of the good that the part of it they pumped into the parties could have done usefully employed.

In their midst, talking animatedly and looking even more beautiful than usual, was Hilary. She was wearing a short bottle-green silk dress and it seemed to Lorimer that she glowed in the light of the big chandelier. Forsyth, on the edge of the gathering, was chatting to two other men. One of them was dark and thick-set and looked like an Italian or, possibly, a Frenchman. The other was several inches taller and fairer skinned, a German, perhaps, or a Dane. Lorimer decided to make for the other side of the room, away from them.

He had reckoned without their host. Forsyth saw him coming and turned, making it virtually impossible for Lorimer to ignore him.

"Come and meet some of our other guests, Gray," he said. "Giovanni,

Piet, this is Graham Lorimer, a colleague of mine. Gray, Giovanni Francetti, Piet van Else."

Lorimer tried to conceal the shock he felt. The Italian was eyeing him curiously, but Lorimer took little notice of him. All his attention was focussed on Francetti's companion. There was more than curiosity in van Else's scrutiny. Clearly he, at least, knew who Lorimer was.

The Dutchman was a bull of a man, about six feet tall and barrel chested, with brown hair, a large nose and ears which laid almost flat against the sides of his square head. But the most noticeable thing about him was his eyes; they were a very pale blue and they gave his face a curiously empty look. It seemed to Lorimer that there was more than a hint of cruelty in them, and he didn't need reminding that this was a man who had had his mistress murdered to protect his own safety.

Beside van Else the plump Italian looked almost genial. Perhaps in many ways he was, and to him the murder of opponents was no more than a step which sometimes had to be taken, of no more significance than selling stock. Perhaps he closed his eyes and ears to what was done and pretended it didn't happen. It was even possible that he didn't know.

A young girl came and asked Lorimer what he would like to drink. He told her a Scotch; he felt he needed it.

"What is your business, Mr. Lorimer?" Francetti enquired.

Before Lorimer could reply Forsyth interposed smoothly, "Gray's my right-hand man."

"Ah, I see." The Italian smiled amiably.

Lorimer told himself that for some reason Forsyth hadn't wanted Francetti to know what he really did. He didn't know what that reason was, but he was pretty sure it wouldn't benefit him. Van Else hadn't smiled. He had gone on looking at him out of those strange pale eyes.

For the next few minutes the four men discussed the shortcomings of air travel, the superiority of certain airlines, music and a new film which had created a minor sensation. There was nothing which could be construed as political, or relating to the reason for their being there.

"We make it a rule not to talk business before dinner on the first evening," Forsyth explained, as if divining what Lorimer was thinking.

Business, Lorimer thought. A euphemism for conspiracy and murder. It was grotesque: these men were here to plot the control of much of Europe's industry and commerce, what they decided would affect in one way or another much of the world, and they were prepared to murder to achieve it—but they might have been successful, sophisti-

cated businessmen relaxing at a cocktail party with no thoughts of anything more criminal than the next takeover bid or the seduction of a
pretty woman. That, of course, was what they were. They weren't
gangsters by birth and upbringing apeing respectability like the *mafiosi,*
they were tycoons who had crossed the narrow divide between legitimate deals and criminality. Perhaps in all of them there was a fatal flaw
which blinded them to everything but their own ambition. A total amo-
rality.

The Italian talked a good deal; he travelled a lot and was knowledgeable about music, and he spoke excellent English. Forsyth played his
part, occasionally drawing Lorimer into the conversation, but van Else
hardly spoke. When he did it was in a strangely flat voice lacking any
expression and with a marked accent. The certainty that the Dutchman
knew about his visit to Amsterdam and his call on Klaasje Wijnen did
nothing to raise Lorimer's spirits.

Francetti was discoursing on a new production at La Scala, and Lorimer looked round the room. The guests had coalesced into small groups
and Hilary was talking to three men a few feet away. There was no one
between them, and, seeing his eyes on her, she smiled.

Reluctantly Lorimer dragged his eyes and thoughts back to his com-
panions. Forsyth had murmured an excuse and was moving off to talk
to others of his guests, leaving him with Francetti and van Else. He
wondered whether the Dutchman knew that he had been indirectly
responsible for Leukens' death. The question seemed unprofitable, and
he turned to the Italian beside him. Francetti was eyeing him with quiet
amusement.

"A beautiful woman, Mrs. Forsyth, yes?" he remarked.

"Yes," Lorimer agreed. He hadn't realised that his expression had
been so revealing, and he hoped Forsyth hadn't noticed it too. "What is
your business, signor?" he asked.

Francetti looked surprised. Perhaps it was vanity; clearly he had
taken it for granted that Lorimer knew. "Chemicals," he replied. "My
company is one of the biggest manufacturers of specialty chemicals in
Europe." He glanced at the man on his left. "Signor van Else, he is in
meat."

"Oh?" Lorimer said, making it sound as innocent and casual as he
could.

"We sell meat all over the Netherlands and Germany," the Dutchman said in his curiously flat voice. "Some we import. Also we slaugh-

ter. We have the biggest slaughterhouses in the Netherlands." Somehow he made the commonplace words sound like a threat.

"Oh?" Lorimer said again.

"You know the Netherlands, Mr. Lorimer?"

"Not very well."

"You have not been there recently?"

Lorimer could see nothing to be gained by admitting he had. "No," he said.

"Italy, perhaps?" Francetti suggested, smiling.

"Not for a long time, I'm afraid."

"That is a pity."

"I would like to go back."

"But of course."

"Do you intend to return to Amsterdam also?" van Else enquired.

Lorimer faced the stare of the Dutchman's light blue eyes. He had said nothing about Amsterdam. "I've no idea," he replied.

"If you do, you must let me know before you come. I will be able to arrange something for you."

Lorimer wondered if van Else's expression ever changed. "Thank you," he said. "I'll remember."

Francetti started telling van Else about a restaurant he had discovered in a small French town and the splendour of its *cuisine*. Looking past them, Lorimer felt a shock of surprise. Standing against the opposite wall was Jenkins' colleague, Clive.

There was no sign that Clive had seen him; he was half turned towards a door a few yards away. Lorimer followed the direction of his gaze and experienced another shock, greater than the first. Standing by the door, as if he had just come in, was Wolf. The Dutchman was looking straight at him. Their eyes met and Wolf started across the hall towards him.

Lorimer felt himself tense. Clive was watching him, his face devoid of expression, giving no sign of recognition.

"You look as if you have had a shock, Mr. Lorimer," van Else remarked. "Is there something wrong?"

"No," Lorimer answered. It was a lie, he thought. Things couldn't be much worse. The one bright spot in a sea of disaster was Clive's presence here. And he couldn't even be sure that that was a plus, maybe Clive was on the other side too.

The fair-haired man arrived at van Else's side.

"I would like you to meet Rutger Wolf," the latter said. He gave a thin, mirthless smile. "He is my right-hand man, Mr. Lorimer. But perhaps you have already met?"

"I don't think so," Lorimer said.

It was the first time he had seen Wolf at close quarters—in the car parked near the Feldhuises' house he had been half obscured by Leukens—and any lingering doubts he had had that Wolf had murdered Rona Smith and McIndoe evaporated. This was the man who had persuaded Hugh Bascomb of the existence of evil. It was not only his hair which was blond, his eyelashes were nearly white, contrasting strangely with his tanned skin, and where van Else's eyes were curiously pale, Wolf's were like empty pools. Looking into them was like gazing into an icy void.

"This is Graham Lorimer, Rutger," van Else said. Almost as an afterthought it seemed, he added, "And Signor Francetti."

Wolf nodded.

Lorimer saw that the Italian looked uneasy. But before he could say anything the people on the other side of the hall began to move towards one of the doors and Hilary came over.

"We're going in to dinner," she said. She looked quickly at Lorimer. "Is everything all right, Gray?"

"Sure, fine," he replied, and wondered if the words sounded as forced to her as they did to him.

Lorimer turned over. The clock on the table beside his bed said ten past seven. It was very quiet; the house had been built solidly enough to prevent any sound short of a minor explosion travelling more than a few yards.

Sliding out of bed, he crossed to the window and looked out. The house faced roughly south-east, so the morning sun didn't reach his room, but a thin mist, little more than a haze, was hanging over the lower slopes of Bheinn Beag. Above it the mountainside was free of cloud, and higher still the sky was a clear, bright blue. It was a typical fine Highlands spring morning, and once the sun had burnt off the haze it would be hot.

Dinner last night had been a relaxed, almost convivial meal. It was obvious that most of the people there were intent on putting serious matters out of their minds for an hour or two and enjoying themselves. Perhaps for them the occasion with its ingredients of intrigue and success brought its own euphoria, Lorimer thought. Again he had the feeling he had had earlier, that these men existed on two levels, one legal, the other criminal, and moved from one to the other easily, almost without noticing the change, like people flying across the equator.

Watching Hilary from the other end of the long table, he had thought at first that she was uneasy. But perhaps it was only the anxiety of any hostess with a large party; long before the end of the meal she appeared to be at her ease. Nevertheless, he suspected that she wasn't enjoying the evening. Her lovely eyes failed to shine and the spark which could illumine her was missing. She was no longer anxious, but neither was she happy. When once or twice their eyes met and he smiled, she barely responded.

After dinner Forsyth had taken the principle guests off for their first meeting, leaving the others to amuse themselves. Lorimer would have given a good deal to know what was discussed behind that heavy oak door off the hall.

Neither Clive nor Wolf had attended the meeting. They had gone off to the billiards room together to play snooker, increasing Lorimer's uncertainty about Clive. He had seen little of Hilary. Soon after dinner she had suggested that if anyone wanted to watch television, there was a set in the library, and shortly afterwards she excused herself and left them. Lorimer suspected that she was deliberately avoiding him. If so, he had only himself to blame.

He had no idea when the meeting had finished; it was still going on when he came up to bed just after eleven. Nor had Clive or Wolf reappeared. He had felt slightly foolish locking his door, but it seemed a sensible precaution and, contrary to his expectations, within a few minutes of getting into bed he was asleep.

That was nearly eight hours ago. Now, when he had washed, shaved and dressed, he went downstairs. The hall was deserted and opening the front door he stepped outside. The air was soft, without a breath of wind, and he could hear the ripple of the burn a couple of hundred yards away. Beyond the far bank the ground was more or less level for about as far again before it started rising, gently at first, then more steeply, towards the bare rock and crags of Bheinn Fhada.

These mountains were among the oldest on earth. Hundreds of thousands of years ago, long before the rising seas had separated Britain from the rest of Europe, they had risen twenty thousand feet and more. What was left were the stumps, like ageing, rotted teeth. Their slopes looked welcoming enough on a morning like this, but on a winter day, with the wind howling round them and thick, cold mist shrouding the peaks, they were a very different proposition. Even today their gentle appearance was misleading; there was nothing friendly about them, they were hard, implacable, taking all a man had to give and yielding nothing in return but their beauty and a sense of achievement for the climber.

Lorimer glanced back over his shoulder at the house and saw a man watching him from a ground floor window. It was Forsyth. The next moment he had gone.

Already the haze was thinning, and looking across the glen Lorimer spotted a man on the far bank of the burn a short distance upstream. The man was walking towards a clump of four or five stunted trees a couple of hundred yards away, but whoever it was was too far off for Lorimer to identify him.

It was early for any of the guests to be about, he thought. But you couldn't judge the men staying here by the ways of normal guests.

At that moment the silence was broken by a shot. The report reverberated round the glen, echoing back from the slopes of the mountains so that it was impossible to tell where it had come from. Lorimer thought it was somewhere higher up the glen, but he couldn't be sure. He had heard enough shots in the past to know that this one hadn't come from a shotgun, it was a rifle shot. And not from anything as light as a .22.

Was there a stalker up there on those bare slopes? Surely not. This was the close season for red deer in Scotland—shooting them was illegal—and, anyway, there were no deer on Iniscaig. Which ruled out poachers too.

The sound of the shot had momentarily distracted Lorimer's attention from the man by the river; now when he looked again the man had gone.

It was impossible; the only cover in that open landscape was the clump of trees, and when Lorimer had last seen him he had been a good two hundred yards from them. He couldn't have reached them yet, and there was nothing else near the burn but tussocky grass and small rocks.

Then Lorimer saw something on the ground where the man had been standing. It looked like a heap of clothing. Shocked and dreading what he would find, he started running towards it.

As he did so the sun finally broke through the haze, flooding the glen with soft light, and he saw another man farther away beyond the trees. The man was covering the ground fast, heading towards the lower slopes of Bheinn Fhada, and he was carrying something. Even at that distance there was no mistaking that it was a rifle.

Once he stopped and looked back. For a second or two the sun was on his face, and Lorimer recognised the Dutchman Wolf. He froze. Wolf must have seen him, he was staring straight at him. Then Wolf turned again and resumed his climb.

Lorimer relaxed a little. Perhaps in his dark clothes and with the sun more or less at his back he had been difficult to see against the Lodge behind him. Wolf had had the sun almost in his eyes.

The wet, peaty ground sucked at Lorimer's shoes, slowing him and making walking hard work, but he had a terrible premonition about what he would find, and he hurried on.

The burn, fed by myriad tiny falls down the slopes of the two mountains, dropped through this part of the glen in a succession of miniature rapids and pools. In only a few places was it more than a dozen feet wide or a couple of feet deep, but it flowed fast, tumbling over the rocks in a flurry of broken water.

The body was lying on the opposite bank, its head and shoulders nearly in the burn. Thirty yards upstream Lorimer found some half-submerged rocks to serve as stepping stones, crossed and walked back. Bending down, he pulled the limp form clear of the water and turned it over. Clive's sightless eyes stared up at him. His anorak was unzipped and there was a bullet hole in the middle of his chest. Blood seeped from it slowly, spreading across the front of his grey T-shirt.

Forsyth must have learnt who Clive was from Jenkins, Lorimer thought. The Welshman trusted him. He had alerted van Else to the danger, and Wolf had lured Clive out here on some pretext, waited in the trees and ambushed him.

SIXTEEN

LORIMER fought back the loathing which welled up in him. Hot, blind anger was a luxury he couldn't afford just now, he had to think. First he must let Jenkins know what had happened—Clive had been his assistant and he would know how to handle the situation.

The nearest phones were at the Lodge, but he couldn't use any of them for obvious reasons. If he went to the village, he could make his call from the hotel. The factory was nearer, but to reach it would mean scaling the steepest face of Bheinn Fhada, and he wasn't equipped for climbing. Nor was he suitably shod, he thought wryly, looking down at his lightweight shoes. There was another consideration: the danger he had been in before was more real than ever now with Clive gone. Moira and her father would shelter him while he talked to Jenkins and worked out what he was going to do.

He peered at the side of the mountain where he had last seen Wolf. There was no sign of the Dutchman now; he must be on the other side of the trees, keeping out of sight of the people in the Lodge while he made his way back there to report to van Else that the job was done.

It occurred to Lorimer that Clive might have been carrying something for Jenkins, and he felt swiftly in the dead man's pockets. But they contained nothing which could conceivably be of any significance, and he straightened up before he remembered that someone in the house might be looking out; he crouched down again in the shelter of the bank.

It was at least four miles from here to the village. That would have been no distance on different terrain, but the first three over boggy ground to the foot of the glen would be hard, slow going. After that the way was across the comparatively level crofts. It would be drier and firmer there, but he would be clearly visible the whole way. Van Else and the others could watch him until it was clear where he was going, then drive down the glen and lie in wait for him at the foot. And there would be no one to see them. He could be shot, his body taken out to sea, weighted and dropped overboard, and he might never be found.

You could think about possibilities like that when the chances of your being personally involved were too remote to merit consideration. Even joke about them. When you were the potential victim it wasn't so funny.

Lorimer's eyes scanned the deserted landscape. There was cover of a sort, but to reach it meant making for the rocky outcrops which littered the side of Bheinn Fhada. It involved no rock climbing, only a stiff haul over rough ground, but it would considerably increase the time it took him to reach the hotel, and time was vital. Nevertheless he had to risk it.

The nearest rocks were a good quarter of a mile away, a single large boulder surrounded by a number of smaller ones. To get to them he would have to cross the level ground on this side of the burn and climb two hundred feet or more up the lowest slope of the mountain. That would have been nothing in normal circumstances, but these weren't normal. And when he reached the rocks he would be only a little nearer the village than he was now.

There was another outcrop farther down the glen. He could see it, a grey column standing out against the pale green turf. If he reached that, he would have made several hundred yards. The only trouble was that those rocks were at least half a mile beyond the others and farther up the mountainside. Moreover until he reached them he would be in full view from the house. He was thankful that the brown anorak and trousers he was wearing would provide him with some sort of camouflage.

Bending nearly double, he started running in a direct line towards the rocks. The marshy ground tugged at his shoes, and peaty brown water, welling up over them, threatened to pull them from his feet. It was like running through thick wet tar and, although he was pretty fit, he wasn't as hard as when he was in full training during the football season. By the time he had covered the first three hundred yards his calf muscles ached.

Then, quite suddenly, the nature of the ground changed. It was drier and less yielding, the turf short and springy instead of the spiky, dark green grass nearer the burn. His feet no longer sank into it, water filling every footprint, and he covered the ground faster. But now it was littered with small rocks, some of them almost buried, and more than once he twisted an ankle painfully. The last thing he needed was to break a leg or sprain an ankle up here, he thought. Do that, and he would be dead.

At the foot of Bheinn Fhada he paused briefly and looked back. There was still no sign of activity at the Lodge, and he turned and started climbing diagonally across the slope.

He didn't mind the exercise. It was an exhilarating morning and the climb was a challenge which in other circumstances he would have enjoyed. He would have preferred to be wearing stouter footwear, but his shoes were just about adequate, and so far he had made good progress.

All the same, it took him longer than he had expected to reach the big boulder. When he did he stopped and leaned against it while he regained his breath. The mountainside was littered with rocks, many more than you could see from a distance, but most of them were far too small to provide any sort of cover. The nearest which might were the six-foot column and its attendant rocks he had seen from the burn, and he set off towards them.

He remembered the column now. He and the others had paused there once on one of their climbs all those years ago. It was a wedge rather than a column, jutting up out of the turf, and presumably harder rock than the rest, so that it had endured when they were worn away, eroded by the winds and rains of centuries. From its shelter he surveyed the way ahead.

Two and a half miles away at the foot of the glen where Bheinn Fhada and Bheinn Beag sloped down to the level ground, the burn turned east towards the shore. Beyond it Lorimer could make out the whitewashed houses of the crofters and, farther away still, the village, a narrow white ribbon at the edge of a deep blue sea. The whole scene was bathed in bright sunlight and he realised that he was hot; it might be only eight o'clock by Greenwich Mean Time, but there was no haze now, and he had climbed several hundred feet fast.

Wolf must be back at the Lodge by this time. He would tell van Else what he had seen, and Forsyth would send out men to look for him. To stalk him like a stag before shooting him. And when it was done they would drag his carcase down to some track and drive it away as men did a dead beast's. A solitary cloud passed across the sun. Its shadow raced across the turf, and for a moment the scene was dulled and the air cooler. Lorimer shivered.

At the foot of the glen, high on the flank of Bheinn Fhada, he could see a group of rocks larger than either of those which had sheltered him so far. If he made it to them, he would have a fast last stretch to the village, downhill at first, then across the flat ground beyond. There would be very little cover, but if he was lucky he just might have sufficient start to reach the hotel before the men from the Lodge could cut him off. It was a pretty remote chance, but he had no alternative.

Pushing on as fast as he could, it took him nearly an hour to reach the rocks. Rarely, he thought, had he felt as exposed as he did working his way across the vast mountainside. Once or twice he paused to look back at the Lodge. He could still see no signs of life there, but by now the house was too far off for him to be sure. Once a small rock crashed past him and went bouncing down the slope. Its sound was exaggerated by the silence before, and Lorimer looked up to see what had dislodged it. But he could see nothing.

Moving across the steep slope was almost more tiring than climbing. Most of the time his left foot was well below his right and his calf muscles ached. His back too, from the strain he was imposing on it.

When he reached the rocks he stopped again for another breather.

The village looked very close from here, the nearest croft almost below his feet. He could see men and women working and, farther off, the straight black scars where peat had been dug.

His right shoelace had worked loose and he stooped down to retie it. As he did so, something struck the rock where his head had been a moment before with a metallic clang. A fragment of stone hurtled away, and at the same instant he heard the shot.

Wolf! he thought. When he had seen the Dutchman heading across the lower slope after shooting Clive he had assumed that he was making his way back to the Lodge. He had counted on it. Since then, in his anxiety to get to the village before anyone from the house, he had almost forgotten him. But Wolf hadn't returned to the Lodge, he had seen him coming to investigate the first shot, guessed that he had seen him, and tracked him along the mountainside. Now he had a clear view of him, and he couldn't wait any longer—in another minute or two Lorimer would be in full view of those houses down there. Already he could see that the nearest man, startled by the shot, had stopped work and was gazing in this direction.

The shot had come from behind and above him. Still bent double and moving cautiously, Lorimer rounded the rocks and peered up at the steep side of Bheinn Fhada. It looked vast from here, a blank wall of rock and grass nearly three thousand feet high and four or five miles long. But somewhere up there was hidden a man who was trying to kill him. The man had a powerful rifle, and he had nothing. Not even a penknife.

There wasn't much cover on that slope, but four or five hundred feet above him and a quarter of a mile to his right was a pile of rocks which at some time had fallen from higher up and settled there. Wolf must be concealed amongst them, it was the only place.

Lorimer looked back up the glen. A Land Rover with four men in it was coming down the track from the Lodge: Forsyth, van Else and the others were moving to cut him off before he reached the village. It was the end, he thought. He had no chance now.

So he might as well go out fighting.

Below him the ground sloped down comparatively gently to a sort of lip twenty yards from where he was crouched. Beyond the lip it fell steeply. If he could make it down the first stretch, keeping the rocks between Wolf and himself, once he got over the edge the fall of the land would conceal him for a minute or so, and by the time he emerged from its shelter he would be another hundred yards or more down the mountainside. With luck Wolf wouldn't realise that he had gone. It was a long shot, but it was better than staying here, a sitting target to be picked off by the Dutchman's rifle.

There had been no more shots. Lowering himself to the ground and murmuring a prayer under his breath, Lorimer stretched out straight and pushed himself off. The next second he was rolling downhill. His speed increasing all the time, he turned over and over across the uneven ground. Rocks projecting from the turf pummelled his body, crunching painfully against his ribs and hips, and tore at the flesh of his hands.

Then he was over the rim. For a moment it seemed to Lorimer as if he were flying, wonderfully free. Rocks no longer battered him. The next moment he landed with a thud that drove the wind out of his body. He gasped. Then he was rolling again, faster than before, hurtling down the mountainside out of control, helpless to slow his crazy progress. All he could do was endeavour to protect his head from the rocks. There were fewer of them here, but when his body struck one the pain was worse. His brain spun dizzily. He told himself he mustn't lose consciousness, that if he did he would be as good as dead, lying here like an injured beast until they came for him.

And somehow he didn't. He had no idea how far he had come; he could see nothing but brief glimpses of the sky interspersed with blackness. Then, with a suddenness which left him gasping for breath, he stopped. He was bruised and sore and he ached all over, but as far as he could tell nothing was broken. He wasn't even cut badly. He had rolled into a depression, a dip in the ground two or three feet deep, and the lower bank had stopped his fall.

For several seconds he laid still, hardly able to grasp what had happened, then, raising himself on his right elbow, he looked back. He was hidden from anyone far up the slope by the depth of the gully and the lip below the rocks. The trouble was that as soon as he stood up he would be visible again. True, he might have a half-mile start, but what use was that against a skilled shot with a high velocity rifle? Nevertheless he had to risk it, and for the first hundred yards or so he would be out of Wolf's sight. After that it would be in the lap of the gods.

He could see the Land Rover much nearer now. As he watched, it turned off the track on to the grass, heading for an iron bridge across the burn, pitching and bucking over the uneven surface. Then something happened. The driver must have misjudged the narrow approach to the bridge; the Land Rover, bouncing wildly, hit the end of the guard-rail on the left-hand side and turned over. As it did so, the driver scrambled out. The next moment it slid into the burn. The driver stood for a moment looking down at the wreck, then, apparently satisfied that there was nothing he could do without help, he started walking towards the village.

Lorimer stood up and began running down the slope towards the nearest croft. He ran upright, because that way he could run faster. Rocks bruised his feet through the thin soles of his shoes and more than once he slithered and nearly fell, but somehow he kept his balance. And so far there had been no shot behind him.

When he reckoned that he had covered a hundred yards he crouched lower and zigzagged from side to side. He was out in the open again now. Once he fell, carried off his feet by the speed of his headlong descent, and he longed to stay there. But he knew that to do so would be fatal and, picking himself up, he raced on. Already he was halfway to the croft: once past the house there would be more shelter.

His lungs felt as if they were bursting and his legs ached more than ever from running down the steep slope, but he daren't slacken his pace. His only hope lay in reaching the hotel before the man from the Land Rover—and before Wolf found his target.

Even as the thought crossed Lorimer's mind, a bullet struck the ground a few feet to his right, followed almost immediately by another just behind it. He turned sharply to his left and ran on. There was no time to worry about the Land Rover's driver, if fortune was on his side he would reach the hotel before the man could hope to on foot.

Another shot plucked viciously at the loose fabric of Lorimer's anorak, leaving a hole where it passed through. The next one . . . he thought, then forced the idea from his mind.

There were two haycocks this side of the house. They might not stop a bullet, but they would provide some sort of cover, and he ran towards them. His breath was coming in gasps which tore his lungs and his heart was pounding. He reached the nearest haycock and paused for a second or two, looking round, before he ran on again.

A man and woman were working a hundred yards away, and it flashed into Lorimer's mind that almost certainly they had a telephone. But it would take time to explain and return to the house, and time was all-important. Also he suspected that Wolf would have no compunction about shooting the couple as well as him if he thought they were a danger. By the time Constable Macdonald had called up reinforcements the Dutchman would be away and there would be nothing to link him or the people at Iniscaig Lodge with the murders.

He had reached the house now, and with a wild sense of joy he saw a bicycle propped against the wall. Grabbing it, he summoned up his remaining strength, swung his leg over the saddle and pedalled off down the track which led to the road and the village.

There were no more shots. Lorimer couldn't believe that Wolf had given up. More likely he was biding his time, planning his next move before coming out into the open.

When he was a boy Lorimer had done a lot of cycling, but it was years now since he had ridden a bike, and at first he wobbled erratically. However the surface of the track was reasonably smooth, and once he had got the feel again he worked up a good speed. When he reached the road the going was smoother and he pedalled faster. The first houses were only a quarter of a mile away now.

Iniscaig had reverted to normal. The caravans and the cars which had been parked near the jetty the last time Lorimer was there had gone and the street was deserted. Half falling off the cycle, he threw it against the wall of the hotel and ran into the lobby. There was no one there. Desperately he rang the bell on the reception desk.

It was a quarter of a minute before Moira appeared. When she did Lorimer thought the sight of no one had ever been so welcome before. She gazed at him in astonishment. He was struggling for breath, there was a gash on his left cheek and his clothes were stained and torn.

"Gray!" she exclaimed. "What are you doing here? What's happened?"

"Have you another phone?" he gasped, hardly able to speak.

"Another one?"

"Private."

"Yes, through here. But why?"

"Can't explain," Lorimer managed to say. His chest was heaving painfully. "Later."

Without asking any more questions, Moira led him through to the MacNeils' living room at the rear of the building.

"It's there," she told him, nodding towards a phone on a bureau by one wall.

"Thanks," Lorimer said.

Moira left him, closing the door behind her, and he picked up the receiver.

It seemed an age before he got through, and when he did they told him Jenkins wasn't there.

"Where is he?" Lorimer demanded. He could breath a little more easily now. "I have to speak to him."

They couldn't say.

Wouldn't, Lorimer thought bitterly. He asked to speak to Wycliffe. "Tell him Clive's dead," he said.

Jenkins' boss remembered him and listened. "Owen's gone to Fort William," he said when Lorimer had finished. "You may get him at the police station. If not, they'll get a message to him."

"Thanks." Lorimer wondered what Jenkins was doing in Fort William.

"Good luck," Wycliffe said.

Lorimer found Jenkins at the police station.

"What's happened?" the Welshman demanded.

Lorimer told him. "Wolf's out there somewhere with a rifle, and one of the men from the Lodge is heading this way," he finished.

"I'll get things moving straightaway," Jenkins promised.

"Thanks." Lorimer knew that whatever Owen did might not be too little, but it would almost certainly be too late. He said good-bye and put down the phone.

Maybe Alan MacNeil had a gun, he thought. If he had, and he let him borrow it and a handful of cartridges, he might be able to hole up in one of the bedrooms and watch the street for Wolf and the Land Rover's driver. He might even be able to hold out until Jenkins arranged whatever it was he was planning. Forsyth and his friends would hardly dare start a shoot-out here in the village, it would bring out most of the population of Iniscaig.

All the same, Owen had better not waste any time getting here. Lorimer went to find Moira.

She was in the lobby, her back to the reception desk and a scared expression on her face. The door from the street was open and standing just inside it, his arms cradling a rifle, was Wolf. The Dutchman was smiling.

Lorimer stopped.

"Who is he, Gray?" Moira asked unsteadily.

"His name's Wolf, he killed Rona Smith," Lorimer replied. His breathing had been almost back to normal, but now it seemed to stop. He was afraid, horribly afraid. His fear wasn't for himself, it was for Moira. If anything happened to her . . .

"It's all right," he said, hoping his fear didn't show in his voice. "He wants me, not you. Go back to the other room."

"But what—?"

"It doesn't matter now. Go."

Moira turned to do as Lorimer had said.

"Stay!" The Dutchman raised his rifle to his shoulder and aimed it at her.

"You don't want her," Lorimer protested angrily.

As if in answer, Wolf squeezed the trigger. In the confined space of the lobby the report was almost deafening. He was only seven or eight yards from them, and if he had been aiming at Moira he couldn't have missed, but at the last moment he had raised the rifle's barrel an inch or two and the bullet tore into the wall behind her just above the level of her head.

Almost simultaneously a voice out in the street shouted, "Wolf! Put that rifle down."

The Dutchman swung round. He was still holding the gun to his shoulder, and now it was aimed lower, at the height of a man's chest. His finger started to squeeze the trigger.

As he did so there was another shot. For a second Wolf seemed to hang in the doorway, as if he were suspended there, then he slumped to the floor, his arms outflung. His rifle clattered on the boards.

Lorimer stared in disbelief. Blood was seeping from a neat hole in the Dutchman's chest.

Moira gasped and put her hand to her mouth, as if to hold back a scream. Then Forsyth appeared in the doorway.

"Just in time," he said.

Lorimer stretched out his legs and drank some more of his host's Laphroig. For the first time in weeks, he thought, he could relax. He still ached like hell and his body felt as if it were bruised all over, but he could bear with that.

They were in Forsyth's study. Outside it was raining hard, but the book-lined room with its dark leather chairs and oak furniture was snug. The other guests had gone, either home thoroughly chastened, or to the mainland under arrest. Forsyth and Jenkins between them had enough evidence to ensure that most of them would be convicted in due course.

"You crashed the Land Rover on purpose, didn't you?" Lorimer asked.

His host smiled wryly. "It was the only way I could think of to shake off van Else and the other two. I knew Wolf was out there with a gun and that he'd be after you and you hadn't one. I guessed you'd make for the village, it was the only place you could go, and the obvious place for a phone was the hotel. I remembered you knew the people there."

None of the three men had been killed when the Land Rover turned over, but two of them, a German and a Belgian, had been flown to hospital in Fort William with fairly serious injuries. Van Else, who had escaped almost unscathed, was under arrest.

"I didn't like shooting Wolf," Forsyth went on. "I'd never fired at a man before. I don't feel good about it now, whatever he was like."

Lorimer understood. He still felt much the same about Leukens' death, and he hadn't intended that. "I'm glad you did," he said.

For the next few moments both men were busy with their own thoughts, and neither of them spoke. Then Forsyth said, "I wasn't sure about you until the other day. You seemed to know too much, and you went off to Amsterdam to see people you wouldn't talk about. It was Jenkins' bloody fault. He plays his cards so close to his chest there's hardly room for him to put his shirt on. All he'd say was that he'd checked you out and you were clean. He didn't tell me he knew you and you'd worked with him before. When I told him about this weekend he suggested I bring you along."

"He didn't tell me much about you either," Lorimer said. If he had, he thought, none of this might have happened. Jenkins had a lot to answer for.

"I didn't know anything about the political side. That was your angle, wasn't it?" Lorimer nodded. "All I was concerned about was their monstrous cartel dominating half the European economy."

"They couldn't do it without the party links," Lorimer said.

"No." Forsyth emptied his glass. "It wasn't true I was against Horwill coming on our boards, I proposed him because I wanted him where I could see him. I went to the meeting that evening to see what sort of hand he made of it."

Forsyth hadn't known about the cartel's political links because only Horwill, van Else and a handful of their closest associates had been involved in them, Lorimer told himself. With their backing, Horwill had controlled Dorn nan Gaidheal and all its activities.

He had been arrested in London before any of his friends could warn him. Soon he would be completely discredited. It would be a terrible shock for Rosalind. There was no logic where emotions were concerned, and Lorimer suspected that she would blame him. For a time, at least. He was sorry about it, but he didn't feel the deep bitterness he would have a week or two ago. He had realised a lot in that terrible moment when Wolf's rifle had been aimed at Moira's heart. One thing was that he no longer wanted to cling to the hope that there might still be a future for Rosalind and him. It had been a dream, and now he had woken up.

"How many of them were involved in the murders?" he asked.

"The same four or five." Forsyth had learnt that from Jenkins after the Welshman had finished his preliminary interrogations. "The rest were prepared to break the law, but they didn't know anything about the way things were worked. One or two of them may have guessed some of it, but I doubt if most of them did even that. A lot of businessmen have tunnel vision."

They saw only their objective and were blind to everything else, Lorimer thought. "Francetti?" he suggested. He rather hoped the Italian hadn't known. He had sat next to him at dinner on Friday night and, despite all the evidence, he had liked him.

"I shouldn't think he even guessed. He'll cheerfully swindle the EEC, but he's no murderer." Forsyth leaned over and poured some more whisky into Lorimer's glass.

"How did you get involved?" the latter asked.

"An old American friend of mine runs a big meat company in Illinois. They do a lot of business with Holland and Germany, and he was worried about some of the deals; he thought his customers were swindling the EEC and he was afraid he might get dragged in if it ever came out. He knew Morgans dealt with the Dutch and he mentioned his suspicions to me.

"Then I was asked to go to a meeting at the ministry. It was very high-powered. There were a couple of Americans there, and it was clear how concerned they were about the way things might go. Politically as well as economically. The American administration might favour a more united Europe, but there were right-wing elements in the States who hated the idea: most of the countries in the EEC have socialist governments. Others didn't want a Europe that was economically stronger than the U.S.A. and could undercut their producers. Some of them were afraid a 'fortress Europe' might shut them out. There was a lot of pressure building up on the White House and the State Department."

Forsyth paused. "Hilary's father has contacts in the Community, he fixed it for me to meet Francetti and Schmidt, the German. They didn't like the way Horwill was working hand-in-glove with van Else and his friends and shutting them out of the decision making. They'd been told I wasn't over-scrupulous, and they asked me if I would come in."

Hilary had lied when she said she hadn't asked him to have lunch with her and go to the theatre in order to find out more about him for her husband, Lorimer thought. She had never been interested in him as a man, only for the danger he might represent. "You asked Hilary to find out what I was doing," he said.

"Yes." Again Forsyth paused. "She's in the drawing room, she wants to explain."

"She doesn't need to," Lorimer said. There was no point, it was all over. Already it belonged to the past.

Nevertheless he went.

"I'm sorry," Hilary said simply. "The other day, when I said there was something I had to tell you and I came to your flat it was to explain. And to apologise. But you were so hard. And when I tried you wouldn't listen." She paused. "I made that up about Robin having a girl in Edinburgh because I hoped it would make you sympathise. Then you might open up."

She looked away for a moment, then turned back and faced him. "It was true I asked you to go to the theatre because I wanted to see you again," she said. "That didn't have anything to do with Robin. And when I kissed you it was because I wanted to do that too."

"It doesn't matter," Lorimer told her. He was surprised how true that was. Hilary had been a dream too.

The beach was deserted and it was very quiet.

"I didn't mean to drag you into it," Lorimer said. "It didn't occur to me there'd be any danger to you, and I didn't know who else to go to."

"I'm glad you came," Moira told him. Her hand found his and crept into it. "It's all over now?"

"Yes."

"So you'll be going back to London."

Lorimer nodded. "Tomorrow."

"Will you come back ever?"

He looked at her. "Would you mind if I did?"

Moira blushed faintly. "No, I wouldn't mind."

They walked a little way without speaking, then Lorimer said, "Your father was telling me he and your mother are thinking of selling the hotel and retiring to live near her folk at Ballachulish."

"Och, they've been talking about that for years," Moira said. "They'll never do it."

"But if they did," Lorimer said. "They'd not be needing you to help there."

"No."

They walked the rest of the way to the village in silence. When they reached the hotel Lorimer asked, "Will you have a room if I can come up in a week or two?"

"I'm sure we will," Moira answered. Her eyes were bright.